JUST ANOTHER SUICIDE

SUICIDE

(or Dare to Love)

DAVENPORT & LEPAGE BOOK 2

by
Judy Ford

Fernie Fazakerley Publications

COPYRIGHT

Just Another Suicide

(or Dare to Love)

Published by Bernie Fazakerley Publications

Copyright © 2023 Judy Ford.

ISBN: 978-1-911083-90-0

DEDICATED TO

The Cheshire Agricultural Chaplaincy
in recognition of its work with the farming community, which has one of the
highest rates of suicide of any occupation.

"Helping and Valuing the whole Farming Community.
A free confidential service offering a listening ear, practical
help, and care to the whole farming community, in a non-
judgemental way."

CONTENTS

Copyright ii

Contents iv

1. Prelude 1

2. Suspicious Death 13

3. Duty Calls 34

4. Day of Rest? 57

5. Case Conference 92

6. Reunion 110

7. Just Another Suicide? 127

8. Cherchez la Femme 138

9. Piecing Together a Picture 149

10. Teenage Diary 166

11. Fathers and Sons 185

12. Cross Examination 209

13. Assembling the Evidence 220

14. Confession 228

15. Case Closed? 240

16. Forgive and Forget? 263

Thank you 277

Acknowledgements 278

Disclaimer 279

CONTENTS

More Books from Judy Ford 280

Glossary of UK police ranks 282

About the Author 284

1. PRELUDE

December 2021

Esther heard voices as she opened the door at the foot of the staircase where she had her room.

'I'll leave you to get on then, Professor Danjuma.' It was Mr Malpas, the head porter. 'If you wouldn't mind locking the room when you're finished and dropping the key off at the lodge.'

'Certainly! I will not forget. Thank you.' That voice was new to her, but somehow familiar. It must be Professor Danjuma, Jibrilu's father. It had the same deep tone, but was less strong – an older man, and one who had learned to be less arrogant and sure of himself.

She looked towards Jibrilu's ground-floor room and saw the porter there in the act of pulling the door closed behind him. He nodded toward her as he passed her on his way back to resume his duties in the lodge.

'Afternoon, Miss Orugun!'

'Good afternoon, Mr Malpas. How are you?'

'Not so bad, thanks. Been to your mothers meeting, I see,' he added, looking towards Esther's blue-and-white Mothers' Union headscarf.

'That's right,' she nodded, smiling back at him. 'We had a very interesting speaker from a women's refuge talking about how difficult it can be for women to escape domestic violence. It made me feel very blessed to be from a home where my father always treated my mother with respect.'

'That's right,' the elderly porter agreed, picking up on a word that was one of his favourites. 'There's not enough respect these days. When I was a boy, I was taught to give up my seat to ladies on the bus, and my dad always carried the heavy bags for my mum. Nowadays, young people only think of themselves and what *they* want. I reckon you Africans could teach them a few things about respect. You understand that the old ways are often the best ways.'

'Oh, I don't know about that! Not all of the old ways are so good. The talk today reminded me about an incident at my church back home. My father is the vicar there. One day, one of the women in the congregation came to him, very upset because her husband had married another woman – a girl, half his age! She asked my dad to talk to him and tell him to send her away. But the man said it was their tradition to have many wives. He said his grandfather had been a tribal chief with ten wives and he was just sticking to the old ways, like him.'

'Yes well, I meant the old British ways,' the porter muttered. 'Respect for authority, churchgoing, minding your language – like you, Miss Orugun. And Mr Danjuma,' he added, glancing back at the closed door behind him. 'I know he was a Muslim, but he was always very polite to me and I never got complaints from the scouts about the state of his room – not like a lot of the young men. It was a crying shame him being killed like that!'

'Yes. I can agree with you on that," Esther nodded. 'Was that his father you were letting into his room just now? I was wondering whether to call and have a word.'

'That's right. He's come to clear out his things. He says he's flying out, back to Nigeria, at the end of the week. Yes, I daresay, he'd be pleased to have you call in and give your condolences. Now, I'd better get on. Can't stand around here chatting all day!'

PRELUDE

Esther waited until the old man had gone past and the door had swung shut behind him, before approaching the room where Jibrilu Danjuma had lived up until his sudden death only a few weeks before. She raised her hand to knock, and then changed her mind abruptly and set off up the stairs to her room instead.

A few minutes later, she was back, standing outside Jibrilu's door with a white envelope clasped in her hand. She stood for a few seconds, her hand poised to knock, her eyes closed.

'Oh Lord,' she prayed silently, 'give me the right words to say to him. Do not allow me to make things worse for him than they already are!'

Then she tapped hard with her knuckles and stepped back a pace to wait for a reply.

The door opened and a man looked out at her. Esther stared back, momentarily lost for words. This could not be Jibrilu's father. He was too young – forty at most, maybe less. And yet, there was something familiar about him. He was tall, like Jibrilu, but slimmer – wiry rather than muscular – and his face …? Something about his eyes and the set of his chin reminded her of the dead postgraduate student. Perhaps this was some relative who had accompanied the grieving father to support him. Not a brother – she knew that Jibrilu had no siblings – a cousin perhaps?

Then the man spoke, not in the northern Nigerian accent that she had been expecting, but in the "received pronunciation" of a native of the home counties. 'Miss Orugun? Can I help you?'

At the sound of his voice, the penny dropped. Of course! The man's face was familiar because she had met him before. This wasn't some member of Jibrilu's family, it was the police officer who had investigated his death. He had interviewed her, because she lived on the same staircase and was a fellow student.

'Inspector!' She tried to gather her thoughts, taken aback at seeing him there. What was his name, now? Lepage! That was it:

Detective Inspector Andy Lepage. 'I'm sorry. I thought … I was looking for Professor Danjuma. I wanted to …'

'Pay your respects?' Lepage smiled back kindly. 'Of course! Come in. I'm just here to help him collect his son's belongings.'

He ushered her inside the room and closed the door behind her.

'Professor! Let me introduce Esther Orugun. She has a room just above here, on the first floor. Miss Orugun – this is Professor Yakubu Danjuma.' The inspector introduced them and then, seeing that Esther was struggling to know how to begin a conversation with the bereaved father, went on, 'I'll just pop back to the car and get those boxes,' and left the room.

'So, you knew Jibrilu?' The professor's voice was deep and resonant, just like Jibrilu's. 'Why don't we both sit down and then we can talk.'

'Thank you.' Esther subsided into one of the two standard-issue easy chairs, identical to the ones in her own room, and sat fiddling with the envelope in her hands. 'I – I … Professor Danjuma-'

'Yakubu, please,' he interrupted. 'I hope that you consider us to be friends. Any friend of Jibrilu's is a friend of mine.'

With a great effort, Esther forced herself to speak steadily. 'Yakubu, I wanted to say how sorry I was about ….'

'Thank you.'

'And I – I – I wanted to apologise.'

'Apologise? Why?'

'I wasn't always very fair towards Jibrilu. In fact, I said some very unfair things. I – I wrote this letter, apologising, but I never gave it to him.'

Esther held out the envelope. Yakubu looked at it for several seconds before putting out his hand and taking it from her.

'Please! Read it!' Esther urged. 'I wish I'd given it to him before … and I should have apologised to his face. It was cowardly to write a letter, but … Well, I'd feel better if I knew that you at least ….' She trailed off into incoherence.

Yakubu opened the envelope and unfolded the single sheet of writing paper inside. He read it in silence and then re-folded it and put it back in the envelope.

'Thank you.' He hesitated and then put the letter into the inside pocket of his jacket. 'Jibrilu spoke of you,' he went on, after a short pause. 'He told me that you had family who were killed by Boko Haram.'

'My aunt and uncle and cousins, yes; but it was wrong of me to suggest that Jibrilu supported them, just because he was a Muslim and-'

'And liked to tell other people how to behave?' Yakubu cut across her. 'Yes. I can see why you were angry with him. He saw everything in black and white and thought it was his duty to point out to people when they were offending against the will of Allah. It is my fault. I'm afraid that when he was a child, I encouraged him to think that way. I was not very religious when I was young, but after Jibrilu's mother died, I became convinced that losing my family was a judgement on me for my lack of devotion. I started praying five times a day and going to the masjid every Friday without fail. It was a comfort to me to feel that I was doing something to …'

'To atone?' suggested Esther timidly.

'Yes. Yes, perhaps that is the right word. I had not been a good Muslim and I think I was not a good husband either. I tried to cover my guilt with religious zeal. And of course, Jibrilu grew up thinking that was all very important – which it is, but not … Allah says, in the Holy Qur'an, "There is no compulsion in religion." And yet Jibrilu always felt obliged to correct those whom he thought were doing wrong.'

5

'You must have been very close,' Esther suggested, unsure how to respond to this unexpected disclosure. 'I can't imagine how you feel now that he's gone.'

'When the police arrived at my office and told me, I did not know how I would go on living,' Yakubu admitted. 'But, Alhamdulillah, this tragedy brought me something totally unexpected. To my utter amazement, I lost one son and miraculously found another!'

He paused dramatically, clearly expecting some sort of reaction from Esther, who was too taken aback to know what to say. What could he possibly mean by this extraordinary statement? Before she could formulate a reply, Yakubu continued, evidently enjoying the opportunity to share his exciting news.

'I can see that you are surprised. I assure you that your amazement cannot be half what mine was when I found out. Allah is indeed great and merciful. That young man who opened the door to you just now – he is my son! A son that I did not even know that I had!'

'Inspector Lepage?' Esther stammered weakly. 'I don't understand. Do you mean that he's been helping you like a son?'

'No, no. He *is* my son, the fruit of my loins.'

'But ... how?'

'I was a student here at Lichfield College forty years ago,' Yakubu went on eagerly. 'I met a young woman here and we fell in love.' Then his face fell and his voice became regretful. 'But I was not honest with her. I did not tell her about my two wives and my baby daughter. When she found out, she was angry with me.'

He paused as if waiting for Esther to respond, so she replied, 'I'm not surprised. I would have been too.'

'Oh yes! I do not blame her: I behaved very badly towards her. She had every right to be angry. But was it right that she never told me about our son, and she did not tell him about me?' He looked towards Esther, who lowered her eyes and said nothing. 'So, we would never have met if it had not been for Jibrilu's death. I lost one son and found another, alhamdulillah.'

'My father says that when God closes one door, He always opens another,' Esther said, realising that he was expecting a reaction from her, and then immediately wishing she had remained silent. This wise saying about life's disappointments and making the most of alternative opportunities seemed trite when applied to the death of a beloved child. However, Yakubu appeared to be satisfied with her words.

'That is very true,' he nodded. 'Your father is a wise man. He clearly understands that Allah always knows best. That is why, although I grieve for the son I have lost, I can still rejoice in the son that I have found.'

Esther was spared the difficulty of formulating an adequate response to this by the return of Inspector Lepage carrying a battered suitcase and two large cardboard boxes, one inside the other.

'Here you are!' he announced, breaking the awkward silence. 'This should be enough for all Jibrilu's things. I'll help you to pack them up and then take everything back to the hotel and you can sort it all out at your leisure.' He spoke cheerfully and perhaps a little louder than was strictly necessary. Was he aware of Esther's unease, and trying to cover her discomfiture?

The inspector put the suitcase down on the narrow bed and opened it, struggling with its rusty hinges. 'This should be big enough to take all his clothes. It's just an old one we've had up in our loft for years. You can keep it. Now, where would you like us to begin? Or would you rather I left you to do this on your own? I'd understand if you don't want ...'

'Thank you, Andy. I'd rather you stayed ... unless you have other things you need to do ...?'

'No, no, I'm free all day. I just thought … I'll take the chest of drawers then, shall I?'

He crossed the room and pulled open the top drawer of a four-drawer chest. Esther watched as he began taking out socks and underwear and packing them into the bottom of the suitcase. Then she turned to Yakubu, who was standing in the middle of the room looking round as if he didn't know where to begin.

'Is there anything I can do to help?'

Yakubu stared at her with an expression on his face that suggested that he had forgotten that she was there.

'Perhaps I could empty the wardrobe?' she suggested gently. 'My father says that I'm good at folding shirts. And I think maybe you would be the best person to go through Jibrilu's desk, in case there are personal papers and stuff in there.'

'Yes,' Yakubu murmured absently. 'Yes. Thank you. You're very kind.'

Esther opened the wardrobe and began taking shirts, jackets and trousers off their hangers, laying them on the bed, folding them neatly and placing them into the suitcase. Yakubu stood watching her for a few moments before walking over to the desk and opening the top drawer.

They worked steadily for about half an hour. Then Inspector Lepage straightened up from the crouching position that he had adopted to reach the bottom drawer, which contained jumpers and sweatshirts. He added the last of these to the suitcase and turned to Esther.

'Is that all the clothes?'

'Yes,' she nodded. 'That's the lot.'

The police officer closed the case and held it down while Esther fastened the two, rather stiff and corroded, catches. He looked towards Yakubu, who had finished with the desk and was now taking down books from the bookcase and stowing them in one of the cardboard boxes. The other box was already full.

'How about we take that box and the case back to the car, while you finish here?' he suggested, obtaining nods from Yakubu and Esther in response.

He picked up the box and fitted it under one arm leaving his other hand free. Esther reached for the suitcase, but he was there first and took hold of the handle.

'It's OK. I can manage both. You go ahead and open the doors for me.'

'Your father seems to be bearing up very well,' Esther said, after the door had closed behind them.

'He told you about that then?' Lepage gave a wry smile. 'I wish he wouldn't.'

'Why?' Esther held open the door that led from the "Hall Staircase" into the college Dining Hall – deserted at this time of the afternoon – and he followed her through, struggling to balance the box while carrying the heavy case in the other hand. 'He's clearly very proud of you.'

'It's all very well for him, but I've got my mum to think about.'

'Oh?'

'She thought she'd seen the back of him forever, and now here he is, large as life! There's nothing for him to be proud of about the way he treated her back then.'

'But he knows that.' Esther hurried ahead to open the door out to the cloisters that ran along the side of Overton Quad. 'He told me about it. He admitted that he treated her badly.'

'He said that?' The inspector sounded surprised. He put the suitcase down on the ground and stood holding the box in both hands and looking at her intently. 'And you believe him? You think he's sincere – not just putting it on?'

'I – I – I've only just met him.' Esther was floored by the question. What did this man want her to say?

They stood looking at one another for several seconds before Lepage shook his head apologetically, swapped the box back into one hand and went to pick up the case again.

'I'm sorry,' he mumbled. 'I shouldn't have-'

'No, no – it's alright.' Suddenly Esther saw him in a new light. This wasn't the confident police authority figure who had questioned her about the circumstances surrounding Jibrilu's death. This was a boy – well, a man, but not so much older than she was herself – who was anxious to know whether he could trust his own father. 'I suppose,' she went on slowly, trying to find something reassuring to say, 'he didn't need to say anything to me about it. He could've made out it was all your mother's fault. I wouldn't have known any different. So, why would he say it, if he didn't mean it?'

'I dunno,' he sighed. 'To make you like him, I suppose. Mum says he's manipulative.'

He shrugged and reached down for the case again., but Esther got to it first, grasping the handle and lifting it off the ground with strong arm muscles. 'I'll take this. That box is too heavy for one hand. Don't worry!' she added, grinning up at him, 'I won't injure myself. I was shot-putt champion at my school three years running!'

She straightened up and stood looking at him expectantly. 'Lead on, Inspector! You know where we're going. I don't.'

'I'm parked just round the corner, in Goose Lane. In fact, thinking about it, the easiest thing would have been for us to have shoved everything out through the window, instead of walking all the way round. And, it's *Andy*, not *inspector*. I'm not on duty now.'

'Thank you, Andy. And you must stop calling me Miss Orugun. My name's Esther. *Miss Orugun* makes me sound like I'm about fifty years old!'

PRELUDE

They made their way across Overton Quad and through the archway that led into the main quad, with its ornate stone sundial and long benches ranged along the walls.

'I suppose you'll be flying out to Nigeria soon?' Andy made conversation as they walked past the porters' lodge and out into the street. 'You said you were going home for Christmas.'

'Yes,' Esther nodded. 'Friday.'

'That's when Yakubu's booked to go. Maybe you'll be on the same flight.'

'We probably will be. There weren't a lot to choose from.'

'I'm taking him to the airport. I could give you a lift too.'

'Are you sure? Won't I be in the way? I mean: you won't be seeing your father again for-'

'I'd really rather not be stuck alone in a car with him for over an hour,' Andy cut in. 'I can't ... I can't be what he wants me to be. Please say you'll come.'

2. SUSPICIOUS DEATH

July 2022

"It's a young man,' PC Gavin Hughes confided to Anna as he led her down the side of a large house in the suburbs of Oxford. 'His father came home and found him hanging from a tree in the back garden. Looks like he did it himself.'

'Did he leave a note?'

'Not that I know of.' Gavin shook his head. 'I had a quick look in his pockets, but most likely he'll have left it somewhere else – in his room, maybe, or somewhere his parents would find it.'

'And where are they now?'

'His mum's out – expected back any time. She's on her way back from London with *her* mum. Dad tried to ring her, but she didn't pick up, presumably driving. Dad's in the house. I told him you'd need to speak to him. And there's a load more of them in there too: a whole lot of brothers and sisters with their other halves and kids. Apparently, they were supposed to be having some sort of family get-together this afternoon. I left Stella Gilbert with them. She's good at quiet sympathy. One or two of the men seemed to be getting a bit restive. We had a hard job keeping them indoors. They wanted to come out and see what had happened. It was good luck we got here before everyone arrived, but even so, the scene's in a bit of a mess. The father got him down, thinking he might still be alive, and tried to revive him before calling 999. He was all for carrying him into the house, but I told him you'd want to see him where he was … which is just here!'

They rounded a dense clump of rhododendrons and Anna nearly collided with Gavin, who had stopped short and was pointing down at the body of a young white man, lying in the leaf litter, his eyes closed and his arms by his sides. He looked almost as if he were asleep. There was a red mark on his neck, where the rope had been, and a graze on the side of his face. Bending closer, Anna saw some smaller marks – scratches which had bled slightly – just below his chin. Better not to touch him. Leave that to the experts when they arrived.

She looked up and saw the noose that had killed him swinging gently in the breeze two feet or more above her head. Higher still, the other end of the rope was wound round a branch, which stood out conveniently in an almost perfectly horizontal direction from the sturdy trunk of a mature apple tree. Next to the rope was propped an aluminium extending ladder.

'And the father got him down by …?'

'He climbed up and managed to get the rope off him.'

'That can't have been easy,' Anna observed, continuing to stare upwards. The branch was a good twelve feet from the ground and the young man's father would have had to support his weight while balancing on the ladder and loosening the ligature round his neck. Eventually, she dropped her gaze and turned back to her colleague. 'The ladder was here – propped up like this – when he came here? When he found his son, I mean?'

'No.' Gavin creased his brow in an expression of puzzlement. 'He said he went and got the ladder from the shed. Over there,' he added, pointing towards a brick-built outbuilding that stood against the high wall at the side of the garden.

'So, how did the victim – what's his name, by the way? – get up there?'

'Dunno,' Gavin shrugged. 'Could he have thrown the rope over the branch and used it to help him shin up the trunk?' Then, seeing Anna's sceptical expression, he hurried on, 'Anyway, you wanted to know his name: it's Rory Quinn. His father's Patrick Quinn. You know – as in Quinn's Superstores.'

'That American who owns a string of supermarkets and hotels? Now I understand why the Chief Super was adamant that I had to come out to this instead of sending a Detective Constable. Presumably he's expecting VIP treatment and a team of officers investigating his son's death, even though by the look of it, it's just another routine suicide.'

'Except for the question of how he got up there by himself,' Gavin pointed out.

'Yes,' Anna nodded, 'Except for that.'

She gave one final look upward at the dangling rope and pondered for a few seconds. Then she turned briskly back to Gavin.

'OK. I'd better go and speak to the father. Perhaps you could take me and introduce us.'

They made their way back round the rhododendron bushes, under the spreading branches of more fruit trees and out on to a sunny lawn bordered by flower beds. As they approached the house, Anna spotted a hot tub on the wide patio that extended across the back of the house overlooked by large Georgian-style bow windows and a pair of glass doors. Her daughter Jessica had been pestering her to get one for them, but the prices were prohibitive.

'Better go round this way,' Gavin, said, as he led her across the back of the house and down the opposite side from the way they had come in. 'The hall's crawling with kids playing by the front door, and there's a whole gaggle of women in the kitchen who'll all be wanting to know what's going on if we go that way.

Mr Quinn's got a sort of office that he runs his business from built on the side of the house down here.'

They rounded the corner of the house. Ahead of them a two-storey extension to the original house filled the space between the front half of the house and the boundary wall. Facing them were a window and a door, which opened almost as soon as they saw it. Clearly, somebody was expecting them.

'Good afternoon, officer. Can I help you?' "Somebody" turned out to be a striking young woman with a tanned face framed by shiny black hair, cut in what looked like a simple style, but which Anna suspected had cost over a hundred pounds. Her black eyebrows were thick and heavy. And her makeup was subtle – or could it be that her skin and lips were just naturally perfect?

'I'm Constable Hughes and this is Detective Chief Inspector Davenport. We were looking for Mr Quinn. He said we'd find him here.'

'Yes, of course. Come in.' The woman stepped out of the doorway and stood waiting as the police officers went through. Then she followed them inside and closed it behind them. 'Please, go through. It's the door on the right.'

They were in a cramped lobby with doors to right and left and a spiral staircase with open treads ahead of them. Anna did as she was told and tried the right-hand door. It opened into a spacious room with light flooding in through the large window that they had seen from outside. A grey-haired man was sitting at a desk, staring into space, turning an expensive-looking pen over and over in his two hands.

'The police want to speak to you again, Dad.'

At the sound of the woman's voice, he gave a start and came out of his reverie. 'I'm sorry.' He got to his feet and put out his hand towards Anna. 'I was miles away. I'm Patrick Quinn, and this is my daughter, Emma – one of my daughters, that is.' He looked towards Gavin. 'I think you've already met my oldest daughter, Róisín? Emma is the next, and then Bianca is the youngest. Emma is my right hand. She almost runs the business these days. I don't know what I'd do without her.' He broke off suddenly and turned back to Anna. 'I'm sorry. I'm rambling. And you must be busy. Sit down – please – and ask me anything you need to know.'

His American accent reminded Anna of old cop-shows from her childhood. She hoped that he was not expecting the frenetic activity and instant results that seemed to characterise the New York Police Department and the Miami Vice Squad.

'Thank you, sir.' Anna sat down on the chair that stood at a second desk, positioned under the window, and swivelled it round so that she was facing Patrick Quinn. Emma pulled up an upright chair and sat down next to her father, looking attentively towards Anna.

'I'm DCI Anna Davenport. I'm very sorry for your loss, and I appreciate that this is a very difficult time for you, but I need to ask you a few questions, and then I'll need to speak to anyone else who was in the house this afternoon and anyone who might know anything about your son's state of mind recently.'

'He didn't do it,' Quinn said quickly. 'He didn't kill himself. Why would he? There was nothing wrong. It's his birthday! We were supposed to be celebrating. Someone must have got in over the back wall. We've had trouble that way before sometimes. He can't have done it!'

'It's alright, Dad,' Emma intervened the moment that Quinn paused for breath. She put her hand on his and half turned so that she could look him in the eye. 'Inspector Davenport has to ask these questions. She has to consider every possibility, but I'm sure she's keeping an open mind.'

'That's right,' Anna agreed, smiling gratefully towards Emma, who seemed surprisingly calm in the face of her brother's sudden death. 'It's all just routine, but necessary if we're going to find out what ha-.' She broke off as the door burst open and two small children hurtled in. A boy of about six and a girl a year or two younger raced across the carpet and flung themselves at the desk where Quinn was sitting.

'Come and play, Grandad!' the boy shouted.

'Daddy's got the Scalextric up in the hall,' the girl added, 'but he can't find all the cars. I want the pink one!'

'I'm sorry guys.' Emma got up and put an arm round each of the children, turning them round gently, but firmly and marching them back to the still open door. 'Grandad's busy right now. He'll come and play with you later.'

'But I want the pink car!' the girl protested loudly.

'And why can't we go in the garden?' added her brother, remembering an earlier grievance, which his father had temporarily placated with the Scalextric set. 'I want to make a den. You promised I could next time we came!'

'Yes, but that's just not possible at the moment,' Emma told him calmly. 'There's been an accident. Your uncle Rory's been hurt – very badly – that's why the police are here,' she added, inclining her head towards Gavin. 'They're going to find out how it happened, and they can't let anyone in the garden until they've finished what they're doing there. So now, let's all go back and see if we can find that pink car for Poppy, shall we?'

She went with them, pushing them gently out through the door and closing it behind them. Quinn watched them go then turned quickly back to Anna.

'I'm sorry,' he apologised. 'My grandchildren – well, two of them. They don't understand what's going on. I suppose someone's going to have to tell them …,' he tailed off in thought, then appeared to bring himself back to attention with a jerk. 'Sorry, you were saying?'

'I was just explaining that we have to investigate and ask questions, some of which may seem a bit personal, to satisfy ourselves – and the coroner – that we've found out what happened to your son – to Rory.'

'Yes, I see that. I'm sorry if I was a bit … anyway, I'm ready now. Fire away.'

'Well, first or all, I'd like you to take me through exactly what you did this afternoon, before and after you found Rory. You were out when he … when it happened?'

'Yes. I went shopping straight after lunch. Only as far as the big Tesco by the Blackbird Leys roundabout. We needed some more supplies for the party. It's Rory's twenty-first today, and he's just graduated – a first class degree from Nottingham University – and, and … Oh my gosh! Ellie! She'll be here any minute! What …? Somebody will have to …'

'Ellie?' queried Anna.

'Rory's fiancée,' Quinn explained. 'That's the other thing we were celebrating. They were making their engagement official. Her parents are bringing her over at about five. What time is it now?' He stared down at his watch, appearing to have trouble focussing his eyes.

'Don't worry, sir,' Gavin intervened. 'That's a few minutes off yet. If you don't need me, ma'am,' he added, looking towards Anna, 'I'll go back out to the front and keep an eye open for them.'

'Yes,' Anna nodded. 'Go ahead.'

Gavin went out. Anna turned back to Quinn.

'Don't worry. PC Hughes will look after her. He lost his own son a couple of years ago, so he knows how it is when … Anyway, perhaps the best thing would be if we go outside. You look as if you could do with some fresh air, and you can take me through how you found Rory when you got back this afternoon, and what you did then.'

Quinn nodded. He got up and opened the door, holding it for Anna to go through and then hurrying past to open the outer door to let her into the garden. They both stepped out into the sunshine. It was hot, even for July, and Anna wished that her suit were made from a cooler material. She took off her jacket and carried it over her arm as they walked slowly across the lawn towards the orchard at the bottom of the garden.

Quinn pointed at the folding tables, which had been put up on the grass, each with its paper table cloth and a small vase of flowers in the centre.

'We were going to have a picnic out here,' he told Anna. 'We thought the kids could sit on the grass and it wouldn't matter if they made a mess.'

'I'm sorry,' Anna said, imagining how it would be if she came home to find that her son Marcus had killed himself. He was just one year younger than Rory had been, and he too was studying for a law degree. 'It must be very difficult for you,' she went on, knowing how inadequate these words must sound, but feeling compelled to say them anyway, 'especially when you were expecting today to be a celebration.'

'Yes,' Quinn agreed. 'That's just it! Rory had so much to look forward to. He had things all mapped out. He'd got a training place at Thompsett and Buckley-'

'The solicitors on Park End Street?'

'That's right. Do you know them?'

'I've had clients of theirs in for questioning,' Anna smiled back. 'But I'm sorry, I interrupted. You were saying…?'

'And then he and Ellie were going to get married as soon as he qualified. She's starting a Master's degree at Cambridge in September. So, it was all going to fit together nicely. That's why I'm so sure that he couldn't have … He had everything to look forward to!'

'Nevertheless,' Anna said cautiously, 'there's no sign of anyone else having been there – not so far, anyway – and young people often hide their feelings from their parents.'

'Not Rory.' Quinn was adamant. 'He told his mother everything. He was a lot younger than our other children. There was ten years between him and Bianca. We thought she was going to be the last and then Rory came along out of the blue when Martina was forty. In many ways, he was like an only child – a bit spoiled and very, very close to his mother. He would never have put her through this – never!'

'I see,' Anna murmured, realising that further argument would only alienate her witness. 'So, getting back to this afternoon, you came home from the shops. What then?'

'I put the bags down in the kitchen and started putting the stuff away. Róisín helped. She was there making a salad.'

'Róisín?'

'Our eldest daughter. We had four children: Brendan, Róisín, Emma and Bianca – and then Rory. Róisín came over early to help get the food ready. She and Colin – that's her husband – only live in High Wycombe, so …'

'I'll need to speak to them too,' Anna told him. 'But, go on: you put the shopping away, and then what?'

'They said they hadn't seen Rory yet, so I went to find him. I thought he ought to be there, seeing as the party was in his honour.'

'I see,' Anna repeated. 'OK. Carry on. Where did you look for him?'

'I called up the stairs, and then, when he didn't come down, I went up to his room, but he wasn't there. He wasn't anywhere downstairs either – the kids made sure of that! They'd been running all over the place ever since they came.'

'The kids?'

'Róisín and Colin's three little girls. They're into everything. When I got back, they were on the stairs, pretending to be mountaineers.'

'I see. And then …?'

'I went outside. Rory likes it down here.' They had now reached the trees and Quinn gestured at them with a wide sweep of his arm. 'When he was little, he used to climb that plum tree over there. Then one day a branch gave way and he fell and broke his arm. Not that that stopped him! As soon as the plaster came off, he was at it again. He was like a monkey. He could throw up a rope over a branch of that big cherry tree and then just shin up it. I thought he might have come down here to get away from everyone. He's shy sometimes, and he's not much good with young children. He never knows how to talk to them or what sorts of things they like doing.'

'So, if he was feeling depressed or worried about something, this might be where he'd go to think things out?' suggested Anna.

'Yes, I suppose so. But hey! You're not suggesting that proves he-? Rory was *not* suicidal! Someone killed him, and I'm going to make damn sure you find whoever it was!'

'Can you think of anyone who might have wanted to harm him?' Anna asked. 'Had he fallen out with anyone?'

'No. Everyone liked Rory.'

'No ex-girlfriends who resented being dropped?' Anna suggested.

'No. He and Ellie had been going out since they were at school together. He never had any others.'

'Jealous rivals then. Someone who would have liked to have dated Ellie?'

'No.'

'What about money? Did he have any debts?'

'Only his student loan, and we were going to pay that off for him.'

'Then why would anyone-?'

'It must have been a psychopath. Or maybe it was envy – someone who resented us being well-off and living in a big house. We have had that before, you know – people accusing us of exploiting our workers and fleecing our customers, begrudging us what we worked hard to get!'

They rounded the rhododendron and stopped a few yards from where Rory's body still lay, the sunshine making dancing shadows over his face through the leafy canopy overhead.

'He was hanging there,' Quinn went on, pointing up at the dangling rope. 'I thought he might still be alive, so I got the ladder and went up and got him down. I told PC Hughes all about it. He wrote it all down.'

'Yes,' Anna acknowledged, 'but I'd like to hear it from you. I'm sorry. I know it must be distressing, but it all helps me to get a picture of what happened. So, you got the ladder and-'

There was a murmur of voices behind them. Anna turned to see two men in the green uniforms of paramedics appearing from behind the dense foliage of the rhododendron bush.

'He's over here,' she told them. 'But there's nothing you can do for him. The pathologist is on his way, so don't move him.'

One of the men bent down and put his hand on Rory's neck, feeling for a pulse. He looked up and shook his head. 'Been dead an hour or two, I'd say.'

'I don't need your expert opinion to tell me that!' Quinn retorted. 'It's been the best part of two hours since I rang for help. What took you so long?'

'I'm sorry. We're very stretched at the moment.'

'Mr Quinn?' Anna intervened, sensing that he might be in danger of venting his frustration at not having been able to save his son on the ambulance crew. Ninety-five minutes from a 999

23

call to the arrival of an ambulance was poor performance, but it had not made any difference to the outcome in Rory's case. 'You were saying …?'

'Oh! Yes, I'm sorry. Like I said, I put the ladder up against the branch and climbed up and carried him down.'

'On your own?' The paramedic who had examined Rory's body stood up and looked at Quinn. 'That must have been quite a task! He must weigh seventy kilos at least.'

'I trained as a volunteer fireman when I was younger.' Quinn sounded defensive. 'I got him over my shoulder, so I could hold up his weight while I got the rope off him. Then I carried him down.'

'OK.' The paramedic nodded, speaking quietly, trying to defuse the situation which had suddenly become inexplicably tense. 'Well done.'

'I gave him mouth-to-mouth and chest compressions,' Quinn went on, speaking earnestly and fixing Anna with his eye. 'But it was no use. I think I knew I was too late, but I had to try!'

'Yes, of course,' Anna nodded. She turned to the paramedics, debating in her mind whether to let them take the body to the mortuary or to make them wait until after the Scenes of Crime team had seen it in situ. It had already been moved, so it hardly mattered – assuming that Quinn's account could be relied upon. 'I think you two might as well go back and wait outside,' she said at last. 'It could be a while before I can let you move him.'

They nodded towards her and murmured words of sympathy to Quinn, then departed. Anna watched them disappear round the big rhododendron.

'He didn't do it! Why don't you believe me?'

She turned to see Quinn crouching down by his son, his right arm outstretched towards him. She stepped across to him, saying urgently, but in a low voice, 'Don't touch him! You could destroy evidence.'

Quinn jumped back, but continued to point towards Rory's right hand.

'Look at his fingernails! Look how they're broken. Doesn't that tell you that he fought back? And that bruise on his face! And there's blood in his hair! Don't you see? An intruder must have got in and attacked him. And then they strung him up to make it look like suicide.'

He looked hopefully towards Anna, willing her to agree with him.

'That's not for me to say,' she replied in a low voice. 'The pathologist will look at all that.'

'We've had trouble before,' Quinn went on eagerly. 'It's open farmland at the back. We've had boys getting in over the back fence and stealing apples. They broke some panes in the greenhouse once. Maybe Rory found them doing damage and tried to stop them and they turned on him.'

'We'll look into all that, of course,' Anna assured him, 'but I have to say that, at the moment, there's nothing definite to suggest that anyone else was involved.'

'You think he killed himself, don't you? You're not even going to consider-'

'I didn't say that. I said that we'll look into all possibilities. At the moment, we're keeping an open mind and treating your son's death as suspicious. Now, you were telling me about the ladder. Where-?'

'Good afternoon!'

Anna broke off and swung round at the sound of Mike Carson's distinctive voice. She had been too intent on her argument with Quinn to notice the pathologist's approach. He stood there, dressed in a scene of crime costume, accompanied by the two paramedics who had been there earlier.

'They told me I'd find my patient back here.' Nearly forty years in Oxford had failed to eradicate the musical tones of his childhood in county Wexford.

'Yes. Mike – this is Patrick Quinn, the deceased's father. Mr Quinn – Dr Michael Carson, the pathologist who's going to examine your son's body to establish how he died.'

'Well, can I draw your attention to his broken fingernails?' Quinn said at once. 'They're clearly defensive wounds. And that bruise on his face. It looks to me like he's been in a fight. And the blood in his-'

'Thank you, Mr Quinn,' Mike said smoothly, 'I'll bear all those in mind.' He looked round at the leaf-covered area where the body lay, then up at the noose still dangling above them with the ladder propped against the branch next to it.

'Mr Quinn brought him down and gave him life support,' Anna told him, 'but it was too late.'

'I see.' Mike nodded. Then he put down his bag next to the body and knelt to take a closer look.

'Mr Quinn,' Anna said, touching him gently on the arm. 'Would you mind going back indoors now? I'll need to talk to you again but …'

'Yes, of course. I'll be in the office.'

Anna watched him go, waiting until she was confident that he would not overhear their conversation before asking the pathologist, '*could* those broken fingernails be defence wounds, do you think?'

'You're suggesting it may not have been suicide?'

'His father is adamant that it can't be. The boy would never have done such a thing, apparently.'

'That's what the relatives often think.'

'I know, but Patrick Quinn has influence. He's best-buddies with the Justice Secretary and he's been seen dining with various newspaper editors. I have to convince him that I've taken his idea that a third party was involved seriously.'

'Well then, I'd say that the damage to his fingers could be a sign of a struggle with an assailant, but that's not the only possible explanation.' Mike turned back to examining the body, turning it over carefully to study the marks of the rope on the neck.

'He was strangled, presumably?' Anna asked.

'Presumably,' Mike grunted, 'but I can't say for sure. There could be other factors. He peered closely at the young man's face. There is some petechial haemorrhaging, but not as much as you might expect.'

'Does that mean he could have been dead before he was strung up?' asked one of the paramedics.

'At this stage, almost anything is possible,' Mike answered drily.

'But, on balance, would you say it's most likely it was the rope that killed him or something else?' Anna pressed him.

'On balance, I'd say that strangulation is the most likely cause of death, but there could be other explanations – and, yes,' he smiled up at the paramedic, 'he could even have been dead before he was *strung up*, as you put it.'

He stood up and started to peel off the latex gloves that he was wearing. 'You might as well take him away,' he said to the ambulance crew. 'He's already been moved, so there's nothing I can see here that I won't be able to examine better at the mortuary.'

'I'll walk back with you.' Anna accompanied him back through the trees and out on to the lawn. 'So, you do think that his father could be right?' she asked. 'It could be murder, rather than suicide?'

'That's for you and the coroner to decide. All I can say is that, from what I've seen so far, the evidence is consistent either with suicide or with some sort of attack. If it *was* murder though, he didn't put up a lot of resistance.'

'Caught off his guard, maybe?'

'Maybe.'

'Perhaps because it was someone he knew?'

Mike shook his head. 'Not my field. I can only tell you what signs there are on his body. He didn't do much to fight back – or he was overpowered quickly.'

'More than one attacker, perhaps?' Anna suggested.

'Or none,' Mike answered, ending the conversation.

As they approached the house Anna became aware of the sound of voices. A moment later, four figures in crime scene suits emerged from the side passage and strode across the patio. Their leader was a tall, dark-haired woman with brown eyes which contrasted starkly with her pale skin. Anna recognised Ruby Mann, an experienced Scenes of Crime Officer whom she had worked with many times before. She greeted her warmly.

'Hi Ruby. Your victim is through there.' She pointed towards the trees. 'You'd better cordon off the whole of that wooded area. I've tried to establish a single path of approach, but the family had already been back and forth a few times before we got here, so …'

'Not to worry,' Ruby replied briskly. 'I gather it's most likely just another suicide, anyway. I doubt there'd have been much for us to find however well preserved the scene was.'

'Don't let the family hear you saying that,' Anna smiled back grimly. 'His father's convinced it must have been murder. He can't believe his son would take his own life.'

'That's par for the course, isn't it? The parents don't want to believe that their child was suicidal, because it suggests they didn't care for him properly.'

'And there are some anomalies,' Anna went on. 'Possible defence wounds, a question mark over how he could have got himself up there without a ladder-'

'But there was a ladder right there,' Mike protested mildly.

'Which his father brought in order to get him down,' Anna explained. 'He told the first officer on the scene that he had to get it out of the shed. So, how did the lad get up into a tree with no branches within reach?'

'I'll keep a look out for any marks on the bark that might give us a clue,' Ruby promised.

'Thanks. Now I'd better go and talk to the family again. Oh! By the way, the deceased's father is Patrick Quinn.'

'Should that name mean something to me?' asked Ruby.

'Think Quinn's Superstores and Quinn's Hotels.'

'And Quinn's Coach Tours of Historic Britain and Ireland?' Ruby added. 'I get the picture. Successful entrepreneur who's used to getting what he wants.'

'That's right. And he's American, so he may have strange expectations regarding how the authorities work here. Everything's much more in the public gaze over there, and everyone's very litigious.' Anna pulled a wry face and then shrugged her shoulders. 'Anyway, I'd better let you get on. Let me know if you find anything interesting.'

She headed back to the annex containing Quinn's office. The room was empty apart from Emma, who was sitting at a computer scrolling through a spreadsheet of figures. She looked up when Anna entered.

'I'm sorry,' she said, getting to her feet. 'My mother arrived back with my grandmother, and my father had to look after them. They're both very upset, as you can imagine. Would you like me to show you through to them?'

'Yes please. But maybe it'll be better to give them a bit more time before I talk to them. I'll need to have a look at your brother Rory's room. Could you show me?'

'Yes, of course. Follow me.'

Emma led the way through the door that connected the extension to the original house. Anna found herself in a spacious hall. An open door on the left gave her a glimpse of the lounge, its deep-pile carpet bathed in sunshine from the large patio doors overlooking the garden and strewn around with Lego bricks and toy cars. A harassed father was walking round and round holding a crying baby in his arms while in the background two older children were having a loud argument over who should have possession of the TV remote control.

'This way.'

Anna followed Emma to the foot of the stairs, dodging to avoid bumping into a small girl who was standing in front of a full-length mirror with her arms out, twirling round to admire herself in a gauzy pink dress, and stepping carefully over the Scalextric set, which now lay abandoned. Children had such a short attention span at that age!

The staircase was wide with highly polished wooden handrails on either side and deep red carpet held in place by ornamental brass fittings. There were six doors opening off the wide landing. All but one – the family bathroom by the look of it – were closed. Emma strode across to the door furthest to the left.

'This is Rory's room,' she announced, flinging the door wide. 'I'll leave you to have a look round, shall I?'

'Yes please.'

'I'll be in the office when you've finished,' Emma told her, reaching out to close the door on her. 'You'll be able to find your way back, won't you?'

'Yes. I'm sure I will. Oh! And … Would you mind …? It would be really helpful if you could make a list of everyone – your family and anyone else who's been at the house today – with who they are and approximately what time they got here. Could you do that for me?'

'Yes, of course.' Emma smiled. 'It is a bit overwhelming when you see us all together, isn't it? I'll draw up a family tree and a timeline of when everyone arrived. Do you want to know about visitors in the morning too, or just from the last time we saw Rory alive?'

'All day, please – and what time your parents each went out, too. And, if you can think of anything that Rory might have been upset or worried about, you might like to jot that down as well.'

'Right you are! I'll get on with doing that, and you come and find me in the office when you're done here.'

Anna stood in the doorway looking round. The first thing that struck her was how tidy it was – much neater than the bedrooms of either of her own offspring! Despite having reached the final year of his degree, Marcus still seemed incapable of putting away his clothes. He simply stepped out of them at night, leaving them lying where they fell, posing trip hazards for anyone unwary enough to attempt to cross the floor in the dark; and there was always a pile of jeans and tee-shirts, back from the wash, stacked on the desk next to empty lager cans and crisp packets. Jessica was better, but the counter that they had built down the side of her room to serve as desk and dressing table combined was never clear of almost empty bottles of nail varnish and mascara, jumbled up with pens and pencils and her ID badge on a long lanyard.

This room, by contrast, had a place for everything and everything in its place. The desk was clear, apart from a laptop computer with its lid closed, the power cable next to it neatly coiled and fastened with Velcro. The duvet had been smoothed out neatly across the bed. The books on the shelves over the desk had their spines precisely lined up. Was this all a sign of obsessive neatness on the part of the occupant or had he tidied his room that day for a particular purpose – part of a ritual of putting his affairs in order before departing this world? Or perhaps his mother was in the habit of coming in and tidying the room for him? He was a spoiled youngest child, after all.

Anna advanced into the room and closed the door behind her. Then she pulled on a pair of latex gloves before picking up the laptop and power cable and putting them into a plastic evidence bag. Was there anything else worth taking away for examination? She reached her hand to open a drawer in the desk, but before she could pull it out there was a knock at the door and Emma reappeared.

'I'm sorry,' she apologised, 'but Rory's fiancée and her parents are here. My father thought you'd like to speak to them.'

'Yes. Thank you. I'll come down.' Anna went out on to the landing, closing the bedroom door behind her. 'I'll send up a uniformed officer to guard the door of this room. I don't want anyone going in there until we've had a chance to look at it properly. Perhaps you could …?'

'Yes, of course. I'll wait here until your officer comes.'

'Thank you.'

Anna paused at the top of the stairs. She could hear Quinn's voice in the hall recounting in some detail how he had returned home to find his son missing from the house, his search for him and the discovery of his body. Looking over the bannister rail, she saw a young woman seated on a long bench attached to the wall near the front door. On either side of her sat a man in his fifties and a woman who looked younger – her parents, presumably. Quinn was standing on front of them, speaking earnestly as if he felt the need to justify his actions, to make it plain that he had done all he could to save his son.

They might as well hear it from him as from her, she decided, taking out her phone from her pocket. It would most likely help him, and it would give her a chance to summon reinforcements. The family would want them out of the house as soon as possible, but she could not let them go without taking statements from each of them. If Quinn was so sure that this was murder then she had to treat it as such until they could be certain otherwise.

3. DUTY CALLS

'So, the trial starts on Wednesday,' Andy said, leaning across to take another slice of pizza from the box that lay on Esther's lap, 'and Yakubu's arriving on Monday to see the show.'

'Don't you mean, *to see justice done for his son*?' she suggested, picking up the final slice and moving the box on to the grass beside her. 'You could hardly expect him to keep away.'

'No.' Andy sighed. 'But it's going to be like tiptoeing on eggshells for me for the next couple of weeks, with him in Oxford and Mum still adamant that she's having nothing to do with him.'

'Aren't you even a little bit curious to get to know him better? After all, he *is* your father too.'

'I know! And I suppose *curious* is about right. I would quite like to know a bit more about him, but I'm not so sure that getting to know him personally – establishing a relationship – would be … Oh, I don't know! It would feel like I was betraying Mum somehow.'

They were sitting in the shade of a large beech tree in the University Parks, their backs leaning against the trunk. Esther rested her head on Andy's shoulder as she chewed on her pizza wondering how to phrase the argument that she felt compelled to put to him next.

'But …,' Esther hesitated. She knew she had to say something, but she knew also that Andy would not really understand. 'Look,' she began again, speaking earnestly in a low voice, 'don't you think it must be more than *just* coincidence? Honestly! What are the chances of your half-brother coming from Nigeria to study in Oxford and then being killed and then you being the police officer in charge of investigating it? I know you think I'm mad, but I'm sure it's all part of God's plan. He's brought your father back into your life for a purpose.'

'By arranging for his son to be killed? I'm not sure I like the sound of your God if that's how he goes on.'

'No, I don't mean that.' Esther thought for a few moments. 'God didn't *want* Jibrilu to be killed, but he was able to use those circumstances as a way of bringing you and your father together – bringing good out of evil. I know you don't believe in that sort of thing, but I've seen it so many times!'

'I don't know.' Andy leaned back and took another bite of his pizza. 'Sometimes I wish I believed the way you do. I'd like to think God was up there, pulling the strings, making everything come out OK in the end. But then, I think about all the senseless violence I see around me in my job, and all the ordinary people who have their homes broken into or their life-savings swindled out of them or …' He sighed, 'and what about Yakubu? His whole family gets killed in a house fire – all except his youngest son – and then *he* comes over here and has an argument in the street with a couple of racist thugs and gets knifed to death! Where was God in all that?'

'I don't know about the house fire,' Esther said cautiously, 'but *I* think that God gave you the abilities you need to be a detective and he guided you to become a police officer and saw to it that you were sent out to investigate when Jibrilu was killed. And he gave all the other people – the forensic scientists and everyone – the skills to find out who was responsible, so that his killers *would* be brought to trial and Yakubu *would* get to see justice done for his son.'

Andy chewed his pizza in silence. Esther did the same, fearing that she had overstepped the mark and was in danger of alienating him.

'What are you going to do, then?' she asked at last, unable to stand the strain of waiting for him respond. 'Surely you and Yakubu are bound to meet. Won't you be giving evidence at the trial?'

'No,' Andy mumbled as he swallowed his last mouthful. 'They'll keep me well away. Anna's going to give the police evidence – and maybe Gavin Hughes, because he was the first officer on the scene. They won't want to draw attention to me having been involved. And anyway, I wasn't – not after we knew about my conflict of interest.'

'Which shouldn't matter, surely? You could hardly be expected to recognise a brother that you didn't even know existed, could you?'

'No, but defence counsels are experts at muddying the waters and confusing jurors' minds. You can bet they'd manage to convey the impression that I must have known and concealed the fact so that I could stay on the case.'

'But even so, what difference would it have made anyway?' Esther argued. 'It's the evidence that counts.'

'But I helped to collect the evidence. Maybe I only followed up on leads that pointed towards the defendants' guilt. Maybe I pressed witnesses to identify them when they weren't really sure. Maybe-'

'But even if you had known that you were investigating your own brother's murder, why would you want to convict the wrong person?'

Andy shrugged and then hugged Esther closer. 'Just because I wanted someone to pay? Because, once I had a suspect, I didn't want to believe I'd got it wrong? Because I needed *closure* above all else? Take your pick! But, getting back to Yakubu, I've arranged to collect him from Heathrow. It seemed simpler than allowing him to arrange a pick-up and then being on the loose in Oxford. I don't trust him not to roll up at our house – or at my grandparents' house – expecting to see Mum.'

'So, you're going to deliver him to his hotel and tell him to keep away from you both?' Esther asked dubiously.

'Not quite. For a start, he insisted on booking his own accommodation. He's gone for an Airbnb flat down Abingdon Road. I suppose at least it's right the opposite side of Oxford from us, but I can't help having a funny feeling that he's up to something.'

'What sort of thing?'

'A self-contained flat, with access direct from the street? No hotel reception watching who he takes up to his room? Maybe he's hoping to get Mum to visit him there – maybe even to stay overnight. I don't know! I'm just uneasy, that's all. She says he's devious.'

'And *I* say you're becoming paranoid,' Esther replied firmly. 'He's probably just saving money by going self-catering.'

'I suppose you're right,' Andy admitted with another sigh. 'Yes, I'm sure you are. After all, Mum only has to say *no*, which I know she would.'

'So, there you go then!' Esther wiped her hands on a paper napkin and reached into her bag for the fruit that she had brought for their dessert. 'Now, would you like an apple or a banana? Or there's enough for you to have both, if you like.'

Andy leaned closer to see inside the bag and selected a shiny green apple. Esther rested her back against the tree trunk as she began unzipping a banana.

'What does your Mum think about it all?'

'I haven't told her yet,' Andy admitted. 'I've been waiting for the right time, but it doesn't seem to have happened yet. I really must get round to breaking it to her this weekend or else the first she knows about it will be reports on the news. Yakubu says that he's had someone from the BBC World Service asking him for an interview already, so it wouldn't surprise me if there were cameras at the airport filming his arrival.'

'And filming you escorting him to Oxford,' Esther nodded.

'She won't be pleased that I'm meeting him,' Andy continued. 'She thinks we ought to have nothing to do with him. I can see her point of view. He did behave very badly towards her, but … Well, you would have thought she might be a bit *curious* as you put it about how he's turned out after all these years too.'

'I'm not a psychologist,' Esther murmured, putting her arm around his shoulders, and holding him close, 'but I'd say she's afraid of losing you. You're always saying how she's devoted her whole life to bringing you up – working full time, no boyfriends, no social life. And now, along comes your father, who's deserted you both before you were even born, expecting to have a part in you. I don't blame her. If you were mine, I wouldn't want to share you either!'

Andy opened his mouth to reply, then stopped short at the sound of his phone. He fished it out of his pocket and gazed down at the screen. 'I'd better get this,' he apologised. 'It's Anna.'

'On your day off?'

Andy scrambled to his feet, swiping the screen to answer the call as he did so. 'Anna?'

'Sorry, Andy, I know you're off duty, but I could do with you at a suspicious death at a house down Kiln Lane. It's most likely just a suicide, but the family are determined that there must have been foul play and I don't have anyone else I can rely on to deal with them sensitively.'

'What about Alice Ray?' Andy asked, naming Anna's trusty detective constable. 'She's always good with families.'

'She's out dealing with a suspected arson, and Williams is still signed off after his set-to with that rottweiler last week, so my team is distinctly depleted. We've been a sergeant down ever since Monica Philipson jumped ship, remember. Look Andy, I really am sorry,' she went on, sensing the inspector's reluctance to answer the summons. 'I wouldn't ask if I could think of anyone else. I was going to try DCI Khan, but he's tied up with that spate of attacks on Asian taxi-drivers, and DI Andrews is on holiday in Italy, so …'

'OK. Don't worry, I'll be right over. It'll take me about half an hour, I'm afraid. I'm in the city centre and I've only got my bike for transport.'

'Not to worry. I can hold the fort until you get here. See you in a bit … and … thanks, Andy.'

He slipped the phone back into his pocket and turned back to Esther, who had finished her banana and was busily gathering up the remains of their picnic and putting things back into her bag. She smiled up at him.

'I'll walk back to the bikes with you.'

'I'm sorry,' Andy began.

'Yes. I know.' Esther continued to smile. 'But you've got to go. I know the score. It's the same with my dad. He's never really off-duty either.' Esther's father was a vicar in the Anglican Church of Nigeria.

'I'm still sorry,' Andy repeated. 'I'd rather stay with you.'

'Yes. And I'd rather you stayed, but I can wait. We could meet up again tomorrow maybe? Now, do you think you could carry the pizza box – just as far as the bin? I've got everything else.'

'Yes.' Andy brightened up. 'Tomorrow afternoon. I'll give you a ring when I've finished with this suspected suicide in Headington.'

'Suicide? That's sad,' Esther said softly as they began their short walk back to the railings where they had padlocked their bikes. 'Who was it? I don't mean names,' she added hastily, 'I mean, were they young or old, a man or a woman and why did they do it?'

'I don't know yet. Anna didn't say. It's a male and it sounds as if he must have done it at home. She mentioned a family, who don't accept that he *did* do it himself, which is why she wants reinforcements. Apparently, they're convinced that it must be murder. That's all I know, and I shouldn't really have told you even that much, so ...'

'Yes, I know. I won't breathe a word to anyone.'

Andy tossed the empty pizza box into a litter bin as they passed. His hands now being free, he reached out his arm and put is round Esher's shoulder. She responded by slipping hers around his waist as they continued along the gravel path. Life had been good, he reflected, during the six months since she returned from Nigeria after the Christmas holiday. If only his father's imminent return did not disrupt it too much ...

***

'I really am sorry to call you out on your rest day,' Anna repeated as she led Andy down the side of the house and into the back garden. 'I wouldn't have done it if I could have thought of anyone else that I could trust to deal with this, and I may not be able to do much after this weekend, because of the Jibrilu Danjuma murder case that's coming up next week.'

'If it's suicide, the police work'll be done and dusted before Wednesday, won't it?'

'*If* being the operative word,' Anna replied, holding back a bramble which dangled down from one of the trees along the route to where Rory's body had been found. 'And *if* we can convince his father of that too. Did I tell you that he's the owner and CEO of Quinn Group? He owns supermarkets and hotels all across Britain and Ireland, and he has friends in high places – including in the press. So, we don't pooh-pooh his theory that a homicidal maniac must have climbed over the back fence or lecture him on the prevalence of suicide among young men.'

'OK,' Andy nodded his understanding. 'I get the picture. Don't worry, discretion is my middle name.'

'Which is another reason that I wanted you here to help me interview the family. The last thing we want is to alienate any of them.'

'Anna!' Crime Scene Manager, Ruby Mann, intercepted them as they emerged from the rhododendron jungle. 'Just the person I was looking for! I've got a couple of things to show you.'

She held up two evidence bags, one in each hand. Anna and Andy bent forward to inspect their contents.

'We found them hidden in the leaves just a few feet away from where he was hanging,' Ruby told them. 'They're surprisingly clean and dry, given their situation, so I'd say they'd not been there long.'

'Temazepam,' Anna read out from the label on a small cardboard box. 'That's a sleeping drug, isn't it? Prescription only?'

'Yes,' Ruby confirmed. She turned the bag round to reveal a label stuck on the back of the packet. 'Prescribed to Rory Quinn back in May. It contained 28 tablets – that's four weeks' supply, which is usually the maximum because it can be addictive if you take it for too long. Both blister packs are empty.'

'OK.' Anna turned to look at the other bag. 'And whisky,' she murmured, studying the empty bottle. 'Coupled with the tablets, this'd make a pretty deadly cocktail!'

'That's what I thought,' Ruby smiled back. 'If you took the lot all at once, you wouldn't need to hang yourself too!'

'OK. Get this little lot off to the lab and tested for fingerprints. We'll need to check them against the dead man's and members of his family – which may be trickier. They seem to want it to be murder rather than suicide, but they won't like the idea that they might be under suspicion themselves.'

'Do any of them have a motive?' asked Andy.

'Not that we know of – yet!' Anna answered, 'but if someone did kill him, my money would be on someone he knew, rather than a random intruder.'

They advanced towards the spot where the rope still hung ominously from the branch, carefully keeping to the single path which Ruby had marked out for the forensics team to use, to avoid trampling over evidence that might be hidden amongst the leaf litter.

'So, he climbed the ladder, tied the rope over the branch, put the loop round his neck and jumped?' Andy suggested, gazing up at the dangling noose.

'Presumably,' Anna agreed, 'except that his father told Gavin Hughes that he had to get the ladder out of a shed to get him down. That, and some marks on his fingers that could be the signs of a struggle, are the only things that suggest that someone else could have been involved.'

'But, if you were staging a murder to look like suicide, why move the ladder?'

'I know!' Anna shook her head. 'It doesn't make sense, does it? But Rory Quinn definitely *couldn't* have put it away, so if he killed himself, he must have got up there without using it.'

Andy walked slowly round the tree, looking for footholds on the trunk or branches within reach. 'There's no way I could get up there without help.'

'Gavin thought he could have thrown a rope over the branch and used that to haul himself up.'

'Mmm,' Andy sounded sceptical. 'I suppose it's possible, but I don't think I could do it.'

'Do you think you two could stop traipsing all over our crime scene?'

Anna looked round and recognised forensic photographer, Janet Kingman. 'Sorry! We were just trying to work out how he got up there.'

'I'd have thought that was obvious.' Janet looked towards the ladder.

'Except that, apparently the ladder wasn't there when he was found, so ...'

'Ah! I see your problem.' She paused for a moment, then shrugged. 'Oh well! That's your department. Now, if you wouldn't mind ...?'

Andy and Anna made their way back to the house.

'What else do we know?' asked Andy. 'Cause of death *was* hanging, presumably?'

'Mike, of course, wouldn't commit to anything,' Anna smiled back. 'And, of course, he didn't know about the sleeping tablets. I'd better give him a ring and ask him to be sure to test for them in his blood. I'd've thought that, if he did take them shortly before he died, it would be another indication that it *was* suicide, but there was no suicide note on his person and I've had a quick look in his room without finding one there either. We've got his laptop and mobile phone, so let's hope there's something on them that'll help us know what was going on in his head. Actually,' she added, 'I'd quite like you to have a look at his room. It all seems a bit odd to me, but you probably know more about what to expect a young man's room to look like.'

'OK. But I'm not so sure that I'll have any better idea than you do."

Emma was ready for them when they got to her office, with a diagram of her family and a list of arrivals and departures at the house throughout the day, complete with names, addresses and contact details. Anna thanked her warmly and congratulated her on her efficiency. Then she led Andy upstairs to where PC Ben Timpson stood, looking rather bored, in front of Rory's bedroom door.

He opened it for them and they stepped through. Andy gazed round at the rows of law books ranged neatly on shelves next to the desk. There were several ring-binders there too, lecture notes he assumed. He turned to see Anna closing the door behind her.

She sat down on the bed and waved her hand to indicate that he should join her. Together, they studied the pieces of paper that Emma had given them.

'OK,' Andy said eventually, 'I think I've got it. The victim's parents are Patrick and Martina Quinn. They have – or had – five kids: Brendan, Róisín, Emma, Bianca and Rory. Brendan is married to Stacey, and they have two kids, a boy and a girl.'

'Theo and Poppy,' Anna added. 'I've met them.'

'Róisín is married to Colin Mills, and they have three little girls. I guess that was one of them we saw in the hall, admiring herself in the mirror.'

'That'd be Layla, the middle one,' I should think.

'Emma isn't married and still lives at home,' Andy went on.

'According to her father, she's his right-hand woman and runs the business with him,' Anna told him. 'She has a flat above the office, so not quite still living at home.'

'Bianca is married to a *Mohammed Dutta*. I wonder how that went down with her parents. I've heard that Patrick Quinn is a strong Catholic. And they also have two children, a boy and a girl.'

'Rory's the youngest by a long way,' Anna commented. 'I rather get the impression that, as a consequence, he was their mother's favourite and a bit spoiled. He'd just finished a Law degree and was about to start solicitor training with our old friends Thompsett and Buckley.'

'The guys who specialise in defending the indefensible?'

'Well, somebody has to do it,' Anna grinned back. 'Everyone is entitled to legal representation, however guilty and recidivist they may be. Anyway, Rory was all set up to work for them, and about to become officially engaged to his childhood sweetheart, Ellie Unwin. It says here that she's a Cambridge graduate and about to start another degree there, which will finish at about the same time as Rory would have completed his legal training.'

'So, he had his life all planned out,' Andy commented.

'Or maybe he'd had it all planned out for him. To my mind, it all sounds a bit too good to be true. What if he didn't really want any of that at all?'

'He had dreams of running away to the circus and shacking up with a trapeze artist, you mean?'

'Something like that. All his siblings are high flyers with degrees from prestigious universities and either good jobs or perfect families or both. He could well have felt under pressure to conform to family expectations.'

'Now, what was it about this room that you thought was strange,' Andy asked, staring round. 'It all looks pretty normal to me, apart from those murals over the bed and along that wall. D'you think he did them himself?'

Anna looked at the walls. Her colleague was right, those colourful scenes painted directly on to the plaster were unusual. Most young people covered their walls with posters of TV stars or music bands – or else campaign posters for whatever cause they happened to be supporting that week!

'If he did, he must be a talented artist,' she commented. 'I wonder why nobody mentioned it. But what I meant about the room being odd was how tidy it all is – too tidy. My son's room always looks as if a tornado has just hit it. This room hardly looks lived in at all.'

'He hadn't been back from uni for long,' Andy pointed out. 'And not all young men like living in a tip!'

There was a knock on the door and Emma appeared, carrying a tray with two bone china mugs, a sugar basin, and a plate of biscuits on it. 'I've got Mamma and Bianca making tea for everyone,' she announced. 'They needed something to do to take their minds off things. I'll put this down here for you,' she went on crossing the room and placing the tray on the desk, 'and then leave you to get on. If you want anything, I'll be in the kitchen.'

'Thank you. I could do with that,' Anna said, picking up one of the mugs, gratefully. 'But, before you go, could you tell us about those?' She pointed at the murals.

'They're good, aren't they? Rory painted them himself. He used to be very good at art. I think he toyed with the idea of doing it professionally, but law is a more secure way of making a living, isn't it?'

Something in the way that Emma said this prompted Anna to ask, 'and who decided that – Rory or your parents?'

'A bit of both, I think, 'Emma shrugged. 'Rory didn't ask my advice.'

'And if he had,' asked Andy, 'what would you have said?'

'Probably that he could do his law degree and still carry on with the paintings and books in his spare time.'

'Books?' queried Anna.

'He drew cartoons,' Emma explained, 'and made them into stories – allegorical ones about climate change and pollution and that sort of thing.' She pointed across the room at the largest of the paintings. It filled the entire wall above the bed. 'See that dragon? It represents global warming. Now have a closer look.'

Anna and Andy went over and peered at the mythical beast. From a distance it had appeared to be simply a colourful monster, resplendent in a scaly coat of red and gold, breathing fiery flames from its fearsome mouth. But on closer inspection, they recognised its face as a caricature of President Trump. The golden scales along its curving spine were pound coins – thousands of them – and all over its body were images of discarded plastic bags, oil rigs, coal-burning power stations, cars and lorries with exhaust fumes billowing from them, and factories with smoking chimneys and ominous waste discharging into rivers. The spikes on its tail turned out to be the heads of various presidents and prime ministers: Boris Johnson, Angela Merkel, Vladimir Putin, Xi Jinping, and several faces that Anna did not recognise. The message was clear: they were all part of the tail of the evil American dragon of climate change denial.

'He's invented his own fantasy world,' Emma told them. 'It's being destroyed by a dragon that keeps breathing out fire and heating everything up. And the animals and birds are trying to fight back, but the dragon is stronger than they are.'

'So, he was an activist?' asked Andy.

'In a sort of behind-the-scenes kind of way,' Emma admitted. 'He didn't go on demonstrations or glue himself to motorways or throw eggs at politicians. It was all just through his cartoons. I think he got some of them published, but I couldn't tell you exactly where. Anyway, if that's all, I'll leave you to get on.'

Anna waited until Emma had left the room and then turned to Andy. 'These sorts of things could make enemies,' she said, 'especially if he posted them on social media.'

'Mmm,' Andy agreed. 'I can't see Trump supporters being exactly thrilled by his depiction of their hero as a fire breathing dragon.'

'Perhaps worse for Boris's followers,' Anna replied. 'He's just part of the tail, following mindlessly along in Trump's wake. Right! That's a job for us to do: scour social media for any signs of death threats or any other sort of trolling. They could be real and indicate that his dad's right and he was killed by an outsider, or they could have tipped him over into suicide.'

'Mmm. Jenny Moorhouse would be good at that. I assume it can wait until Monday?' Andy had wandered over to the desk and was going systematically through the drawers. 'There are lots more drawings in here.'

'Bag them all up and we'll take them away. I want to get an expert in radicalisation to have a look at it — and at his social media activity. I don't know much about environmental activism, but presumably you could be sufficiently fanatical to be a danger to society.'

'Or to attract attention from people who *think* you are,' Andy nodded. 'I'll take some photos of these murals too. For all we know, there could be some hidden message coded into them.'

Anna looked at her watch. 'OK, I think we're done in here. We'd better get on with interviewing everyone so that we can let them go home. Do you think you could take the fiancée while I talk to Rory's Mum?'

By the time they had taken brief statements from everyone and done more in-depth interviews with Ellie, Martina and Emma, Andy was feeling both tired and hungry. His pizza in the park felt like a distant memory. He stood waiting while Anna thanked them all for their patience and for agreeing to have their fingerprints taken for elimination purposes. She had just told them that they were free to go and turned round to speak to him when his phone rang.

It was his mother.

'What happened to you?' she demanded. 'I've just had Nana on the phone saying you never turned up to help them get those things down out of the loft. Where were you?'

'Oh! I'm sorry, Mum. I just forgot. I was called out to a suspicious death and I-'

'But you're off duty this weekend!'

'I know, but we're two officers down at the moment and there wasn't anyone else. But I should have rung Nana and Gramps to let them know.'

'You know they need the cot and high chair down before Fiona comes on Monday,' Amanda Lepage was not to be mollified. 'They were banking on you doing it today.'

'I'll go round as soon as we've finished here,' Andy promised. 'I think we're nearly done. We've just got to-'

'No,' his mother cut him off. 'I've promised you'll do it tomorrow. We're both invited to Sunday lunch. I said we'd be there at about twelve fifteen – after they'll have got back from church – and then you'll go up in the loft for them straight after we've eaten.'

'OK. Thanks. That sounds great. I really am sorry.'

'Just make sure you don't get called out again tomorrow. It must be possible to tell them you have prior commitments.'

'Don't worry. I'll be there.'

'Oh! And we'll need to take the car. The drive band has broken on Nana's sewing machine and she's in the middle of running up some new curtains for the room where the baby's going to be sleeping. I told her we'd lend her mine.'

'That's fine. I won't let you down.'

Andy ended the call and looked apologetically towards Anna who smiled back. 'Put the blame on me, if you like. I shouldn't have called you on your weekend off. But I am glad you came. And not just because Patrick Quinn's a powerful man with connections, who could make trouble for us if we cock up. If it was my son hanging from that branch, I'd want to know why too!'

'Even if it was obviously suicide?'

'Especially, if it was suicide.' Anna shook her head sadly. 'OK, Andy, you'd better get off home and patch things up with your mum. I won't bother you tomorrow, but if you could manage to get your notes of those interviews written up in time for a team meeting at eight on Monday, I'd really appreciate it. I'm just going to have another word with Emma, and then I'll call it a day too.'

Andy rode his bike back along Kiln Lane towards the ring road. His home lay just beyond, in Headington Quarry. He passed Lewis Close, named after the famous author of *The Lion the Witch and the Wardrobe* who had live there, and the Risinghurst Community Centre. Then, a few yards further on he spotted a familiar figure on the pavement. It was his old boss, DCI Jonah Porter, moving briskly in his electric wheelchair.

Andy slowed to a standstill and waited with one foot on the kerb until Jonah came alongside him.

'Hello! How're you doing?'

'Andy! What brings you to this neck of the woods?'

'I've been visiting a potential crime scene - a suspicious death.'

'Oh?' Jonah's eyes lit up at the prospect of some excitement in his neighbourhood. 'Tell me more.'

'There isn't a lot to it,' Andy shrugged, wondering if he should have been more circumspect. Jonah was supposedly retired from the police now, but he had never settled into a life of leisure and took every opportunity to get involved in any investigation that interested him. 'Just another suicide – all routine stuff.'

'*Just* suicide!' Andy felt Jonah's icy tone like a body-blow. 'It's never *just* suicide – not for the victim – or their family!'

'No, of course not. I didn't intend to – I only meant, there isn't anything much to investigate. Typical scenario: young male, feeling under pressure to perform, maybe a bit of a drink problem. Like I said, all just routine.'

'The day you start seeing the death of a young man as "just routine" is the day you ought to start thinking about changing careers,' Jonah observed gravely.

'Look, I'm sorry,' Andy protested with rising frustration. 'I put it badly. I'm tired and I've just had my mum on the phone tearing me off a strip for not helping my Nan with something I promised to do this afternoon and I just want to go home and try to make peace with her, and now you …. Yes, I *know* it's a tragedy for the family. I've been tiptoeing round them all on eggshells all evening trying to avoid upsetting them with questions that just have to be asked. But you can't blame me if I'm just the tiniest bit resentful of being called in on my weekend off to investigate a death that almost certainly isn't a crime just because the victim's father is a big noise with connections and can't believe he wanted to kill himself!'

Andy mounted his bicycle again and put his foot on the raised pedal, ready to start off again.

'Goodbye, sir! Enjoy the rest of your weekend.'

'Andy! Wait!' He heard Jonah calling after him, but didn't turn his head or slow down. He was stung by the criticism, all the more so because he knew that it was not totally unjustified. But it was only the sort of thing that his police colleagues said all the time. You couldn't afford to get emotionally involved in every case. If you did, you'd never survive in the job. And he'd behaved impeccably in front of the family – as Jonah knew full well he would have done! What right had he to speak to him as if he were still his sergeant – or more like some newly-qualified constable? It was way out of order!

***

Meanwhile, Anna was thumbing her notes, preparing for her final interview with Emma Quinn. She glanced down at her watch. Was that the time? She had better let Philip know that she would be later home than she had told him to expect. When she took out her phone to text him, she was greeted with a series of messages demanding, with increasing impatience, to know where she was and why she was not responding.

Sighing, she sent a brief note apologising for not replying before and promising to be home within the next hour or so. Phil must have been waiting for her response, because before she could put the phone away, he had already sent another text accusing her of caring more for her job than for him.

Anna angrily composed a reply pointing out that her job was a whole lot easier than living with someone who had plotted behind her back to take the whole family off to live in Devon, and that if he couldn't cope with her being late home, perhaps he'd better go back there and live with his mother. For several seconds, she stood there, with her finger poised to press *send*. Then, sighing, she deleted the words and put the phone back in her pocket. She would deal with Philip later.

The interview with Emma was short and straightforward, mainly confirming information that she had been given by other members of the family. Anna thanked her witness again for her time and patience and handed her a business card.

'If you want to speak to me about anything or if you think of anything that might help us with finding out exactly what happened to your brother, you can ring this number any time. If you don't get through to me, there'll be a member of my team there who can help.'

'Thank you.' Emma took the card and put it in the pocket of her well-tailored jacket.

'If your father's free, I'll just let him know I'm going.'

'Of course.'

Emma led the way to the lounge, where Patrick was sitting drinking tea with Martina and Róisín while three small girls sat or lay on the floor watching a cartoon on a large television screen. Anna bade them all goodbye, repeating her condolences at their loss in words that had begun to sound very hollow after so much use, and then left, going out through the front door, past the uniformed constable at the garden gate and into the road outside.

She took out her phone as she approached her car and found yet more texts from her husband expressing his increasing frustration at her continued absence and lack of adequate response, and reminding her that they were supposed to be going out together that evening. Bother! She had forgotten they'd got tickets for the Playhouse. No wonder Phil was getting agitated. She was about to ring him to apologise and assure him that she was on her way now and they would just make it in time, when yet another angry text came through. He just couldn't let it rest for a moment, could he?

Fighting down the temptation to let rip, she sent off a brief reply, merely stating her expected time of arrival. The trouble with Phil was that he wanted everything planned out; he couldn't cope with the uncertainty that was inevitable in a job like hers. It wouldn't be the end of the world if they arrived a few minutes late for the play, for goodness sake! What was it they were going to, anyway? She couldn't remember. It must have been Philip's choice. Probably some highbrow stuff that she wouldn't even understand.

She drummed her fingers on the steering wheel as she waited for the lights to change to allow her out on to the ring road. On the face of it, this was a straightforward case of a young man overwhelmed by anxiety for his future falling into a state of depression in which the easiest way out was to end it all; but was that just too simple? In the absence of a suicide note, they couldn't afford to rule out foul play – especially when his father was so convinced that his son had been murdered. He would never forgive them if they failed to investigate thoroughly and then evidence to that effect turned up later. And there was the question of who could have moved that ladder …

She pulled out into the stream of traffic, accelerating to pass a lorry carrying bricks and giant bags of sand. If he *was* killed, who could have done it? Whatever his father might say, there was no sign of intruders. And, if the sleeping pills and alcohol were implicated in any way, it was far more likely to have been a family member or a friend who could have persuaded him to take them than a random stranger.

But then, what motive had any of them for killing him? Jealousy, perhaps, because he was their parents' favourite? But all his siblings were grown up with families and careers of their own, why would this matter to them now? Unless it was something to do with inheritance. How had Patrick Quinn distributed his vast wealth in his will? And was his wealth as vast as it seemed? If the business was in fact on the brink of going under, could Patrick – or indeed Emma – be hoping to cash in on any insurance that there might be on Rory's life?

No! She was getting into the realms of fantasy now. Anna sighed as she backed the car into the drive. She was too tired to think straight. Better to try to forget the case until the morning when she would have Andy and the rest of the team to bounce ideas off.

By the time that she had got out of the car, Philip was there on the doorstep waiting for her. He already had his coat on ready to go out. He held out a small rectangular package.

'You'd better eat these in the car. I assume you haven't had dinner? I cooked a roast, but at least that was OK to make sandwiches out of.'

'I'm sorry Phil. I didn't realise you'd gone to so much trouble.' Anna stood gazing down guiltily at the rounds of brown bread in their cling film wrapping. 'And I did genuinely forget about the play. I'm sorry,' she repeated. 'I really am.'

'Well, never mind,' her husband grunted. 'Just give me the keys and get in. If we get off now, we might just make it before the first act's over.'

Anna chewed her sandwiches in silence as Philip drove through the busy streets towards the city centre. She felt bad about forgetting that it was their wedding anniversary and that they had planned an evening out at the playhouse to celebrate. Not that they had all that much to celebrate! Philip's return after his three-year absence had been very much a mixed blessing as far as she was concerned. Yes, it was nice to have another adult to share the child-care responsibilities; but it had rather spoilt her close relationship with their daughter Jessica, who made no secret of her hostility towards her father.

'Look, Anna,' she glanced up and saw Phil's knuckles turning white as he gripped the wheel fiercely, 'do you want to try to save our marriage or not?'

Anna hesitated, trying to think of a suitable response to this outburst.

'Oh!' Philip went on. 'I see.'

'No, you don't!' Anna protested. 'Of course, I'd like things to go back to how they were before-.' She stopped. She had been about to say, 'before you ran out on us,' but realised in time that this was hardly going to help to pacify Philip, who had clearly been brooding on her failures for several hours. 'It's just that it's complicated.'

'It seems simple enough to me,' Philip retorted. 'It's just how we agreed it was going to be twenty-one years ago: I work from home and look after the kids so that you can carry on with your job. I'm keeping my part of the bargain, but you don't seem interested in anything except your work.'

'That's not fair! I took time off to take Donna to her hospital appointment last week. I went with you to her parents' evening last term. I picked up Marcus from the station the other day. I-'

'But when do you ever do anything with *me*?' Philip interrupted. 'You're always very happy to demonstrate how well you can manage to look after the kids without me, but you never seem to want to be with *me* or to do anything for *me*! I'm just a useful domestic servant to have around when you're too busy with your precious job to look after your family and Jess isn't available to step in.'

'Thus speaks the man who happily ran off back to his mother to get away from me and the kids,' Anna muttered just loud enough that she could be confident that Philip would hear while pretending to herself it was merely a private observation.

'That's right! Throw that back in my face, the way you always do! I've told you a thousand times, I wanted us *all* to move down there together. The kids would've loved it if we'd all gone.'

'Maybe if you had had the decency to consult us first, instead of making all the arrangements and expecting us to just jump when you said.'

'I would've done if you'd ever been there to consult, but you were always too busy working or too tired to talk or–'

'OK, Phil,' Anna cut in, 'you've made your point. I'm sorry about this evening. I should have remembered about the play and our anniversary, and I should have let you know sooner that I'd be late. And I will try to make things work between us. But I've just been talking to a father who came home this afternoon and found his son dead in their garden, and that isn't something you can just rush away from. They were supposed to be having a party this evening, not giving statements to the police.'

She crumpled up the cling film and tossed it into the pocket on the inside of the car door.

'Now, let's stop arguing and try to enjoy our romantic evening out together, shall we?'

4. DAY OF REST?

Father Damien Rowland, parish priest of St Cyprian's Roman Catholic church, was up early as usual. He came into the sanctuary through the connecting passageway from the presbytery and made his personal devotions in front of the blessed sacrament before walking briskly down the aisle to the back of the church to unlock the door in readiness for the early mass.

To his surprise, when he threw open the double outer doors of the porch there was already someone waiting to be let in, although the service was not due to start for forty minutes.

'Father! Have you heard the news?' It was Deirdre Carr, a devout widow and a stalwart of St Cyprian's.

'I don't know. What news would that be?'

'About poor Martina Quinn's youngest. It was his birthday yesterday but, when the party was just about to start, they went to look for him and found him hanging there from one of the trees in their garden. Did they not call you to give him the last rites?'

'No.' Damien shook his head. 'I've not heard anything about it. Are you sure you've got this right? You know how things can get blown out of proportion when gossip starts.'

'Now, Father, you know I wouldn't be telling you anything unless I was sure of my facts,' Deirdre chided him gently. 'Martina rang me herself last night. She's on the coffee rota this morning, but she doesn't feel up to it and she was hoping I'd stand in for her. She told me Rory must have gone down there and done it while she was off collecting her mother from London for the party.'

'I see.' Damien thought for a moment and then stepped back, gesturing to Deirdre to follow him. 'You'd better come through to the vestry.'

They walked together up the aisle, pausing to genuflect before the altar on their way to the small door at the side of the sanctuary that led to the vestries. Damien cleared a pile of tattered hymn books off the single chair in the small room and signalled to Dierdre to sit down, while he perched on a small table strewn with candle-ends and photocopied notice sheets.

Deirdre sat down with her capacious black leather handbag on her lap. She opened it and took out a jam-jar.

'I don't think they want visitors,' she told Damien, 'but I'm sure *you'll* be welcome. So, I wondered if you could give them this. It's some of my home-made lemon curd. I made it yesterday. I've got some for the church stall too. It isn't much, but I thought ... well it shows that we're thinking of them, doesn't it?'

'Indeed it does,' Damien agreed, taking the jar and putting it down on the table next to his breviary. Deirdre's answer to every eventuality, was generous helpings of whatever culinary delights she had most recently produced. 'Thank you for telling me about this. I'll pay them a call this afternoon.'

'And could this mass be for the rest of the poor lad's soul?' Deirdre asked. 'It says on the notice board "Parishioners intentions" and that would be mine.'

'Of course. This mass will be for ....' The priest hesitated, trying to remember the name.

'Rory,' Deirdre prompted. 'He's just back from college – Nottingham university, I think it was.'

'Yes, of course, Rory! I remember him well. He was one of the first kids that I prepared for communion. A very bright spark, but easily put down – not a lot of confidence. As I said, this morning's early mass will be for Rory and his family. And I'll see that Martina gets your lemon curd. Now, I must prepare the altar and get robed up for mass or we'll be late starting.'

'Of course, Father.' Deirdre got up and walked purposefully back out into the church, satisfied that she had done her duty as a Catholic and as a friend of the bereaved family.

Damien pondered on Deirdre's news as he wriggled into his alb, shaking it down over his shoulders and smoothing it out over his cassock. The death by suicide of a child was devastating for any parent, and Martina was not the most robust of women mentally. He remembered Rory clearly now. A rather shy boy, but determined, in a rather diffident sort of way, always trying to match up to the achievements of his siblings. He'd been very disappointed not to have got in to Cambridge, but that could have been more to do with his girlfriend having a place there than parental expectations. And Nottingham was a good university. One of Damien's cousins had gone there and done very well.

He reached out and picked up the thick cord with which he fastened the alb at the waist, forcing himself to concentrate on the vesting prayers as he tied it securely.

Rory hadn't been to mass since Easter, but that wasn't surprising with him being away at university. When he was at home, he usually came with his mother to the eleven o'clock service. Patrick Quinn wasn't so regular and neither was the girl who still lived at home – what was her name now? Elsa, was it? He must be getting old; his memory was like a sieve these days. Emma! That was it. And there were two or three other siblings, all a lot older than Rory. Damien hardly knew them because they were already teenagers or older when he came to the parish.

He slipped his chasuble over his head, muttering the prescribed prayers, 'O Lord, who has said, "My yoke is sweet and my burden light," grant that I may so carry it as to merit Thy grace.' What could have caused Rory to have wanted to die? Only last week Martina had been talking about his engagement and his new job. She was so pleased that he would be living at home again, until they got married, which wouldn't be until he'd finished his solicitor's training. His fiancée was a local girl, a Catholic but her family worshipped at St Aloysius in the centre of town. They'd met at school. It was all perfect, from Martina's point of view.

Could that be the problem? Was his mother directing his life too much. Did Rory feel trapped on a path that he no longer wanted to follow? So sad if he could see no way to break free except to take his own life. Damien fell to his knees and offered up a quick private prayer for the troubled young man and his grieving family. Then he scrambled to his feet and sat down at the table to scribble an addendum to the intercessory prayers that he had prepared the night before and slipped inside his Sunday missal. He knew better than to try to ad lib. There was nothing worse than getting a name wrong or saying something misleading in front of a congregation of elderly gossips!

To be fair, although the attendees at the early mass on a Sunday did have an average age of over seventy, they were not all either elderly nor prone to gossip. As Damien stood at the front of the church surveying his flock, he was pleased to see a welcome addition in the form of a young woman with clear blue eyes and a wisp of fair hair peeping out from beneath a lime green headscarf. Lucy Paige must be home from her course at Liverpool University. On either side of her sat her mother, Bernie and her stepfather, Peter. At the end of their pew, in the space reserved for wheelchair-users, their friend Jonah seemed to be engrossed in something on the computer screen that was his constant companion and source of information. Studying the liturgy or the Gospel of the day, perhaps? Or, more likely, looking into some police investigation that he was taking an interest in. He was still finding it hard to settle into retirement from Thames Valley CID!

'Good morning!' Damien announced, with sufficient authority to quieten the low hum of talking among the cluster of parishioners sitting on the back row, friends who always used the Sunday service as an opportunity to catch up on one another's news. 'Before we begin the mass this morning, I have some sad news to share with you. I'm sure that many of you know the Quinn family. Martina and Patrick have been regular attenders at St Cyprian's for longer than I have. I'm afraid that their son Rory was found dead yesterday. I don't know any more than that, but I'm sure that you will all share my sorrow at hearing about their loss. This mass will be for the eternal rest of Rory's soul.'

Damien lowered his gaze, preparing himself mentally to begin the liturgy, but not before he had seen Jonah's eyes widening slightly and his face taking on an expression of increased interest. He would be wanting to know more about this, possibly suspicious, death at the end of the service.

Sure enough, Jonah managed to manipulate things so that he and his friends were the last to leave and he was able to cross-examine Damien on the subject of the death of Rory Quinn without holding up the small queue of parishioners filing past on their way home. After the main mass of the day there would be coffee and biscuits served in the Parish Centre, but the congregation at the early service liked to get away promptly. Many of them continued the tradition of fasting before mass and would be hungry for their bacon and eggs.

'I'm sorry to hear about this Rory Quinn,' Jonah began conversationally. 'He was only quite young, I gather?'

'Just back from university,' Damien confirmed.

'I suppose you'll have known him quite well?' Jonah continued innocently, 'being his parish priest?'

'He didn't share any secrets with me, if that's what you're fishing for,' Damien smiled back. 'In fact, I hadn't seen much of him since he went to uni. Just Christmas and Easter, really.'

'And his parents hadn't been worried about him, at all?' Jonah persisted. 'His mother would have confided in you, wouldn't she?'

'Not necessarily. A lot of people prefer to keep that sort of thing private.'

'Even from the man to whom they have entrusted the *cure of their souls*?'

'Jonah!' Peter interjected. 'Lay off, can't you?' Like Jonah, he was a retired police officer, but unlike his friend he was not constantly on the lookout for an excuse to get back into the thick of a new investigation.

'I think I remember Rory,' Lucy put in, cleverly assisting her stepfather by introducing a diversion. 'Didn't he take his first communion at the same time as me?'

'That's right,' Damien nodded. 'It was a first for me too! You provided quite a baptism of fire for a green young priest in his first parish – so many awkward questions. I complained to my old seminary tutor about it, but he just quoted Psalm 8 at me and told me to lighten up and show a bit more humility.'

'Psalm 8?' queried Lucy.

'Out of the mouths of babes and sucklings,' quoted Bernie. 'He meant that you may have had a point when you asked awkward questions.'

'That's right,' agreed Damien, grinning round at them. 'And he was right, of course. I always feel that I learn far more at my classes than the kids ever do! And often the questions are more important than the answers.'

'But getting back to the Quinns,' Jonah persisted. 'I gather they live quite close?'

'Down Kiln Lane,' Damien confirmed

'But I don't know how you know,' Peter added suspiciously. 'Nobody mentioned it.'

'The big house with the stone lions on the gate post?' Jonah asked, ignoring his friend's intervention.

'Yes,' Damien admitted. 'Apparently, Patrick had it built after he made his first million. I've only visited a couple of times. It's a bit intimidating, having to use the intercom to ask them to open the gates for you. But I suppose they must be afraid of burglars. I imagine they've probably got some valuable stuff in there.'

'Anyway, we'd better be getting home,' Bernie said firmly, giving Jonah a warning tap on the shoulder. 'My friend Stan's preaching at our other church this morning and I don't want to miss him. And Father Damien will want some time to relax before the next mass.'

Jonah opened his mouth to ask the priest another question, then thought better of it and pressed a button to move his electric wheelchair forward and out into the sunny car park. Lucy hurried after him. Bernie and Peter nodded their goodbyes to Damien before joining the procession.

'How *did* you know where the Quinns live?' demanded Peter, as soon as they were out of earshot of Father Damien. 'You've never met them, and Father Damien definitely didn't mention it until you brought it up.'

'I'm a detective. I deduced it.'

'Deduced it from what? Where was your evidence?'

'Alright, I'll come clean.' Jonah was clearly enjoying himself. 'I bumped into Andy Lepage last night, on my way back from the corner shop. He'd been attending a suspected suicide. He told me that the victim's father was, and I quote, *a big noise with connections*, and he was cycling down Kiln Lane. I've noticed that big house with the lions at the entrance before and it's obvious that whoever lives there must have a penny or two, so I made an educated guess and Father Damien confirmed it. Elementary, my dear Watson!'

'Very clever,' muttered Peter. 'But you do know that this is all none of our business, don't you?'

'Fancy you knowing the boy, Lucy!' Jonah said, ignoring Peter's remark. 'What was he like?'

'Honestly, Jonah, you are incorrigible!' Bernie protested. 'Lucy was only nine. What do you expect her to remember?'

'Lucy?' Jonah repeated.

'Like Mam says,' Lucy sighed, 'I was only nine at the time, and Rory was even younger, I think. He seemed young to me, anyway. He was very polite and eager to please. He always put his hand up when Father Damien asked a question, and usually he got the answer right – unlike me!' she added with a chuckle. 'But he was mortified if he didn't or if Father Damien seemed to be criticising him in any way. That's all I remember. It was a long time ago.'

***

'Was the play good?' Jessica Davenport asked her parents when she came down to breakfast and saw them sitting opposite each other in silence. She recognised the signs. There was another row rumbling on – or maybe just the same one from yesterday, when Dad was so put out at Mum being delayed at work on what he insisted was "our special day". Did they really believe that she and Marcus didn't notice? Even little Donna could tell. She looked round from her special chair that gave her the support she needed to sit up to the table and smiled towards her big sister, but did not speak.

'It was very … interesting … different,' Anna replied cautiously. She was trying to be honest without openly criticising Philip's choice of entertainment.

'I don't see how you can have an opinion, seeing as you slept through most of the second act,' Philip muttered sullenly.

'That's not true,' Anna made an effort to keep her voice steady. 'I may have dropped off for a few minutes, but I didn't miss anything.'

'Because there wasn't anything *to* miss, I suppose?' Philip's voice rose a little before he remembered Jessica and Donna and forced it into an angry mumble. 'You've made it perfectly plain that you'd rather we hadn't gone. I did *try* to get you to choose what we did, but you were always too busy. You told me to decide.'

'Yes.' Anna poured herself another cup of coffee. 'And I'm perfectly happy with your choice. It was a good play. I enjoyed it. I was just a bit tired after yesterday's caseload, that's all.' She turned to Jessica. 'I'm going to make myself some toast. Shall I put some on for you too?'

'No thanks. I'll just have cereal. And then I thought I'd take Donna to the park. Give you a bit of peace and quiet.'

'Would you?' Anna put a slice of toast into the toaster and pushed the handle down. 'That would be great. I need to prepare for tomorrow's team briefing and I'd really like to have a look through the Jibrilu Danjuma file too. The court case starts this week.'

'No problems!' Jessica said cheerfully. 'We'll have a great time in the park, won't we Donna? It looks like another gorgeous day. We could take a picnic and stay out all day, if you like.'

'Would you?' Anna repeated gratefully. 'It's not that I wouldn't rather be playing with you,' she added, going across and kissing little Donna on the cheek, 'It's just that there's so much I need to do before tomorrow morning.'

'Well, if you two have got all that sorted, I suppose I might as well ring Jim and see if he can give me a round of golf this morning.' Philip got up, leaving his coffee cup half full, and headed for the door. 'I'll have lunch at the clubhouse – that is unless you need me for anything this afternoon,' he added sarcastically as he left the room.

'No thanks, we can manage,' Anna answered, addressing the closed door.

The toast popped up. Anna took it back to her place and sat down.

'I am really grateful to you for looking after Donna today,' she assured Jessica. 'I really don't know how we'd manage without you.'

'Don't be silly. That was the deal, remember? When Donna was born. You're on duty this weekend and I'm not. So, I'm in charge of childcare. Dad takes over tomorrow when we're both working – although I bet we'd be able to manage between us perfectly well, with the breakfast club and the after school club – and you've got a long weekend off next week, so you'll have the pleasure of Donna's company for three whole days then, and I'll be able to go out with my mates. Simples!'

'Simples! Simples!' Donna joined in, copying the catch-phrase from the popular TV ad.

'Unless I get called to give evidence in court on Friday. The Jibrilu Danjuma murder trial starts on Wednesday.'

'We'll cross that bridge when we come to it!' Jessica continued to speak cheerfully. She enjoyed looking after her young sister and revelled in her mother's dependence on her support. They were alright, the three of them – and Marcus too, she supposed, if he stuck around – they didn't need Dad. If he wanted to stay, it had to be on their terms.

They heard heavy footsteps descending the stairs followed by a clatter in the hall as Philip put down his golf bag. The front door opened and then closed again with a bang.

'I've finished.' Donna announced, putting out her arms to be lifted down from her chair. She had been born with spina bifida, which affected her ability to move her legs, so she spent most of her waking hours in a wheelchair, which she had become surprisingly adept at manipulating with her hands.

Anna and Jessica both got to their feet, ready to help.

'No, I'll take her,' Anna said, stepping forward and grasping her younger daughter under the arms. 'You eat your breakfast.'

She moved Donna on to one hip and picked up her toast in the other hand. 'Come along, young lady! Up to the bathroom with you and let's wash those sticky fingers!'

Anna sat at the kitchen table diligently typing up the notes that she had taken at the Quinn family home the previous day. The house was silent, apart from the gentle swashing sound of the dishwasher. The girls were no doubt enjoying themselves in the park. Marcus had come down late and disappeared almost immediately on a mission to meet up with some mates. She had the house to herself.

Philip would no doubt be grumbling to his golfing buddies about her unreasonableness and telling them that she'd better watch out or he'd go off again down to Devon. But he never would! He might get frustrated with family life and resentful of her job, but he had discovered that it was better than the constant demands that his mother had made on him when he was living down there. And his sister had moved in with her, after that fall she'd had. She and Phil had never got on.

Anna drained her coffee mug and dragged her thoughts back to her work. Who else was in the house at the time when Rory Quinn must have died? She scrolled through her notes on the screen. Martina had left for London a couple of hours earlier. Patrick was out shopping – or so he said. On the face of it, it looked as if-

The ringing of her mobile phone cut off Anna's train of thought. She looked down at it, lying on the table next to her laptop. The number was an unfamiliar one.

'Hello? DCI Davenport here.'

'He-he-he-hello,' came a female voice, sounding very young and very nervous. 'It's Ellie – Ellie Unwin – Rory's ... I ... I was at his hou-hou ... I was at his house yesterday. You said to te-te-te-telephone if I th-thought of anything that ...'

'Yes, Ellie, I remember.' Anna did her best to sound reassuring and sympathetic. 'You were very brave – and helpful.'

'Well ...'

'Yes?'

There was a long pause.

'Have you thought of something?' Anna suggested gently. 'Something we should know about?'

'I'm not sh-sh-sure.'

'That's OK. Why don't you tell me anyway?'

'We-ell ... I'm sorry, M-Mum and D-Dad will be back soon, I c-can't talk now.'

'Maybe we could meet up somewhere,' Anna suggested quickly, 'if you'd rather your mum and dad aren't there – a coffee shop, maybe, or ...'

'Port Meadow!' Ellie suddenly sounded more decisive. 'I'll leave a n-n-n-note to say I'm t-taking the dog for a walk. She could do with one, anyway. I'll m-meet you in the car p-p-p-park at the end of Walton Well Road in t-t-ten minutes.'

'OK. At least, you'll have to give me a bit longer than that. Can we say …,' Anna consulted her watch, 'quarter to twelve?'

'Great!' Ellie's relief was palpable. 'See you th-there then.'

Anna sat for a minute staring down at her phone. What could it be that Ellie was so anxious to tell her, and which she was equally anxious for her parents not to hear?

Ellie was already there when Anna pulled into the car park at the southern end of Port Meadow. She was sitting on a bench holding the lead of a bored-looking basset hound. She got up when she recognised Anna and walked over to the car.

'This is B-Bessie,' she said, pointing down at the dog.

'Hello Bessie!' Ann smiled down at her new acquaintance, speaking in that special tone reserved for young children and animals. 'Have I kept you waiting? We'd better give you that walk you were promised, hadn't we?'

They set off through the kissing gate and walked briskly along the path. Ellie allowed Bessie to pull her extending lead out to its full length, but did not let her run free. 'I'm always afraid of her ch-ch-chasing the ponies,' she explained. 'She d-d-did once. Not that she had any chance of c-c-catching them!'

'No, I don't suppose she did.' Anna agreed, watching the dog's waddling gait.

They walked on in silence for several minutes.

'You said you had something to tell me,' Anna ventured at last.

'Yes.'

Anna waited.

'P-p-p-promise you won't tell Rory's m-mum and d-dad?'

69

'Well, until I know what it is, I can't absolutely promise,' Anna replied cautiously. 'But I'll only do so if it's absolutely necessary – to keep someone safe, for example.'

'Oh. OK. Well, here g-goes then!' Ellie took a deep breath and began speaking, looking ahead all the time, and walking a little faster. 'Rory was experiencing s-s-same-s-sex attraction. He t-t-told me about it while we were st-st-still at sch-ch-chool. He said he knew it was wrong and he was f-f-fighting it, but he wanted me to know in c-case I'd rather not carry on going out with him.'

'And you told him you didn't mind?'

'Of c-c-course! It wasn't his f-fault, was it. And at least he'd been s-s-straight with me.' Ellie appeared to be unaware of the irony in her choice of adjective.

'And nobody else knows about this?'

'N-not here in Oxford, I'm sure, but I d-d-don't know about at uni. That's why I th-thought you ought to know. I have a f-feeling that he may have s-someone s-special in Nottingham.'

'A boyfriend, you mean?'

'Yes, I s-s-suppose th-th-tha-that's what you'd c-call it. I d-don't *know* – it's just a f-feeling I got from some things he said. But if there *is* someone then he ought to be t-told about … I mean, it wouldn't be f-fair if he doesn't find out until …'

'Yes,' Anna nodded. 'You're right – and it was very kind of you to think about that.'

'So, can you f-find him – if there is a him – and let him know?'

'We'll certainly do our best,' Anna promised, 'but it may not be all that easy. You don't have a name, presumably?'

'N-no. He n-never said anything definite – it was just a f-feeling I got.'

'Did he ever talk about his friends at uni? If we could find them, they might be able to tell us.'

'He sh-sh-shared a house with some g-guys in his final year. He t-talked about them sometimes.'

'And can you remember their names?' Anna asked, after waiting several seconds for Ellie to continue.

M-Max and Adam. Max B-Bishop and Adam … Adam … F-F-Francis. And M-Max had a girlfriend l-living there too. I th-th-th-think she was c-called G-G-Grace.

Anna wrote all these names down in her pocket book.

'And did you meet any of them – when you visited Rory in Nottingham, perhaps?'

'N-no. I n-never went to Nottingham. And he never came to C-C-Cambridge either. Our mums wouldn't have l-liked it,' she added,' looking round at Anna for the first time and giving a wry smile. 'Th-they would have been afraid we were up to *hanky-p-panky*, as they c-c-c-called it!'

'Well, we'll certainly look up Max and Adam. Was there anyone else you can think of?'

'I d-d-don't th-think s-' Ellie suddenly broke off and seemed to be thinking. 'I-I'm not sure,' she resumed after a short pause. 'but I *think* there was someone called Jamie that he was c-c-c-close to. He n-never really talked about him, b-b-but … One time he s-said something like, "J-J-Jamie would have loved th-that!" and then he went red and started talking about something d-d-different.'

'Mmmm,' Anna murmured in agreement. 'That does sound a bit as if Jamie could've been more than just a friend, doesn't it? And you've no idea what Jamie's other name was?'

'No.' Ellie shook her head, 'L-like I s-said, Rory d-d-didn't want to talk about him.'

'OK. Thanks for telling me about this. I'll try and track this Jamie down.'

'Th-th-thanks. And you won't tell Rory's mum about any of this, will you? She – she – she'd be *so* upset if – if – if she knew!'

***

After a rather frosty breakfast-time with his mother, who was still clearly narked about his having let her parents down, Andy spent the morning in his room, typing up the notes that he had made of his interviews with the Quinn family. He kept a close eye on the clock, making sure to be downstairs, with hair combed and clothes neat, in good time for the short drive to his grandparents' home. His mother looked him up and down with a critical eye and flicked a small fleck of dander from the collar of his jacket before nodding her approval.

'And I hope you've got your phone switched off,' she said, as they closed the front door behind them. 'I don't want you getting called away before you've got those things down from the loft for Gramps. If you don't do it, he'll have a go himself and he can't afford to have a fall at his age.'

'Don't worry. Anna knows the score. She's promised not to call me out today.'

'Well, she'd better not, that's all I can say.'

Andy was relieved that Nana and Gramps were more forgiving.

'Come on in!' Gramps called out, flinging the front door wide and beckoning them through.

'You've timed that just right!' Nana called out, coming out from the kitchen, wiping her hands on her apron. 'Lunch is just on ready. Go and sit down in the dining room and we'll bring it through.'

Andy had to admit that it was a good lunch. Nobody cooked a leg of lamb quite as well as Nana – not even Mum. And as for her chocolate chip sponge pudding …! Either the good food or Nana's cheerful conversation thawed Mum's mood towards him too, and things were back to normal by the time he finished his after-lunch coffee and turned to Gramps.

'Now, I'd better get up in the loft and get those things down for you.'

'I'll come up with you and help. I know where everythi-,' Gramps began, but his daughter intervened.

'Oh no you won't. You sit back down and leave it to us. Andrew will be able to find everything easily enough, and he can pass the things down to me.'

After a bit of argument, Gramps finally gave way, merely insisting on coming up to the landing to show them how to open the loft access and get down the ladder. Then he consented to go back to help Nana with the washing up, while Andy climbed up into the roof space to fetch all the paraphernalia that they would need for a visiting infant.

He soon found the high chair that had been his when he was a baby, and handed it down to his mother, who was waiting at the foot of the loft ladder. A plastic baby bath followed, together with a bag of bath toys. Then he looked around for the most important item of all: his old cot. Where was it?

For several minutes, Andy stumbled around in the dim light of his torch. The loft was piled high with items that were *bound to come in useful one day*, making it difficult to see what there was at the further end. Was that the cot mattress sticking up above that tower of cardboard boxes? Yes, he was almost certain that it was!

He clambered over a pile of bulging carrier bags in an effort to reach his prize. One of them slid sideways knocking him off balance, and, in trying to right himself, he knocked against a stack of cardboard boxes dislodging the top two, which then disgorged their contents in an untidy heap.

'What happened?' Andy's mother called anxiously up the ladder. 'Are you alright up there?'

'Yes. Don't worry, I've just knocked over a couple of boxes, that's all,' he reassured her. 'I've found the cot. Stand by and I'll hand it down to you in a minute.'

He cleared a path through the plastic carrier bags (which turned out to contain old curtains and cushion covers) and managed to reach the cot without further mishap. He was soon handing it down, piece by piece to his mother, who took the components and stacked them neatly on the landing.

'We'll need the cot sheets and blankets too,' Nana called up through the access hole. 'They're in a red suitcase. It should be next to where you found the cot.'

'OK. I'll have a look.'

Andy made his way back to where he had located the cot and, sure enough, there was an old-fashioned suitcase leaning against one of the beams that supported the roof. He checked inside before staggering back with it to the loft entrance.

'Be careful,' he warned his mother, who had put up her arms to receive it. 'It's heavy. I'll try to slid it down the ladder so you don't have to take all the weight at once.'

He lowered it carefully through the small hatch, keeping hold of it for as long as he could before finally releasing it into his mother's hands.

'That's everything now,' Nana called up. 'You can come down now.'

'And you can help us to put the cot up,' Mum added, leaning against the ladder and peering up into the darkness above.

'In a bit,' Andy called back. 'I'd just better clear up the mess I made knocking over those boxes.'

He went back and set the two boxes upright, ready to replace their contents. It turned out that they had held some of his old exercise books from Primary School. Fancy Nana and Gramps keeping those! There was his project on the Norman Conquest! And here was a pile of maths workbooks. And this was the book where they had to write their weekend news every Monday. He opened the blue cover of the exercise book and began to read.

DAY OF REST?

On Saturday Mum was working so Nana took me to the park. I played on the swings and the slide. On Sunday I went to Junior Church with Nana and Gramps. We drew fish and listened to a story about Jesus. Mum was working.

He turned the pages. Every weekend seemed sadly similar. This must have been while Mum was doing her Open University course, trying to improve her prospects of getting a good job to support him better and to afford a home for them together. Sighing, he put the book back in the box and started gathering more of them together. It must have been hard for Mum, working and studying and trying to look after a child at the same time. Thank goodness she had had Nana and Gramps to help her.

He had almost filled the first box when he came across something a bit different. It was a diary: a page-a-day one, with a padded PVC cover and a lock – the sort you might give someone for a Christmas present. Had it been his? He didn't remember it. No! Nobody would have given this to a boy – not with that picture of flowers and horses on the front. It was a girl's diary, somewhere for a teenage girl to write her secrets.

He tried the clasp. It wasn't locked. *This diary belongs to Amanda Lepage.* It was Mum's diary! Of course! She must have left it behind when they moved out of her parents' house, just like his old exercise books and artwork; and Nana and Gramps put them all up in the loft for safekeeping. Andy closed the book and put it to one side. Mum might like to read it, to see what she was doing in … He opened it again to check the date: 1982. Two years before he was born. She must have still been at school then, studying for her A' levels and hoping to go to Oxford University … and working as a cleaner at Lichfield College.

Andy's hand hovered over the page, wondering whether to turn it and read the entries. It must have been round about this time that she met Yakubu Danjuma, the postgraduate student with whom she had fallen in love. It would be interesting to read anything she had written about the romance.

And unforgivably intrusive.

He closed the diary and refastened the catch. He would take it with him, but not to show to Mum. This wasn't the right time to revive memories of those days – not with Yakubu about to arrive back in Oxford.

He sighed as he put the diary down in one of the few clear spaces on the dusty floor. He still hadn't told her about Yakubu! Last night, with her so angry about his having let down her parents, had definitely *not* been the right time, and now time was running out …

He hurried to collect the rest of the books that had fallen out of the box, shining the torch round to check that he had found them all. He didn't want to leave any trip hazards lying around, just in case Gramps were to come up here. A stray exercise book, unnoticed in the dark, could easily send him flying, possibly down through the open trap door to the floor below.

That seemed to be the lot, and both boxes were nearly full, confirming that their contents had been restored to them. There was just that shoebox, lying on its side with the lid off. Had that also been in one of the boxes? Andy righted it and looked more closely at bundles of paper that had fallen out. It was piles of those old aerogramme letters that people used to use: thin paper folded and sealed without an envelope to reduce weight and save postage, bound together in small packs. But they weren't the same as he remembered Nana using for her letters to her sister in Canada. They had been a different colour and … and they didn't say *Nigeria* in the corner!

These must be letters from Yakubu to Mum! He must have written to her during the vacations when he went home to his family. Fancy her keeping them all these years! You would have thought she would have destroyed them after he let her down so badly.

He slipped one out from the elastic band that held it. The band immediately broke sending Andy scrabbling around on the floor to collect all the letters together again. There were about ten of them in that bunch, and there were … He counted: twelve bundles, making over a hundred letters in all. He must have written to her almost every day!

Andy's heart was beating fast as he debated whether or not to open the aerogramme. It couldn't do any harm after all these years. Mum need never know. Yakubu was his father, after all. Andy felt sure that he would be pleased to know that the letters had been preserved and happy for his son to read them. But they were addressed to Mum. And love letters should be private …

'Haven't you finished yet? Gramps needs your help with the cot.'

'Sorry!' Andy called back through the hatch to his mother. 'I won't be a minute.'

He hastily removed some of the exercise books from one of the boxes and replaced them with the diary and the air letters. Then he put the books back on top to conceal his booty, folded down the flaps of the box over them and carried it across to the ladder.

'I found these old school books of mine up there,' he explained, as he descended with the box clasped in his arms. 'I thought it might be fun to have a look at them sometime. I'll just take them out to the car, he added, setting off downstairs without pausing. 'Then I'd better get myself cleaned up a bit. I'm covered with dust.'

***

Esther blinked as she emerged from the gloom of the church into the bright sunshine, greeting the vicar and saying a few words, before joining the stream of worshippers making their way to the church hall for coffee and biscuits. She took off her cardigan and hung it over her arm. Now that the sun was high in the sky, it was overpoweringly hot outside. The thick stone walls of the mediaeval church certainly had benefits in such a hot summer!

She took out her phone, which she had switched to *silent* during the service, and immediately noticed that she had a missed call from Andy. With a sinking feeling in her stomach, she stepped to the side of the path and returned the call. He answered immediately.

'Esther! I'm so glad you rang. I wanted to talk rather than just leaving a voicemail. I'm so sorry-'

'But you won't be able to meet me this afternoon after all,' Esther finished for him. 'I understand, and it's OK: your work is important.'

'It's not work this time – or, at least, it's because I got called into work yesterday that I can't make it today. I completely forgot that I'd promised to call in at my grandparents' house and do a few things for them yesterday evening; so now I've got to go round there for Sunday lunch and do them this afternoon.'

'I told you: it's OK,' Esther repeated.

'I'll ring you again when I'm home from Nana's. Maybe there'll still be time for us to … or maybe after dinner?'

'That would be nice. But, Andy, please – it really is OK. You don't have to keep apologising.'

'But I want you to know! I want you to know that I'd rather be with you. I don't want you to think …. Anyway, I'd better go. Mum's hardly speaking to me today, after I messed Nana and Gramps about yesterday, so I mustn't make us late. I'll ring again later, like I said.'

Esther stood staring down at her phone. To her surprise and annoyance, she found herself blinking away tears. Why had Andy's change of plans affected her so much? OK, so she had been looking forward to spending another afternoon in his company, but it wasn't as if they had been separated for months. They'd seen each other only yesterday, for goodness' sake!

She slipped her phone into her handbag and turned back down the path. She could not face making polite conversation with the well-meaning white ladies who would be eagerly trying to make her feel at home in their church. She would go back to her room and look through her notes from last week's laboratory work, and then have lunch in Hall and spend the afternoon back in the labs, working on her DPhil project.

Once she was out of the churchyard, she quickened her pace, walking briskly through the narrow back streets of the ancient city. It wasn't Andy's fault, she told herself firmly. He couldn't help it. It was his job that made him such an unreliable companion. And his job was important. It was making a difference to real people's lives.

But it wasn't his job calling him away this time – or only indirectly. Was that the difference? Was that why she couldn't prevent the resentment bubbling up that he hadn't put her first? Which was ridiculous, because the needs of his elderly grandparents obviously had to take precedence over their ... their what? Love life? Courtship? Or was it just ... They'd never actually talked about what their relationship was or how it might be developing.

She turned in at the entrance of her college, passing the Porters' Lodge and coming back out into the sunshine of the main quadrangle. It was a beautiful day. She had enough to eat, clothes to wear and a roof over her head. And she was being paid to do research that might one day help to produce more food for some of the people in the world who were less fortunate than she was. What more could she demand from life? Why was she being so unreasonable? Why could she not dispel these feelings of irritation at having her plans for the afternoon disrupted? Why did she feel such antagonism towards Andy's mother for having insisted that he put his grandparents first?

That was it, wasn't it? Andy's mother! What had Andy told her about their relationship? Why hadn't he arranged for them to meet yet? Was he afraid that his mother would try to split them up if she knew she had a rival for his affection? Was that how he came to have reached his late thirties without getting married or leaving home? He never spoke about any other relationships. Could that really be because she was the first?

Preparations for serving lunch were well underway when she passed through the grand, but rather gloomy, oak-panelled hall on her way to the inconvenient little staircase that led off it to the rooms where the college housed its international postgraduate students. Kitchen staff and teenage part-timers called cheerfully to one another as they set up the self-service buffet and put out pots of salt and pepper on the tables. Had Andy's mother ever done that, when she had been a schoolgirl earning a few pounds while she studied to become a student herself?

There was no doubt that she deserved his loyalty. She had given up her hopes of an Oxford degree in favour of caring for him; and then worked hard to gain the good job that she now had at the university library because she wanted to be able to provide the best for him. But surely, she must recognise that she could not keep him to herself forever? If she cared for him – and not just for her own sense of power over him – then she must realise that he needed to break away and forge his own life apart from her.

Esther clumped up the narrow spiral staircase in her Sunday best shoes. What was it she'd said to Andy yesterday when he was complaining about his mother not wanting him to have anything to do with Yakubu? "If you were mine, I wouldn't want to share you either!" That was it! And she had been secretly hoping that he would immediately hug her and tell her that he *was* hers. But he hadn't. And he probably never would. Because he would never be anyone except Amanda Lepage's little boy!

***

'It's Father Damien – from St Cyprian's. I wanted to express my condolences and to ask if there's anything I can do for you at this sad time.' The parish priest spoke awkwardly into the intercom next to the high wrought iron gates that kept intruders out of the Quinn family home.

'Of course, Father,' came back the muffled reply. 'I'll open the gate for you now.'

There was a click and whirr and then the massive gates began to move, turning slowly as powerful electric motors rotated them inwards creating a space wide enough to admit a sizeable vehicle – or a man in a wheelchair and his entourage of friends, scurrying beside him.

'Hello again, Father!' Jonah greeted Damien. 'Thank you for dealing with the gates for us. We thought we'd come and offer our condolences – and one of Peter's famous blackcurrant pies. After all, we are neighbours and Lucy was a friend of Rory's.'

At the sound of this familiar voice, Damien turned and stared. He hadn't noticed Jonah following him along the road as he walked the short distance from the presbytery. Now, here he was smiling up at the priest from his wheelchair, with Peter, Bernie and Lucy standing behind him looking rather shamefaced.

'No, Jonah, you can't do this,' Peter protested. 'You haven't been invited. They only opened the gate for Father Damien – not for you too. Come back out and wait your turn.'

'If they say they'd like us to leave, we will do,' Jonah promised, propelling his chair further up the drive towards the house. 'But there can't be any harm in asking them face-to-face, now that the gates are open anyway. Oh, come on, Peter! Lighten up, can't you?'

'When they see you in that ruddy chair of yours, they won't dare to tell you buzz off,' Peter muttered, hurrying after his friend. 'You take advantage of people's sympathy, and it's not fair – not when they've just lost their son.'

'And I wasn't ever one of Rory's friends,' Lucy put in, 'so don't try to use that to wangle your way in.'

'*Neighbours* is stretching things a bit, too,' Bernie added.

Jonah, predictably, wasn't listening to any of their protestations. He had reached the front door and was smiling up at Emma Quinn, who had come to let in Father Damien.

The others watched as her expression of surprise softened at whatever words he was using to explain his uninvited presence. She came out and sat down on the highest of the three steps that led up to the main entrance of the house, so that she was facing him at his own level. Then she stood up and pointed to the path that ran across the front of the house and down the side to the kitchen door and the back garden. Jonah set off along it, while Emma came forward to greet Father Damien and his companions.

'Father! It was good of you to call. Mamma was so pleased when I told her you were coming.' She looked round at the others, who were shuffling their feet in embarrassment and trying to think of appropriate words to explain why they were there. 'And it's very kind of you to come too,' she said politely. 'I didn't know that we had a police hero living so close.'

'We usually try to avoid people finding out,' Bernie told her with a wry smile. 'I'm sure you can appreciate that publicity can be a nuisance at times!'

'Oh yes!' Emma agreed. 'We try to keep a low profile when we're at home too. Now, let's go round the back and I'll introduce you to Mamma. Dad's out, I'm afraid. He's gone for a walk. He's ... I've never seen him so shaken up about anything before – not even when his mother died. I'm Emma,' she added, 'Rory's sister, and you are …?'

'His minders!' Bernie replied, jerking her head in the direction of Jonah as he disappeared round the side of the house. 'My name's Bernie, and this is my husband, Peter, and my daughter, Lucy. Technology goes a long way these days, but at the end of the day, Jonah isn't quite as totally independent as he'd like you to believe.'

'I can imagine,' Emma nodded. 'I remember the news reports when it happened, and, to be honest, I thought at the time that in his place I'd have been asking to be taken straight off to Dignitas. I was gobsmacked when we watched him on that *Inspirational Lives* programme and it turned out he'd even gone back into the police. I would never have thought it was possible.'

'Oh, he gets by,' Peter told her.

'With a little help from his friends,' Lucy added with a grin.

'Yes,' Emma nodded. 'That was something else I remember from the programme. You were in it too, weren't you?' She turned to Bernie. 'You gave up your job to look after him.'

'I took early retirement,' Bernie corrected her. 'It's not the same. And being personal assistant to a DCI meant that I got to see a lot of very interesting police work from the inside. So I wasn't really giving up anything.'

'And having Jonah living with us gave me plenty to talk about at my interview, when I applied to study medicine,' Lucy chipped in.'

'But hadn't we better go and rescue your mother from his clutches?' Peter suggested. 'Knowing him, he'll be subjecting her to in-depth questioning about all the circumstances leading up to your brother's death. He just can't help himself!'

They followed the path down the side of the house and into the back garden. There on the patio were four well-cushioned cane garden chairs grouped round a table with a large sunshade in its centre. Jonah's wheelchair was drawn up to the table and he was in conversation with two women: one in her early sixties, slim, dark-haired and brown-eyed; the other two or three decades older, shorter and plumper, with grey, almost white, hair. On the table lay a box of tissues, a hardback book, a rosary of purple beads and a partially-completed garment in rainbow wool with knitting needles sticking out of it.

'My mother, Martina, and my grandmother, Giovanna,' Emma introduced them. 'Mamma, these are Inspector Porter's friends: Bernie, Peter and Lucy. I expect the inspector's already told you that they live just round the corner.'

'Indeed he has,' Mrs Quinn answered. 'And look at the lovely fruit pie that he brought with him for us. All the neighbours have been very kind,' she went on, looking towards Father Damien, 'even though we don't really know any of them. It makes you realise how much we're missing these days, with all our security measures and going everywhere in the car.'

'That's right,' her mother grunted in a husky voice with a strong Italian accent. 'Nobody knows their neighbours in a place like this. Not like back home in Cosenza – or even in the old days in London. When I came to England to join Salvatore, we had nothing! We lived in two rooms and Salvatore made money selling ice-cream from a bicycle. But those were happy times. And why? Because we knew all our neighbours and we all helped each other.'

'Apart from the ones who told you to go back to Italy!' Martina commented.

'What's that?' Her mother asked sharply. 'Speak up! I don't like all this mumbling.'

Damien remembered that Giovanna was rather deaf and realised that Martina had deliberately lowered her voice so that her mother would miss her remark.

'I was only saying, Mamma, that things haven't really changed so much. See what good neighbours we have here!'

'Indeed!' Father Damien agreed before Giovanna could argue with this statement. 'And I have an example of that right here.' He held out the jar of lemon curd that Deirdre had given him. 'Deirdre Carr asked me to give this to you and to tell you that she'd like to pay you a visit, but later, when you've had time for the terrible news to sink in. She didn't want to intrude too early.'

'Dear Deirdre!' Martina took the jar and set it down on the table, as she dabbed her red-rimmed eyes with a tissue. 'She is always so kind!'

'We used to call her Auntie when we were little,' Emma added. 'She used to give us presents every year on the anniversary of our baptisms.'

'It's so sad that her husband died before they had any children,' Martina went on. 'She's always loved children. She'll be-,' she broke off, taking hold of Damien's arm and looking up earnestly into his face. 'You will keep an eye on Deirdre, won't you? She was very fond of Rory.'

'I'll call round to see her later this afternoon,' Damien promised. 'But right now, I'm here for you and your family.'

'Thank you, Father. I'm sorry I wasn't at Mass this morning. I just couldn't face going out. I'd have felt that everyone was looking at me.'

Damien sat down next to Martina and gently took her two hands in his. 'We dedicated the early mass to the rest of Rory's soul. It was Deirdre's idea.'

'Thank you, Father. And ... and he will be alright?' Martina lowered her voice again. 'My grandmother is convinced that he'll go to hell because he killed himself. She's ninety-nine and in a home in Italy, but she's been on the phone constantly, worrying my mother with her stories of doom and gloom. I've told her

God will forgive him, but she says that's impossible unless he repented before he died.'

'With the greatest respect to you grandmother,' Damien replied, in an even lower voice, 'she is not a theologian. Don't worry: God loves Rory just as much as he did on the day he was baptised or when he took his first communion. Don't you remember Jesus talking about gathering us together like a mother hen gathering her chicks under her wings? You didn't stop loving Rory when he did what he did, and neither did God. God is like the best mother that anyone could have – don't you ever forget that.'

Emma busily moved more chairs into the circle and motioned to everyone to sit down, while Damien continued to comfort Martina, and Peter tried to break the ice with Giovanna by asking about the knitting, which she had picked up, perhaps as an act of defiance to show that she knew that her daughter was deliberately excluding her from her exchange with the priest.

Jonah sat in silence, listening in on both conversations.

He learned that Rory's youngest sister, Bianca, was expecting her third child in November, which would make Giovanna a great grandmother seven times over. But Bianca still hadn't had her older children baptised, because she was married to a Muslim and they were allowing the children to make up their own minds about their religion when they were older.

Martina was sure that Rory had been hiding something from the family in recent months, but she had no idea what it could be. She had guilt feelings for not having talked to him about it, whatever it was. Perhaps, if she had, he wouldn't have killed himself. That must have been because he didn't think anyone cared, mustn't it?

Patrick and Martina were very lax with their children. Giovanna's father would never have allowed her to consort with any young man who wasn't a good Catholic. Róisín was just the same: her husband called himself an agnostic, which was just a protestant that didn't bother going to church.

Martina knew that she tended to spoil Rory because he was the youngest. Maybe that was why he found going away from home difficult. Was Father Damien sure that he wouldn't go to hell for killing himself? That was what her family had always taught her.

Giovanna's grandchildren all thought she was going gaga. They mumbled and whispered so that she wouldn't hear, but she knew that's what they were saying about her. And Martina didn't discipline them for their disrespect. She would never have been allowed to speak about her elders the way they did!

Patrick was sure that Rory must have been killed by an intruder, but that wasn't what the police thought, Martina was sure – unless Patrick knew something that he was keeping from her. Which he might do. He always tried to protect her from anything that might worry her. It was very provoking, but she tried not to let it show.

At this point, Jonah couldn't resist asking, 'and what do the police say about the intruder theory?'

'Oh! They're being very polite about it,' Martina replied. 'Everyone is being very polite and sympathetic and not contradicting Patrick, because he's a bereaved father and has a right to any ideas that make him feel better, but I don't suppose they're taking it seriously. There's a woman in charge. She interviewed me. She asked about the tablets Rory had to help him sleep when he was taking his exams. And she wanted to know how much he usually drank and whether he liked whisky. That must have been because she thought it was suicide, mustn't it?'

'Oh suicide!' Giovanna broke in, catching this single word as her daughter raised her voice a little. 'Don't talk to me about suicide! Your great uncle Riccardo committed suicide back in …

nineteen forty-eight it must have been. I was only a little girl, but I remember it so well! He was on the run from the police. I never knew exactly what for, but whatever it was, he decided that he would rather die than be arrested. So, he shot himself in the head. My mother was frantic with the shame of what her brother had done. And I remember the parish priest coming round – we all lived in my grandmother's house at that time – and saying that he could not have a Catholic funeral because he died in a state of mortal sin. Oh, the trouble that caused! Oh–'

'There's no question of Rory being denied a funeral,' Father Damien put in quickly. 'The Church has come a long way since then in our understanding of mental illness. Taking one's own life is still a serious business, but we now appreciate that Despair isn't so much a mortal sin as a symptom of a disordered mind.'

'And that's important for you to remember too, Martina,' Bernie put in earnestly. 'If Rory did kill himself, it's absolutely not because you didn't do all the right things. I know it's hard, but do try not to blame yourself.'

'Anyway,' Peter added, getting to his feet, 'It's time we were going. I'm sure you'd rather have some time alone with Father Damien.'

'I'll see you out,' Emma volunteered. 'Thank you so much for coming – and for that delicious-looking pie.'

'It was no trouble – really,' Peter assured her. 'And do let us know if there's anything else we can do.'

'If you want to find out how the police investigation's going,' Jonah added, 'I know the officers in charge. So just tell me if you've got any questions about it and I'll….'

'Jonah!' Bernie rebuked in a low growl, bending low over his chair so that none of the Quinn family would hear. 'Leave them alone, can't you? None of this is any of your business.'

They made their way round to the front of the house, from where Emma was able to open the gates to let them out, using a pocket remote control. By the time they had reached the road outside, Jonah was already keying Andy's number into the mobile phone attachment on the arm of his chair.

'Yes?' Andy answered grudgingly. Jonah had interrupted him in the job of secreting the diary and letters that he had brought back from his grandparents' loft in his room. It was not easy to choose a place where his mother was guaranteed not to stumble across them. It was very good of her – although totally unnecessary – to come in to clean and to change his sheets, but it did impact on his privacy.

'I just thought I'd touch base regarding your suspicious death,' Jonah answered cheerily. 'I'm just leaving the Quinn place now. It's quite a mansion, isn't it? Not a very likely scenario for a random killing by a chance intruder!'

'No,' Andy agreed warily. 'But what on earth were *you* doing there?'

'Being a good neighbour. Expressing our condolences through the medium of one of Peter's excellent fruit pies.'

'Oh. So why are you ringing me?'

'I thought you might like my help with the case. I could cast an experienced eye over the evidence, give you some pointers on where to go next, that sort of thing.'

'So, you still think it is a *case*?' Andy asked suspiciously. 'I suppose Patrick Quinn has been filling you with ideas about an intruder climbing over the back fence and randomly attacking a fit young man and stringing him up from a tree without leaving any sign of a struggle?'

'No, I haven't met Patrick Quinn yet. We spoke to Rory's mother and one of his sisters – and his grandmother was there too. And, interestingly enough, they all accept the suicide theory.'

'So much for Patrick trying to protect his wife from thinking her son killed himself!' Andy was becoming interested in spite of himself. 'He was convinced she wouldn't be able to cope.'

'And you think that's the only reason he's trying to convince you it was murder?'

'Yes — well that and the ladder. That *is* a bit of a mystery. Anyway, I've got to go,' he added quickly, sensing that Jonah's interest had been piqued and he was about to ask for more details. 'I promised Mum I'd help her get the curtains down in the front room to wash them, and I'm already in the dog house with her after being late home yesterday.'

He ended the call, put his phone back in his pocket and turned back to the task of finding a hiding place for his mother's diary and the letters from Nigeria. Of course! He crossed the room and opened the wardrobe. He reached past the jackets and trousers hanging neatly from the rail and pulled out a black drawstring bag. It held the tripod that he used to hold his camera on the increasingly rare occasions when he had time to indulge in his hobby of birdwatching. There was no possible reason why Mum would ever look in there.

He pulled the top of the bag open and pushed the diary inside, shaking it down to the bottom. Then he picked up a handful of the letters. That was funny! These ones didn't seem ever to have been opened! He laid the pile down on the bed and took one in both hands, testing the seal by attempting to lift the flap. Then he turned it over and examined the postmark. What was the date? He went over to the window where the light was better. 1985. So Yakubu was telling the truth when he said that he had continued to write to Mum after he went back to Nigeria for the last time!

And Mum had refused even to open his letters.

Or, could it be that she had never seen them? Could Nana and Gramps have intercepted them and hidden them from her? They were addressed to their house. And he had found them in their loft. Had they deliberately tried to make sure that there was no chance that their daughter would be reconciled with the man who had deceived her into bearing his child?

Andy walked back across the room and gathered the letters together. He put them into the bag and drew the string tight before returning it to its place at the very back of the wardrobe.

5. CASE CONFERENCE

Anna arrived late to work the following morning, after another row with Philip, which had upset Donna and made her uncooperative at breakfast. She walked into the open plan office where her team was based and found Sergeant Alice Ray already busily typing, a half-empty coffee mug standing on the desk beside her.

'Alice! I'm glad you're here. How did you get on with that arson you were looking into?'

'All done and dusted!' Alice reported. 'Surprise, surprise! It was our old friend Tom Brierly, off his meds and on the razzle. The usual thing – he just enjoys watching things burn. At least nobody got hurt, but I hope the owner of that warehouse is well-insured!'

'That's good. You can help me with a suspicious death that came in over the weekend. It looks like a straightforward case of suicide, but the family are convinced it's murder and even if they come round to accepting that he did it himself, they'll want to know why. The victim's father is-'

'Patrick Quinn of Quinn's Superstores,' Alice finished for her. 'I know. One of the uniforms told me about it when I came back here on Saturday night. I've been having a look into the family – just an internet search for stuff that's publicly available.'

'On your Sunday off?'

'I was at a loose end. Monica was on duty and it was either that or cleaning the fridge!'

'Well, I hope Monica was more understanding than Phil would have been when she came back off duty and found that the fridge was still dirty! I suppose it must be easier when you and your partner both work unsocial hours.'

'She hasn't noticed yet,' Alice smiled. 'With any luck, she'll have forgotten about it for long enough that I'll be able to claim that the mould must just have grown back quicker than usual! But, getting back to the Quinns, Brendan, the oldest of the siblings, has form.'

'Oh?'

'Two cautions while he was at university: one for disorderly conduct and one for common assault. I found it on Wikipedia and I've just been checking on the database now, and they are both genuine. He seems to have had rather a short fuse and got into fights quite regularly back then. Monica thinks he might well have bullied his brother and that could have contributed towards low self-esteem and suicidal ideation.'

'Hmm! It's an interesting theory, but I'm not that keen on officers becoming amateur psychologists. It's at least equally likely that he would have been fiercely protective of his little brother.'

'And Brendan has also taken part in demonstrations outside abortion clinics. He's got a bit of a reputation for extreme pro-life views.'

'Presumably associated with his Catholic upbringing,' Anna murmured thoughtfully. 'His grandmother was fiddling with a string of what I assume were rosary beads all the time I was talking to them.'

'Yes,' Alice agreed. 'And Catholics think suicide is a mortal sin – I got that off Wikipedia too. So, it's not surprising they don't want to admit that Rory Quinn killed himself.'

'And it is *just* possible that they're right. There *were* some marks on his fingers that could have been defensive wounds and then there's the question of how he got up there by himself. We're going to have to treat this as a potential murder until we can prove it's not. Now, I'm just going to pop to my office to boot up my computer and check my emails and then I'll brief the team. Can you get them all together in here ready?'

Anna walked briskly up the stairs to her private office. There she first turned on the power to her computer and then inserted a pod into the new coffee maker that she had recently purchased. She needed a stiff dose of caffeine to get her going after a disturbed night. Donna had developed a cough that had kept the whole family – except for Marcus, who could sleep through anything – awake until the early hours, when exhaustion finally allowed her to drift off into a restless slumber giving the rest of them a few hours of peace.

There was nothing of note in her inbox – unless you counted the message from Jonah offering his assistance with the Quinn case, should she require it. What was he like! Right now, if *she* had got forty plus years of service, as he had, and could have afforded to take early retirement, she'd have jumped at the idea – and she wouldn't always be hankering after coming back! But Phil's freelance work was too erratic to be relied upon to pay the mortgage – even if she weren't on the verge of telling him to eff off back to his mother's house in Devon – and she had only nineteen years' worth of contributions in the pension scheme.

Sighing, she picked up the mug of black coffee and headed back down to meet the team.

Andy was at the front of the room flicking through slides on the large display screen. He had reproduced the family tree that Emma had given them, incorporating photographs of each of the adults who had been present at the house on Saturday. There was also a map showing the location of the property and a larger scale one with possible entry points for an intruder marked in red. Why did everyone except Anna apparently have plenty of time for supererogatory work? Why didn't they all have the long lists of unfinished DIY jobs and household chores that she had?

She walked to the front of the room and put her mug down on the desk. She stood in silence looking round at the team of officers and staff, some engrossed in their computer screens, others indulging in banter. Gradually the chatter subsided as, one by one, they looked up and saw her there.

'I'm sure you've all heard by now that we have a suspicious death to investigate,' she began. 'The victim, Rory Quinn, is the son of Patrick Quinn, the owner and CEO of Quinn Group, so we can expect some press interest in the case. It looks like a fairly typical suicide: young man, possibly under the influence of alcohol. But his family insist that he wouldn't have done it, and we have to take that seriously. Quinn will have a massive PR department at his beck and call that will make things extremely difficult for us if we ignore them and it turns out to be murder after all. Mike Carson's doing the PM this morning. That may possibly give us a clear answer one way or the other. Until then, we're focusing on finding out why he might have killed himself, while keeping an open mind about the possibility of foul play. Everything clear so far? OK, Andy, take us through what happened.'

Andy got up and addressed the room. 'This is the Quinn family home,' he told them, pointing at a photograph of the house in Kiln Lane. Security is good as far as access from the road is concerned: high walls, wrought iron gates operated from inside the house. But the back garden has farmland behind it, with just a close-board fence to keep people out. According to Patrick Quinn, they've had trouble in the past with kids getting in and scrumping apples. His theory is that someone climbed over the fence, lay in wait for Rory and killed him. He was found hanging from one of the big apple trees near the bottom of the garden.'

At the click of a button, the house was replaced by a shot of the noose dangling from the tree. More clicks brought up images of Rory's body lying in the leaf litter, views of the garden from various angles and finally Emma's family tree.

'Here we have the Quinn family,' Andy continued. 'Patrick Quinn and his wife, Martina, have five children: Brendan, Róisín, Emma, Bianca and Rory, who was the youngest by ten years. He and Emma were the only ones still living with their parents. The other three are all married with children of their own and living at various locations, all within a couple of hours' drive of Oxford. Alice has been doing a bit of research into their background.'

He sat down and Alice walked forward to take his place.

'Patrick Quinn is an American citizen,' she told them as a photograph of the multi-millionaire appeared on the screen behind her. 'He's been living in Oxford since 1978, when he came over here on a Rhodes Scholarship. His business empire began with a programme of package holidays for Americans wanting to come to Britain and Ireland to find their roots. As his name suggests, Patrick traces his own ancestry back to Irish immigrants who left County Galway during the potato famine.'

She glanced towards Andy, who advanced the slides to bring up a new photograph.

'Quinn met his wife, Bianca, while they were both studying in Oxford. She was born in London, but her parents were Italian immigrants who came over here in the fifties. Believe it or not, her father started out as an ice-cream seller!'

'Which just goes to show that stereotypes aren't always wrong,' Andy smiled.

'Brendan, the oldest of their children, was quite wild in his youth,' Alice resumed, 'acquiring a couple of cautions for getting into fights while he was a student. But he seems to have settled down now and he's a consultant opthal- ... ophthalmolo- ... He's a senior eye specialist at the Bristol Eye Hospital. He and his wife, Stacey, have two children aged six and four.'

'And they were all at the house on Saturday,' Andy added. 'The whole family were round to celebrate Rory's twenty-first; but most of them – including Brendan – didn't arrive until after Rory was dead.'

'The oldest of the girls is Róisín,' Alice went on. 'She's a teacher, married to a man called Colin Mills, who she met when they were both at Cambridge University. He's a teacher too. They have three daughters: Grace, Layla and Willow. Rory's youngest sister, Bianca, is also married. She has two children, a boy and a girl.'

'And another on the way,' Andy added. 'Bianca's husband is a British-born Muslim of Bangladeshi descent. They met at the School of Oriental and African Studies in London, and he's now got a research job at the university here.'

'Which just leaves Emma,' Anna put in. 'She's the middle one and a very calm and efficient young woman, good at keeping her head while all around her are losing theirs, as my old boss, DCI Porter, would have put it.'

'She's Chief Operating Officer for the family business,' Alice added, 'and expected to take over as CEO when her father retires. She has a first-class degree from the LSE and an MBA from the Saïd Business School.'

'She still lives in the family home, but she's got a separate flat above the office where she and her father work,' Andy explained. 'She seemed to be in charge of the whole show when we were there on Saturday, but that may just be because her parents were in shock after their son's death.'

'The other person who comes into it, although she didn't arrive at the house until after Rory was dead, is his fiancée, Ellie

Unwin,' Anna went on. 'They've been together since they were at school and they were supposed to be becoming officially engaged at the party on Saturday. She came to see me yesterday with some additional information that she didn't tell us on Saturday, but we'll come to that later. Carry on, Andy, take us through the sequence of events on Saturday.'

'As far as we've managed to piece together – mainly based on a timeline that Emma produced for us – this is what happened,' Andy told them, bringing up a schedule of times on the screen. 'The family – that's Patrick, Martina, Emma and Rory – got up between seven and eight o'clock. Emma had breakfast in her flat, and the others ate in the kitchen of the main house. At half past eight their regular cleaning lady came round. She comes every Monday, Wednesday and Friday morning. This was an extra visit to help get things ready for the party. She worked until eleven thirty and then left.'

'And her name?' asked Joshua Pitchfork, a young detective constable, who was conscientiously taking notes.

'Mrs Rosie Simms.' Andy glanced down at his notebook and then back at the screen. 'At nine o'clock, Rory went out for a run. He does this every day. Nobody noticed what time he got back, but he was definitely there when his mother set off for London at about eleven thirty. She was going to collect her mother to bring her to the party. Patrick, Emma and Rory had lunch together, and then they went their separate ways. Emma went back to the office and Patrick went out to get some last-minute provisions for the party. They both assumed that Rory went to his room, but they didn't check. That was the last they saw of him alive.'

Andy paused to check his notes and scroll the timeline upwards.

'During the course of the afternoon, the guests start to arrive. Róisín and her family are first, sometime between two and two thirty. Then about half an hour later, Bianca and her family join them. Patrick Quinn returns shortly after three. He goes up to Rory's room to fetch him down, but he's not there. A few minutes later, he discovers his body hanging in the orchard at the bottom of the garden and he calls the emergency services.'

'I interviewed him,' Anna intervened. 'He told me that when he got back, Róisín and Bianca were in the kitchen making a salad, and the children were playing in the hall with their dads. Emma was working in the office, which is an extension built on the side of the house with a door through from the hall. Patrick put the bags of food he'd bought in the kitchen and went to look for Rory, first in his bedroom and then in the garden. Apparently, he often used to go down to read a book at the bottom of the garden. He liked to get away from everyone.'

'Even when it was his birthday party?' queried Alice.

'Reading between the lines, I think he probably didn't find social occasions very easy,' Anna replied. 'I'm sure his father would deny it, but he seems like a bit of a loner to me.'

'Mmm,' Alice murmured thoughtfully. 'That figures. It sounds like his family knew that. I mean: you'd have expected a much more lavish twenty-first birthday party for Patrick Quinn's youngest son, wouldn't you? I'd have expected a glitzy do at the Ritz – or at very least the Randolph!'

'They do seem to be a surprisingly normal family,' Andy agreed. 'It's a big house, but that's about the only thing that makes them any different from any of us. I'd have expected them to bring in outside caterers at the very least.'

'Getting back to Patrick Quinn's account of what happened,' Anna said firmly. 'He found Rory hanging from the apple tree and went to the shed to fetch the stepladder. He climbed up and managed to get the loop of rope off over Rory's head. He tried to revive him using mouth-to-mouth and chest compressions, but he didn't respond. He called for an ambulance and then went indoors to warn the family to keep the children away from the garden.'

She paused to scan further down her interview notes.

'He's adamant that Rory would never kill himself. In his opinion, it must have been an intruder getting in over the back fence. He told me they've had trouble in the past with teenagers coming over to steal apples from the trees and sometimes doing damage. And they regularly received hate mail from nutters who objected to Patrick's public support of the campaign to overturn Roe v. Wade.'

'But there's no sign that I could see of anyone having got over the back fence recently,' Andy put in.

'And his father couldn't think of anyone who could have wanted Rory dead,' Anna agreed. 'According to him, he was very popular and had no enemies.'

'Like practically every murder victim we've ever come across,' Alice mumbled.

'His theory,' Anna continued, without acknowledging the interruption, 'is that it was a random attack by a chance intruder. I can't honestly say that I buy that idea at all. If it was a killing, it must have been someone he knew, someone who could persuade him to co-operate enough to get him down there, probably with a hefty dose of sleeping tablets and whisky inside him, and-'

'Why do you say that?' interrupted Alice. 'The whisky and the sleeping tablets I mean?'

'We found the empties lying under the leaves near where his father laid him down,' Anna told her. 'And I think I could smell alcohol on him. If it wasn't for the problem of how he got himself up to that branch without a ladder, I'd be ruling out anything other than suicide already.'

'There was no suicide note either, presumably?' Alice queried.

'No. Not on his body and not in his room either. I looked for one and Andy searched his room too. His father had already been in there before we got there and he's sure everything was just as usual. Well …,' she looked down at her notes. 'He pointed out this, lying on the bed, which he'd never seen before. He thought Rory must've brought it back with him from uni.'

She brought up a photograph on the screen.

'What is it?' asked Alice, staring at an elaborately carved length of wood lying on a plain blue duvet cover.

'It's called a love spoon,' Andy informed her. 'It's a traditional Welsh design. Apparently, they're something that men give to their sweethearts. Maybe he'd bought it to give to his fiancée.'

'And he'd got it out ready to hand it to her at the party,' Anna agreed. 'But, with Patrick Quinn having drawn it to our attention as something new, we've sent it off for fingerprinting, just in case. Anyway, to summarise, Patrick Quinn is very keen to tell us that his son was deliriously happy at the prospect of settling down in Oxford with his childhood sweetheart and excellent prospects in a prestigious solicitor's firm. He's determined not to entertain the possibility of suicide – which is going to make our job quite tricky if that's what it turns out to be.'

'Even more tricky if our findings are inconclusive,' Andy observed in a low voice.

'Mmm,' Anna nodded. 'Anyway, now it's over to you, Andy. Tell us what you found out from Emma when you spoke to her.'

'Emma was like your perfect witness,' Andy informed them. 'She was very calm and very systematic. She told me that she was working in the office all morning and during the afternoon until the guests started arriving. I asked her what order they got there in and she said that Róisín and Colin were first, and then Bianca and Mohammed. I was a bit surprised about Mohammed – I

101

mean it was a funny name for ... well I wasn't expecting one of Patrick Quinn's daughters to have married a ...'

Andy felt his cheeks burning as he floundered in his efforts to avoid any suggestion that he was biased against Muslims or ethnic minorities. Not for the first time, he was grateful that his darker skin tone masked his blushes.

'Apparently Bianca is very interested in Islam and she studied it at uni, which is where they met – like Alice said. Mohammed is a Muslim, but, according to Emma, he's very broadminded. He hasn't tried to make Bianca convert, but Emma reckons that's how it will probably turn out in the end. I think she's rather looking forward to seeing the sparks fly if that happens.'

'That's interesting,' Anna commented. 'Did she expand on who would be making those sparks?'

'Emma reckoned that Brendan would go ballistic. She said that Patrick would also be angry, but would come round in the end. She thought that Martina would be upset, but ... the way she put it was *blood is thicker than water*, so I guess she means that their mother would do anything to avoid a rift in the family.'

'OK. Go on.'

'Mohammed works at the university here in Oxford. He's researching into ...,' Andy peered down at his notes before reading out carefully, 'Qur'anic exegesis (whatever that is!). Bianca has a part-time job coaching undergraduates in the same faculty. They live in Summertown, in a big house that Daddy bought them for a wedding present. Apparently, he was planning to do the same for Rory and Ellie.'

'It must be nice to have a rich daddy who can buy you a house, instead of having to save up a deposit and then work to pay the mortgage,' Alice muttered.

'Brendan didn't arrive until after the police. PC Gilbert has that down as 16.03,' Andy resumed, filling the silence that followed Alice's observation. 'His wife, Stacey, was a nurse working with him when he was a registrar at Moorfields. She's now a fulltime wife and mother. Emma made it very clear that she doesn't have any time for women who conform to that sort of stereotype. She was much more approving of the way that Róisín and Colin organise their lives. They're both part-time Chemistry teachers and they share childcare responsibilities equally. They've got three little girls: Grace, Layla and Willow. Bianca's kids are called Abraham and Maria; and Brendan's are Theo and Poppy.'

'That makes seven grandchildren altogether,' Anna murmured, 'with another on the way.'

'And Rory was godfather to five of them,' Andy added. 'Bianca's two haven't been christened. She and Mohammed are leaving it up to them to choose what religion they want to be when they're older. That's a bit of a sore point with some other members of the family, according to Emma.'

'Which ones?' asked Anna sharply.

'Brendan mainly, I think. I got the impression that the older generation aren't desperately happy either, but they're being more polite about it. Emma seems rather amused by the whole thing.' Andy shook his head. 'I can't really make her out. She seems so detached from it all. It's as if all this is happening to someone else – as if she's an outsider looking in. You wouldn't think it was her little brother who'd just been found dead in her back garden!'

'Maybe it hasn't sunk in yet,' Anna suggested, 'or maybe that's her way of coping. Everyone reacts differently to sudden bereavement. It's handy for us that there's someone who can tell us about the family without dissolving into tears or wasting time protesting about how ridiculous it is to suggest that Rory killed himself. You've learned far more than I got out of talking to Rory's parents. But go on, I interrupted you.'

'I asked her how they all got on as kids. She said there were the usual sibling rivalries, but Rory wasn't really part of that because he was so much younger.' Andy looked down at his notes. 'Here's what Emma said about them. "Brendan was always giving him advice, which he resented, I think – or I would have done in his place, anyway! Róisín spoiled him – she was 15 when he was born and she loved mothering him. Bianca may have felt pushed out when she stopped being the youngest, but she didn't ever show it. She's very generous and kind – much the nicest of us!" I don't think Emma likes Brendan much.'

'Maybe he was in the habit of giving her advice too,' Anna suggested with a smile. 'I know my two would have resented that.'

'Maybe. Anyway, next I asked her how Rory seemed that day. She said he wasn't any different from usual that morning. According to Emma, he's never been exactly care-free. He's always been trying to live up to family expectations – although they've all tried to make it clear that he didn't need to compete with his older siblings. Arguably, they all went to better universities than he did. He applied to Cambridge, but didn't get in. He seemed a bit happier during his last year at Nottingham, but it didn't last after he came home again this summer. Maybe he wasn't looking forward to becoming a solicitor. Their parents didn't exactly pressurise the children into their careers, but it was pretty clear that they were expected to get good degrees and professional jobs. Rory liked to be out-of-doors. He volunteered with conservation charities and went walking and camping.'

'It sounds as if his dad would have done better buying him a farm to run, instead of pushing him into a solicitor's office,' Alice grunted.

'I asked her about the pictures on his walls,' Andy continued. 'She said yes, that was his other great passion. I got the impression that Emma thought it was a pity that he hadn't gone to Art College instead of studying law. So, I asked her if his parents pressurised him into that, but she said it was entirely Rory's decision.'

'I wonder ...,' mused Anna. 'Some people are very clever at forcing other people to choose the option that they want them to.'

'Then I asked her about Rory's friends. I don't get the impression that he had many – or maybe he just didn't bring them home or talk about them to his sister. The only name she came up with was a Jamie, who was at Nottingham with Rory. She mentioned him because he's coming to Oxford next term to do a teaching certificate at Brookes[1].'

'A bit of a loner then?' suggested Anna.

'I don't suppose his family would agree with that. I asked Emma if she could think of anyone who might bear him a grudge and even she was sticking to the line that he was popular with everyone. When I pressed her, she admitted that she wouldn't have known if he'd upset anyone in Nottingham, but she didn't think it was likely. So, I moved on to the hypothesis that someone might have attacked Rory to get back at his father or at the family business. She said "no" and then later she talked about a disgruntled employee who claimed unfair dismissal saying that they'd discriminated against him because he was white and British and working class. Obviously had a chip on his shoulder. He pulled out of the employment tribunal, presumably on the advice of his lawyers, but carried on making threats against Patrick.'

'Did Patrick report him to the police?' Anna asked sharply.

'Nope!' Andy shook his head. 'I don't think any of them took it seriously. Emma seemed to think he was all talk. And this was

---

[1] Oxford Brookes University

back in 2019, so if he was going to do anything, he'd probably have done it by now.'

'All the same, we'd better follow up on this. What was his name?'

'Jack Lampard. I haven't had time to look to see if he's got form.'

'Jennifer can do that.' Anna looked across at a civilian member of staff, sitting unobtrusively behind a computer screen, listening diligently to Andy's account. Their eyes met and Jennifer Moorhouse nodded briefly. 'Thanks Andy. Now sit down and I'll tell everyone about what I learned from Martina and, more significantly, from Ellie.'

Andy returned to his seat, passing the clicker over to Anna as she came forward to take his place.

'This is Martina Quinn,' Anna began, pointing at a new face on the screen. Mrs Quinn was a handsome woman with jet black hair and dark brown eyes. Expertly applied makeup – or possibly cosmetic surgery? – made her look younger than her sixty-one years. 'She confirmed what we already knew about her movements on Saturday: she left for London about 11.30 and didn't get back to the house until half past four. When she left, Rory was in his bedroom, Emma was working in the office – in Martina's opinion, she works too hard – and Patrick was in the kitchen checking what food they still needed to buy for the party. Martina drove straight to her mother's house in Clerkenwell. That's where she herself grew up. Her father set up his first restaurant there. She wishes that her mother would come and live with them, but she doesn't want to move away from her friends.'

Anna paused and smiled round at her audience. 'I get the impression that Martina feels that she knows what would be best for everyone in the family, and is somewhat frustrated that they keep ignoring all her good advice.'

'Welcome to my world,' Jennifer smiled back. 'Harriet and Lydia have always ignored me when I've so much as hinted that perhaps they're heading off on a course of action that is possibly not the ultimate in good ideas. That's what motherhood is all about: you work your socks off trying give them all the things you never had as a child, and they repay you by accusing you of ruining their lives!'

'Mothers aren't always all that good at taking advice themselves,' Andy muttered. Then, louder, 'I'm sorry - I've just got a few things going on at home at the moment. And that reminds me, I'll have to go at about two this afternoon to pick up Yakubu Danjuma from Heathrow.'

'And I'm most likely going to be tied up with the Danjuma trial from Wednesday afternoon onwards,' Anna nodded. 'So, let's do our best to get this business wrapped up by the end of tomorrow. It looks like suicide, but, for the family's peace of mind, we need to establish that for sure. Alice! I'd like you to track down this Jamie. Nottingham university ought to be able to point you in the right direction – or it may be quicker to contact Oxford Brookes, if he's registered on a course there. Jennifer, once forensics send back Rory's phone and laptop, I want you to go through all his calls, social media activity and documents, in case he's hidden a suicide note there somewhere. Josh, I'd like you to get in touch with Rory's tutor and see if they know anything about his state of mind while he was at uni. And maybe you could talk to his new employer too. Did they have any qualms about taking him on? Or had he expressed any reservations about joining the firm?'

The detective constable stood up, as if to go. There was a general atmosphere of movement in the room as everyone prepared to begin their assigned tasks. Anna waved them back into their places.

'Before you all go, I need to tell you about what Rory's fiancée told me yesterday.'

'Yesterday?' queried Alice.

'She rang me and said she had something else to tell me,' Anna explained. 'On Saturday, in front of her parents, she toed the party line, like the rest of the family: Rory was happy and looking forward to his good job and his marriage; he didn't have any enemies; no signs of depression etc., etc.'

'And yesterday?' prompted Alice.

'Yesterday, she rang to say that she hadn't been entirely honest. Mind you, even then I wasn't totally convinced. There was something about her relationship with her parents that made me wonder if the marriage to Rory wasn't as much to please them as because that's what Ellie really wanted. She's an only child and her parents must have both been in their forties when she was born. I think her mother in particular was anxious to have some grandchildren while they were still young enough to enjoy them. Ellie has a quite marked stammer, which her mum may have been afraid would put boys off. That was what brought them together apparently. It was when they were at high school. Ellie was being bullied and Rory stood up for her. They'd been going out together since they were thirteen.'

'In that case, it wouldn't be surprising of one or other of them had got cold feet about the wedding by now,' Alice observed.

'That's what I thought,' Anna agreed, 'but according to Ellie, they were both … well, I don't think happy is necessarily the right word, content with it is probably nearer the mark. Ellie talked as if it was an arrangement that suited them both, but not because they were madly in love, just because … Well, the way she put it was that things would be simpler for them both. And it was still some way off. She's starting a Master's degree at Cambridge next term and there was no question of them getting married until she'd finished that. I think they may both have been kicking the can down the road to avoid awkward questions from their families.'

'What sort of questions?' asked Andy.

'That's what I'm coming on to. When we met yesterday, Ellie told me that Rory had confided in her that he was gay – or maybe bisexual, *experiencing same-sex attraction* was how she put it. And he'd mentioned a Jamie in Nottingham who seemed to be a particularly close friend. If he and Rory were lovers, then things might have got very complicated once he was living in Oxford too.'

6. REUNION

'Bismillah al rahman al rahim.' Yakubu Danjuma leaned forward, bending so that his head almost touched the floor of the departure lounge. *In the name of God, the most Gracious, the most Compassionate.* As he raised his head and rocked back on his heels, he wondered why he was saying this traditional blessing. Was he really dedicating his actions to God and declaring his acceptance of whatever outcome God should send? Or was this hypocrisy? Were his true reasons for travelling to Oxford merely selfish ones? Was this outward show of religious devotion a self-deluding smoke-screen to prevent him from admitting his true desires?

'Final call for Virgin Atlantic Flight VS412 to London Heathrow!' Yakubu scrambled to his feet, picked up his bag and reached into his pocket for passport and boarding card. 'Bismillah al rahman al rahim,' he repeated softly as he stepped forward and presented them at the gate. Now, like many of his fellow-passengers, he was calling upon God to keep him safe during the flight. Planes did not often crash, but there was no point taking any chances!

He fastened his seatbelt and leaned back, waiting for take-off. Around him, other passengers fussed with coats and bags. Which items should go in the overhead lockers and which would fit under the seat? Would this be needed on the journey or only on arrival in London? Yakubu gazed out of the window, watching the last few cases being loaded into the hold. Not long now.

The cabin crew walked down the aisle, shooing the last few still-standing passengers into their seats, and checking that the lockers were firmly closed and seatbelts were fastened. Down below, the luggage trolley drove away across the tarmac. The pre-recorded safety announcement began and the plane slowly started to move away from the terminal building. The six-hour flight had begun.

Yakubu handed over the debris from his lunch to the waiting steward and turned his attention back to the thesis that he had brought with him to read during the flight. The other examiners had both already sent in their reports and he was under pressure to finish his, but he had been finding it hard to concentrate recently. A long flight should have been the perfect opportunity to get the job finished, but somehow his mind kept straying to thoughts of what was going to happen after he arrived in Oxford.

Sighing, he opened the roughly-bound manuscript at the page that he had been reading before lunch. 'To establish the result, we first prove the following lemma.' *What result? What was it that the student had stated was the aim of this section?* Yakubu studied the lemma, trying to remember what each of the variables in the formulae signified. He flipped back to the previous page, seeking to refresh his memory. 'As θ varies from 0 to 2π ...' *But what did θ mean, in this context?*

It was no good! He turned back to the beginning of the chapter and started again. To be fair to the student whose work he was examining, he must be thorough. It wasn't good enough to skim through the pages hoping that things would become clearer as he read further.

He read solidly for ten minutes, occasionally underlining sentences or making marginal notes with a pencil, and jotting down potential questions for the viva in a small spiral-bound notebook. Then his mind started to wander again.

What was he expecting to get out of this visit to his old university town? Justice for Jibrilu, he supposed. And answers to the question that had been gnawing at his mind ever since the police had brought the awful news to him that his son had been killed – why? Why had a perfect stranger taken out a knife and killed an innocent young man? What had Jibrilu done to offend them – apart from being a black man who wasn't afraid to intervene when he saw a thirteen-year-old boy being bullied.

That was something! At least Jibrilu had died trying to do the right thing. *He* had nothing to be ashamed of. Unlike his killers. If Yakubu had his way, they would all be sentenced to death! But there was no death penalty in Britain. Life imprisonment, then. And more important, they needed to admit what they had done – to recognise how wicked they had been – to express regret. And to answer that question – to tell him, Jibrilu's father, *why* they had killed his son!

That was why it was so important for him to be there to watch the trial. He needed to see them there in court, and to hear their response to all those questions for which he needed answers. What exactly happened that night? Why did they use a knife when Jibrilu carried no weapon? Were they remorseful about what they had done?

But Andy had warned him not to expect too much from the trial. They could not be forced to give evidence. That would be up to their lawyers, who might decide that their case would be better served by their keeping silent. He had told Yakubu that most of the facts in the case were undisputed, which meant that most of the time would probably be spent in complicated legal arguments over the distinction between murder and manslaughter and the degree of culpability attached to those who were involved in the incident but did not actually wield the knife. Andy had warned him that … Andy had said …

Yes, Andy! Yakubu looked down at his watch – the one that his own father had bought for him to celebrate his having won a scholarship to study in Oxford all those years ago, and which he had passed on to Jibrilu at that proud moment when he had followed in his footsteps. It was not long now before he would be seeing Andy again. Andy. Detective Inspector Andy Lepage. His son! It was still difficult to believe. Allah was indeed gracious and compassionate! How else could it have been that the death of his son Jibrilu had been the means of his discovering this son that he had not even known he had?

And then there was Mandy – his Mandy! Except that he should not call her his any longer. She had made that quite clear. He must see her again. He must speak to her. He could not be in Oxford and not see her and speak to her! He must try to persuade her to allow him back into her life. If only things had been different, all those years ago! If only he hadn't permitted his parents to push him into that early marriage. Zubaydah had been beautiful and submissive, but she had not been his choice; and she had been a dutiful spouse, not a real companion – not someone that he could speak to as an equal, someone with ideas of her own – not, in short, someone like Mandy.

Things would have been so different if he had been free to marry Mandy. She would have leapt at the chance, there was no doubt about that. She had been prompting him to ask her for months before his scheduled departure date. And it was only a few days before he left Oxford for the last time that he finally plucked up the courage to explain to her why he could not stay in Britain and settle down with her. He would never forget the look on her face when he told her that he was already married, that in fact, he had two wives and a baby daughter, that he had a duty to them to return to Nigeria. Disbelief at first – then a kind of horror and repugnance – and then anger, raging anger, white-hot and unquenchable.

Did she know then that she was carrying his child? What would he have done if she had told him? Would that have been enough to give him the courage to follow his heart? What would his duty have been, if he had known? If he had divorced Zubaydah and Jamilah, and married Mandy, he would have been able to find work in Britain, which would have paid well enough for him to send money back to Nigeria to support his ex-wives and his little daughter. They had all been happy enough living with his parents during the three years that he had spent in Oxford; they would not have missed his presence. And if he had not returned to his job at the university, they would never have moved into that house with the faulty wiring, and the fire would never have occurred and they would all have still been alive!

Except for Jibrilu. If Yakubu had never returned to Nigeria, Jibrilu would never have been born. Most likely Jamilah would have married again and had children by her new husband, but there would have been no Jibrilu – no bright, ambitious young man eager to follow his father into a career in academia. And nobody to hear the cries of a scared young boy faced with taunts and threats from a group of racist thugs! Jibrilu was a son to be proud of – the boy's parents had told him that.

But Andy Lepage was also a son that he could take pride in. Mandy had done a good job of raising him on her own. Detective Inspector was a senior rank, wasn't it? He must be good at his job to have got so far.

Yakubu reached inside his jacket and pulled out a small photograph. Two of the corners were bent and the picture was faded with age, but her smiling face still looked back at him with the same intensity that he remembered from all those years ago. They'd gone into one of those automatic photo booths together one day. Four pictures: one of each of them separately and two as a couple, hugging one another close on the little bench seat, giggling with the pure joy of being together. Did Mandy still have the one that she had kept of him? Probably not, considering that she seemed determined to erase him from her life and her memory.

He stared down at the picture in his hand. She looked so young! But then she was young – only seventeen in this picture or perhaps just turned eighteen. Her parents had been worried about the age difference between them. He could see it in their eyes, but they had said nothing. He would have been more direct if a child of his had been forming an unsuitable relationship, but they were trying not to interfere.

Or perhaps they were afraid that their disapproval would only push their daughter further into his clutches. Mandy had said as much the day she invited him back to her house for the first time. When he suggested that her parents might not approve of him, she had laughed and told him that they knew better than to try to keep them apart. They knew that would only make her more determined to stay with him.

Was that all he was to her? An act of defiance? An attempt to get her parents' attention by finding the most outrageously unsuitable boyfriend that she could? Except that they had seemed to like him. Was that just politeness? Or did they invite him to their house so often because they preferred him to meet Mandy under their supervision – or the scrutiny of her younger sister, Jennifer?

Little Jennifer! She had only been twelve when they met for the first time. She had been openly curious about him, asking all the questions that the adults in the family were embarrassed to broach. She was clearly excited by the idea of her sister going out with a black man and interested in what the implications might be for the future.

'If you get married and have children, what colour will they be?' she had asked, to her parents very obvious discomfiture.

Mandy had laughed and told her that she would have to wait and see. And Mrs Lepage had said firmly that this was all a long way down the line and Mandy had her degree to finish before even thinking about getting married.

Sighing, Yakubu but the photograph back into his jacket pocket. Poor Mandy! Things had worked out so differently from what she had expected. She'd laid it all out before him at that last meeting that they'd had before he left Oxford for the last time. Once they were married, he would be allowed to live in Britain as the spouse of a British citizen. And he could easily get a job there with his doctorate from Oxford.

And, after she finished her degree in Oxford, they could decide whether to make their permanent home in Britain or in Nigeria. She was longing to go there and meet his family.

That had been the point at which he broke the news to her that his family included two wives and a little daughter. For one insane moment he had dreamed of Mandy agreeing to become wife number three – a hope that was viciously smashed to smithereens by her tears of misery and rage. How could he do this to her? How could he have lied to her all this time?

He hadn't lied. She had never asked him if he was married.

She shouldn't have needed to ask! He had deliberately deceived her! How could he?

Because he loved her.

Is that what he'd told his two wives? Did he love them too?

Not the way he loved his Mandy. That was different – something he'd never felt for anyone before. And she had loved him; he was sure of that. She had even been willing to leave her home and go with him to Nigeria – but not as one wife out of three!

What should he have done? Mandy's parents no doubt would say that he should never have formed a relationship with their daughter. That he should have told her that he was already married. His own family would probably have said the same. His father, in particular, hated all kinds of lying and deception.

But his parents were partly to blame for the situation that he found himself in! They had "encouraged" him to marry Zubaydah, as a favour to her father, who was struggling financially. And then, when Zubaydah fell ill after Samirah was born, they had suggested the perfect solution to his problems: marry her sister! Jamilah had cared diligently for her sister and her niece. He could never have managed without her. Certainly, without her, his DPhil in Oxford would have been out of the question!

'Professor Danjuma!' At the sound of his name, Yakubu scanned the row of waiting taxi-drivers clustering around the exit from Passport Control. There he was! His son!

'Andy!' He hurried forward, his cabin bag slung over his shoulder so that he could use his walking stick in one hand while pulling his trolley case with the other. 'It's so good to see you again!'

'I'll take that, sir.' Andy reached out for the trolley case. Yakubu meekly handed it over, but frowned at the formal greeting.

'Yakubu, please. I know that you cannot call me *father*, but at least let us be on first-name terms.'

'OK.' There was still no warmth in Andy's voice. He was merely carrying out a duty, perhaps an unwelcome or even an unpleasant one.

They spoke little during the journey to Oxford. Andy appeared preoccupied and Yakubu soon gave up his attempts at conversation after receiving little more than grunts in reply. A detective inspector was bound to have things on his mind. Perhaps he was in the middle of an important case. Perhaps that was the explanation for his apparent resentment at having to take time out to collect his father from the airport.

'This must be it,' Andy said at last, pulling up outside a tall mid-terraced house in a side-street off Abingdon Road. 'I'll drop you off here and then find somewhere to park.'

He put on the hazard warning lights before getting out and going round to open the door for Yakubu. 'I'll have to hurry you, I'm afraid. We're blocking the road.'

Yakubu got out, then turned to reach inside for his stick and small bag. As soon as he was ready, Andy closed the door and hurried back to the driver's side. An impatient motorist behind beeped her horn. Andy waved apologetically and then drove off, leaving Yakubu standing on the pavement looking after him.

He took out the piece of paper on which he had printed out the instructions for accessing the flat that he was renting. There was a key-safe next to the front door. He punched in the combination and it fell open. Inside there were two keys on a small key ring. One was for the front door of the house, the other would allow him into his flat. But once he was inside with the doors locked behind him, how would Andy be able to let him know when he needed to be let in?

He opened the door and stepped inside, waiting for his eyes to adjust to the darkness of the hallway. In front of him a steep staircase led upwards. To the left of the stairs the original hall had been blocked off with wooden panels. There was a door with a yale lock, which was presumably the entrance to the ground floor flat. That was where the owners of the house lived, he remembered. The flat that he was renting was on the second floor. He hesitated, wondering whether to ascend now or to wait for Andy. Would the owner mind, if he left the front door open while he went up to find his accommodation? What if whoever was occupying the first-floor flat were to come back and close it, shutting Andy out? He turned back and stood anxiously on the doorstep, watching for his son's return.

After a few minutes, which felt like hours, there he was, walking briskly with the trolley case trundling noisily behind him on the uneven pavement. When he got to the front gate, he stopped to push down the handle of the case so that he could pick it up and lift it over the step onto the black-and-white chequered tiles of the path to the front door.

'OK, where now?' he asked as he climbed the two steps into the house.

'It's upstairs,' Yakubu answered. 'The second floor.'

'Right.' Andy looked up at the steep stairs and then back at Yakubu. 'Give me that bag,' he ordered, reaching out his hand for the small bag that Yakubu had slung over his shoulder. 'Then you go first and I'll follow. Take your time,' he added. 'There's no rush.'

'Yakubu opened his mouth to protest that he was not so old that he could not carry his own luggage. Then he changed his mind and meekly handed over the bag. Holding tightly to the handrail and leaning heavily on his stick he made his way slowly up the stairs. A light came on automatically as he reached the landing. He walked along it, past another locked door and two doorways that had been blocked up with sheets of plasterboard, to a second flight of stairs. Panting with exertion, he hauled himself up. Another light magically came on as he reached the top, revealing a small square landing with a door up a single further stair on the left.

'Looks like you're up in the attic,' Andy observed, putting the case down. 'Not exactly ideal, but I suppose it's only for a week or so.'

'I booked for a month,' Yakubu told him. 'You said that trials were sometimes delayed or adjourned.'

'Yes,' Andy nodded reluctantly. 'I suppose that makes sense.'

'And I wanted to be here in Oxford for longer,' Yakubu went on. 'I was hoping that we might spend some time together – to get to know one another.'

'Oh! Well, we're very busy at the moment. I don't get a lot of free time.' Andy looked down at his watch. 'In fact, I really ought to be getting back to work now. So, if you could open the door, I'll just bring these bags inside and then leave you to get settled in.'

Yakubu inserted the key and turned the lock. The door swung open and he stepped inside. There were no windows in the living room, but the strong July sunshine shone down through a skylight high up in the sloping ceiling.

Andy followed him in and put the bag down on a square table in the centre of the room. 'Looks like you've got everything you need,' he observed, gazing around the room. 'Cooking facilities over there, TV, sofa.'

He prowled around opening doors and peering into cupboards. 'They've left you some teabags and sugar, but there's no milk. If you make a list, I could get you some supplies, to save you having to lug them all up those stairs.'

'Thank you. That's very kind. Or perhaps we could go shopping together?'

'That's the bedroom.' Andy continued to explore the flat. Despite his earlier words, he seemed to be in no hurry to leave. 'Shall I put your case in there? It's a bit small, but after all, it's only for a few weeks.'

Getting no reply from Yakubu, he closed the bedroom door and continued his investigation of the facilities. 'Oh! There's another bedroom here. So, you have a choice. This one's a bit bigger, but it faces on to the road, so it could be noisy. Now, there must be a bathroom somewhere ... Oh, I see, this isn't a cupboard, it's ...' He opened a narrow door in the corner of the living room. 'No bath,' he reported, 'but a shower is probably better really. I'll put your case in the front bedroom. It'll be more convenient, right next to the bathroom. I'd better go now. If you email me across that shopping list, I'll bring the stuff round sometime this evening.'

'Thank you, but ....' Yakubu moved across to bar Andy's way out. 'But ... there's something else first.'

'Oh?'

'I – I was hoping ... I chose a flat with two bedrooms because ... I would like you to stay here with me.'

Andy's surprise was palpable. He stared at his father for several seconds before answering.

'But that's ridiculous! Why would I ...? What about Mum? She'd go ballistic!'

'She's had you for thirty-eight years,' Yakubu reasoned. 'Is it so much to ask that you give me four weeks of your time, to get to know you? You are my son – my *only* son, now. Don't I have a right–?'

'You lost any rights you had over me the day you walked out on Mum and went off back to Africa – to your two wives! The ones you never even had the decency to tell her existed!'

Andy took a pace towards the door, but Yakubu stepped in front of him again. 'Please! At least stay here with me until the trial is over.'

'I'll come and pick you up every day and take you to the court,' Andy promised. 'And I can talk to Victim Support about getting you some counselling.'

'I do not need counselling!' Yakubu spat out angrily. 'I need to have my son with me. I need ….'

'You need a replacement for Jibrilu,' Andy finished for him. 'But I can't be that – and I wouldn't if I could. I'm sorry that you lost your son – truly I am – but I can't, and won't, try to fill his place. You've got to learn to accept that.'

He took a step to one side, trying to skirt round Yakubu to reach the door, but his father side-stepped too and remained blocking his way out. It would be easy for the younger man to push past him. Those muscular arms would have no trouble simply lifting Yakubu's frail body out of the way.

'Listen to me,' he pleaded, putting out his arm and resting his hand on Andy's shoulder. 'I am not the fool you take me for. I am not looking for a new son to replace Jibrilu. I love him far too much to think for a minute that anyone could do that! I want – I need – to know you better because you are my own flesh and blood. And, more important, your mother is my Mandy, the love of my life!'

'Whom you deceived, seduced and then abandoned,' Andy cut in. 'And all while she was still in her teens.'

'I know. I know. But now I would like the chance to make amends.'

'As far as Mum's concerned the best way you can do that is to get back to Nigeria the moment the trial is over.'

'Oh Andy! My son! Have you never been in love?' Yakubu sighed. 'I have a pain in my heart.' He took his hand off Andy's shoulder and placed it in a fist on his chest. 'Here! There is an emptiness that only my Mandy can fill. You cannot imagine how difficult it is for me to be here in Oxford, so close to her, and yet with no prospect of seeing her, speaking to her, holding her in my arms again! And you are the only link that I have with her. I am begging you. Come and stay here. Spend some time with your old father, before it is too late!'

'I suppose if I don't, you'll go off on your own trying to track mum down at work or something,' Andy grunted ungraciously. 'OK. I'll come for a few days – but that's all! I'm not being your go-between with Mum. She's made it quite clear she doesn't want you back in her life, and I don't blame her. Now, I've got a lot of work to catch up on, so I probably won't be back until late. I suggest you order a takeaway for your dinner. I saw a pile of leaflets next to the TV. There'll be phone numbers in them.'

'Thank you.' Yakubu stepped aside, and Andy hurried past him and out of the door. 'You can have no idea how much it means to me to see you and have you here with me.'

Yakubu gathered up the packaging from his Indian meal and walked slowly over to put it in the bin under the sink. He was tired and stiff after his long journey, but his mind was restless. He wandered into the bedroom and stood gazing down at the street below. The light was fading and some of the street lamps had come on. How long would it be before Andy got back? He had warned that he might be late. Lots of work to do, he had said, but more likely putting his departure off until the last minute to appease his mother. Was she really as determined to keep them apart as Andy made out? Or was that just a convenient excuse for him to keep his father at arm's length?

At last, there he was! He had a rucksack on his back and carrier bags in both hands, which he put down on the path when he reached the house. He stood there, fumbling for something in his pocket. Yakubu waved, but could not catch his attention, so he turned away from the window and headed out of the flat and downstairs to let him in. Flinging the front door open wide, he saw Andy standing there with his mobile phone to his ear. He looked up as Yakubu approached.

'I was just ringing you to let you know I was here,' he said, putting the phone back in his pocket and picking up the bags of shopping. 'Let's go inside and put this little lot away, shall we?'

'Let me help.' Yakubu reached for one of the bags, but Andy kept hold of it and strode inside. He was halfway up the first flight of stairs by the time that Yakubu had come into the hall and closed the door.

The climb to his attic accommodation seemed even further and steeper than it had earlier in the day. By the time he reached the first-floor landing, Andy was out of sight. Yakubu stood, breathing heavily, gathering his strength for the next ascent. Luckily, in his haste to get down to let his son into the building, he had failed to close the door of his flat. He would take his time and allow Andy to start unpacking and settling into the smaller bedroom at the back of the house.

When he reached the flat, he found Andy putting away packets and cans in a wall cupboard above the sink.

'There's milk and butter in the fridge,' he informed Yakubu, 'and some ham for sandwiches tomorrow. I always take a packed lunch to work with me, because I never know where I'll be. There's plenty for you too, if you want it or ...' he stopped. Yakubu's face must have given away his uncertainty about the offer of ham for his lunch.

'Thank you,' he said as graciously as he could manage, 'that's very thoughtful of you. I don't eat ham, but don't worry abou-'

'Of course! I should have thought,' Andy interrupted. 'I forgot Muslims don't eat pork. I'm sorry, I should have remembered. I got some cheese as well. Will that be OK?'

'Everything is just splendid,' Yakubu assured him. 'Now, let me make us each a cup of tea while you unpack and make yourself at home in your room, and then we can have a nice evening together.'

'OK.' Andy picked up his rucksack from the table and carried it into the bedroom.

Yakubu filled the kettle and put teabags into two mugs. Looking in the wall cupboard, he found a packet of digestive biscuits, which he took out and placed on the table.

'You do understand that this is just for a night or two – while you get settled in and the trial gets going.' Andy was back. He did not seem to have taken long over unpacking.

'That's a pity,' Yakubu sighed as he poured boiling water on to the teabags. 'I had hoped …, but I suppose it was too much to expect that you could have much pity for your old father after … How is you mother?'

'Not at all happy about me being here – and I don't blame her.'

'Perhaps if we were to meet …?' Yakubu suggested.

'Out of the question,' Andy snapped back. 'And I do wish you wouldn't keep on about it. Just forget it, can't you?'

'I'm sorry.' Yakubu picked up the mugs and carried them over to the table. 'Sit down and drink your tea. You must be tired after your long day. I've brought some photographs of Nigeria to show you. Pictures of my home and the university where I work and some of your aunts and cousins.'

'I'm sorry. Maybe another time. I've got to go to Coventry tomorrow to interview a witness, and I need to make plans for getting there and so on.' Andy picked up one of the mugs and carried it into his bedroom, leaving Yakubu staring at the closed door.

Yakubu sat down at the table and drew the other mug closer to him. The tea was too hot to drink, so he sat there staring into it. This was not how he was hoping that things would be. He reached out for the packet of biscuits and spent several minutes struggling to get it open. Then he got up and started across the room with the biscuits in his hand, intending to use them as an excuse to visit Andy in his room. He got to the door but hesitated with his arm outstretched towards the handle. Then, sighing, he returned to his seat. He must be patient or he would lose what little goodwill there was between them.

Two hours later Andy had still not emerged. Yakubu found more mugs and made more tea. Then, with a mug in one hand and the packet of biscuits in the other, he boldly entered his son's bedroom.

'I thought this might help the work along,' he announced.

Andy was sitting on the bed with a laptop computer next to him. At the sound of Yakubu's voice, he looked up and quickly pulled the pillow on top of a pile of airmail envelopes that were also lying beside him on the bed.

'Thanks.' He closed the lid of the laptop and got to his feet. 'I'm pretty well done now, so I'll come through and join you. You had some photos you wanted to show me, didn't you?'

7. JUST ANOTHER SUICIDE?

While Andy was preparing to drive to the airport to meet his father, Anna was hurriedly eating a late lunch in her office. When her phone rang, she reached out for the receiver, struggling to swallow a mouthful of the cheese and pickle sandwich that Philip had prepared for her the night before. Her somewhat indistinct greeting was answered by Mike Carson's musical brogue.

'I've finished the PM. I'll get the report off to you when I get time, but you asked about alcohol and sleeping tablets, so I thought I'd let you know: we found both of them in his stomach – quite large quantities, but not enough to kill him, or at least not before the rope round his neck did the job.'

'So, it's definitely suicide? He took the drugs and then hanged himself?'

'Now you know that *definitely* isn't a word in my vocabulary,' Mike teased, 'and there are a few contra-indications. Nothing *definite* you understand but ...'

'And they are ...?' Sometimes Mike could be quite infuriating.

'Those broken fingernails that the father pointed out have traces of his own skin under them, and the marks on his neck look like attempts to untie the noose while he was hanging there.'

'So, now you're saying that someone else strung him up and he tried to get loose?' demanded Anna. 'Which is it?'

'I'm saying that I can't be *definite* about it.' She could visualise Mike's smiling face as he said this. 'On balance, I'd say it's most likely that he did it himself and then, either changed his mind or else instinctively tried to free himself while he was woozy with the effect of the booze and the sleeping tablets. I'm afraid that's the best I can do for you. I've taken some blood samples and sent them off for toxicology tests. That may tell us how much of the drugs were absorbed, which will give an idea of what effect they would have had. For example, he wouldn't have been able to climb that tree if he was already unconscious because of the sleeping tablets he'd taken.'

'OK. Thanks Mike. Let me know when those results come through.'

She hardly had time to put the phone down and take another bite of her sandwich before there was a knock at the door and Ruby's head appeared round it.

'Sorry, I didn't realise this was your lunch break. I just popped in to let you know that both the whisky bottle and the temazepam box were clean – no fingerprints at all.'

Ruby came in and closed the door behind her.

'So, if Rory took them himself, either he or someone else wiped them afterwards,' Anna murmured thoughtfully. 'Was that because someone else gave them to him and they didn't want to be implicated, do you think? You hear a lot these days about groups online egging each other on to kill themselves. Could this have been something like that, but in-person rather than online?'

'Don't ask me – you're the detective!' Ruby answered with a little laugh.

'I'm not getting far with detecting what happened here,' Anna smiled back. 'I'm almost certain it was suicide, but why he did it is a real mystery. He seemed to have everything going for him.'

'Depression's a funny thing,' Ruby remarked. 'And young people often try to hide their feelings – especially from their parents. And if he was prescribed sleeping tablets, that suggests he wasn't as happy and relaxed as all that, doesn't it?'

'I suppose so. We haven't got confirmation on the prescription. It must have been his doctor in Nottingham who gave it to him and he hasn't had his registration transferred back to Oxford yet, so I'm waiting on the Nottingham police to check it out with his GP. The sticker on the box looked genuine enough but ...'

'Now, the other thing I thought you'd like to know is that the only fingerprints on Rory's laptop and phone were from Rory and his father.' Ruby broke in on Anna's thoughts that a murderer seeking to add to the appearance of suicide could easily have printed the label on the tablet packet. She looked up with a questioning expression.

'His father? So could he have been using Rory's computer – maybe checking out what he'd been doing on it?'

'Difficult to say. The prints were mostly on the case, not the keyboard. So, maybe he just picked it up to move it out of the way or something. Anyway, our IT bods have unlocked the phone and I've left it with Jen Moorcroft to have a look at. She said you wanted her to see if he could've left a suicide note there. The laptop is proving a bit more of a challenge for them, but I should be able to get it back to you later today – I hope.'

'Thanks,' Anna mumbled though another bite of sandwich.

'Oh! And you wanted us to see if we could find any evidence of intruders getting into the garden. There *are* some loose boards in the back fence and plenty of footwear marks in the ground beyond it, but nothing definite to say that anyone has been through or over the fence recently.'

'When you say *loose boards*, what exactly ...?'

'It's a close board fence with slats mounted vertically on two horizontal rails. Three or four adjacent ones were only attached at the top, so, if you wanted, you could push them aside and crawl through. You'd have to be quite small though – a child or a small woman. I doubt if many men would be able to squeeze through.'

'So again, there could have been an intruder or there may not have. Just like he could have hanged himself or he could have been strung up by someone else – maybe after being drugged with whisky and sleeping tablets.'

'Our knot expert says the hanging was an amateur affair. Whoever did it didn't know how to make a proper hangman's noose. He reckoned it wouldn't pull tight enough to kill anyone right away.'

'That fits in with Mike Carson's idea that he may have had time to break his fingernails trying to get it off,' Anna commented.

'Now, what else can I tell you?' Ruby went on. 'Oh yes! We found some blood on one of the lower branches of the tree where he was hanging. I've sent samples off to the lab for DNA testing. They may well only be from the victim, but you never know.'

'Thanks. Let me know when the results come back.'

'Well, that's about it.' Ruby turned and put her hand on the door handle. 'I'll leave you to eat your lunch in peace now.

Anna only just had time to finish her sandwich and take a bite of the apple that Philip had packed with it to ensure that she ate her *five-a-day* quota of fruit and vegetables, when her mobile phone began ringing. She put down the apple on the desk, swallowed hastily and answered the call.

'Is that Mrs Davenport?' asked an unfamiliar voice with an official-sounding manner.

'Yes. I'm Anna Davenport. What is it?'

'I'm afraid there's been an incident.'

'What's happened?' Anna's heart raced. She leapt to her feet and started pacing the room. 'Is that the school? Is Donna alright?'

'No. This is PC Bailey, Thames Valley Police. I'm ringing about your husband.'

'Philip?' Anna felt a moment of relief knowing that her daughter was safe and then a jumble of thoughts began bouncing around in her head. What had happened to Philip? What had he done? Who would pick up Donna from nursery school?

'Yes,' the voice confirmed. 'I'm sorry to have to tell you that we pulled your husband Philip Davenport out of the river this afternoon.'

'Drowned?' Anna's voice rose and she forced herself to sit back down at her desk. 'How? What happened?'

'No, no,' the voice became apologetic and a little flustered. 'I'm sorry, I should have explained better. He's quite alright. Just swallowed rather a lot of water. We've got him here at Sandford Lock, being checked over by a paramedic, just in case. I was hoping you might be able to come and collect him – and bring him some dry clothes.'

'OK. I'll have to go home first to get the clothes. It'll be about half an hour – will that be OK?'

'No problem. I'll be waiting for you outside the King's Arms.'

'But how did it happen? Phil swims like a fish. He grew up by the sea. His mum always said he could swim before he could walk.' In her confusion, Anna found herself gabbling incoherently.

'A witness said he just stepped off the side and sank. He'd filled his pockets with heavy tools from the car: spanners, wrench, pliers, measuring tape, that sort of thing.'

'You mean he was trying to kill himself?'

'I'm afraid it looks that way. Fortunately, a member of the public saw him go in and called us and meanwhile a couple of people from the pub managed to get him out. And, like I said, there doesn't seem to be any serious damage done.'

'I see.' Anna stood in the centre of the room, her phone held to her ear, suddenly unable to move or speak. Philip had tried to kill himself! But why? He'd never said anything that would suggest he had had suicidal thoughts. Things had been difficult for him since he came back to live with them again, but no more difficult than for her or the kids. And if he didn't like it, he could always have gone back down to his mother's house in Devon.

'Are you still there, Mrs Davenport?' The constable's voice jolted her back to the immediate situation.

'Yes. I'm sorry. I'll start off right away. I'll be with you in about half an hour.'

However, half an hour later, Anna was still battling with the traffic on the congested Woodstock Road, heading north towards her home in Kidlington. Perhaps she would have done better taking the longer route westwards through Botley and round the by-pass, but it was too late to worry about that now. There were roadworks on the roundabout and a lane closure that was causing the traffic to back up. She should have remembered that.

She glanced down at the clock on the dashboard. Donna would be coming out of her pre-school in less than an hour. Phil should have been picking her up. How irresponsible of him to get himself into this mess without any thought for what would happen to his little daughter! Anna would have to do it, but there was no possibility of getting home and then to Sandford and back in time. Phil would just have to wait!

Constable Bailey was sympathetic when she rang him a few moments later, using the hands-free phone connection in her car. He told her that the pub landlord had found some dry clothes for her husband and he was now settled in the bar with a pint. Would it be easier for Anna if he brought him home in the squad car, instead of waiting for her to get there?

Fighting down her indignation at the thought of her husband relaxing in the pub while she was forced to take responsibility for their daughter's welfare at the same time as still supposedly being on duty and in the middle of a potential murder investigation, Anna agreed to this suggestion. She would drive straight to the pre-school and be there in good time to meet Donna as soon as she was released. With luck they'd arrive home shortly after Phil and PC Bailey.

One problem solved – but Phil would hardly be in a fit state to be left in charge of Donna until Jess got home. So, that would mean more time lost from Anna's working day. When was she ever going to find time to prepare for the trial? It was due to start the day after tomorrow. Not that she'd be called to give evidence before the second day at earliest, but she needed time to re-familiarise herself with the evidence. Phil knew that this was a busy week for her! And he was the one who had insisted that they didn't need to employ a childminder. *He* could look after Donna outside of her nursery school hours. So what was he doing jumping into the Thames with weights in his pockets?

Was it her fault? Had she driven him to take his own life? Had she been too hard on him? Should she have done more to make him feel welcome and appreciated when he returned from his escapade in Devon? Should she have tried harder to persuade Jessica to tone down her hostility towards him? Should she at least have noticed that he was depressed and encouraged him to seek help?

This must be how Patrick and Martina Quinn were feeling. Only worse, because Rory was their son and they had a duty of care towards him that she did not have for Phil. Rory was young and impressionable. Phil was a mature man who ought to know better than to abandon his responsibilities in that cavalier fashion!

Anna felt her indignation rising again and fought to get it under control, telling herself that she was not being fair. Phil must be stressed out and not thinking straight. He could not be held accountable for his actions. In his own twisted mind, it must have seemed that they would all be better off without him. She must try to be sympathetic and understanding.

She felt out of place outside the school gates, waiting for the nursery class to be dismissed. All the other mums seemed to know one another. They chattered and laughed about things their offspring had done or said, and swapped ideas for birthday parties or outings. And most of them seemed so young! Well, apart from a few who must surely be grandmothers caring for children whose parents were out at work. Or was she fooling herself and these were really her own contemporaries – other women who had given birth later in life?

After what felt like an age, the doors opened and children began pouring out, shouting and laughing as they sought out their parents and grandparents. Anna was relieved to hear a particularly ancient-looking woman being addressed as "gran" by a freckled redheaded boy. At least there was no reason for her to suspect that she looked as old as that!

'Mummy! What are *you* doing here?' Donna appeared, rolling down the ramp from the school door in her wheelchair amidst a group of her friends. 'Where's Daddy?'

'He's … not very well. You'll have to make do with me.'

'OK. Carry this.' Donna held out a large piece of sugar paper covered with pasta shapes stuck on with glue.

'That's nice,' Anna said admiringly, taking hold of the picture and gazing down at it, feigning rapt attention while inwardly impatient to get off home. 'Now let's get back to the car, shall we? I'm parked just down the road. Would you like me to push you?'

'No. I can do it, now you've got my dinosaur.' Donna propelled her lightweight wheelchair forward, scattering children to left and right as she skilfully weaved her way across the playground to the gate. Thank goodness they had managed to buy this new chair, so much easier for her to handle than the heavy, clunky one provided by the health service!

'Your dinosaur?' queried Anna as she hurried after her daughter.

'That's right.' Donna suddenly stopped in her tracks and pointed at the paper in her mother's hand. 'It's a triceratops. There are its horns – look!'

Anna studied the pasta picture, which she had assumed was an abstract design. 'Oh yes! I see. Sorry! How could I have missed those?'

When they arrived home, Anna was surprised to see Philip's car on the drive. Had he driven himself home in the end? But no, PC Bailey was there, evidently looking out for her arrival, because he opened the door before Anna had time to get Donna out of the car.

'Need any help with that?' he called out as she lifted the wheelchair out of the boot.

'No thanks. We can manage – can't we, Donna?'

'Yes,' Donna nodded, leaning forward to help her mother pick her up from her car seat. 'Daddy usually collects me, but he isn't very well, so Mummy's doing it today. Why are you here?' she added, staring at PC Bailey's uniform. 'Have you come to see Mummy?'

'In a way. I drove your Daddy's car home for him. Like you said, he's not very well. And I *would* like a word with your Mummy before I go.'

'Hi Mum!' At the sound of her son's voice, Anna twisted round and saw Marcus coming down the ramp from the front door. 'Dad's upstairs getting changed. I'll look after Donna, if you like.'

'Thanks.' Anna stared at him in bemusement. Marcus rarely left his room these days, apart from meals or to go out with his mates. He had never volunteered to care for his little sister before. He left all that to Anna and Jessica, apparently seeing it as women's work, despite his own childhood in which Philip had been his primary carer.

Donna, too, looked surprised but followed her brother meekly down the hall into the kitchen. Anna turned to PC Bailey.

'How is he? And what happened exactly?'

'I suggest we step back inside. Your neighbours are probably already wondering what a police officer's doing at your house. No point giving them any more grist for the local rumour mill.'

Anna followed him inside and closed the door, but smiled at his concern. 'They'll think it's to do with my work. I'm a DCI. This isn't the first time I've had uniformed officers calling round. But you haven't answered my question.'

'Sorry Ma'am. I didn't realise.' The young officer blushed red. 'I haven't been in Oxford long. I got a transfer from West Midlands.'

'I guessed.' Anna waited expectantly.

'Like I said on the phone, it looks like he filled his pockets with all the heavy things he could find in his car and then just walked off the edge of the path by Sandford lock. The paramedic said there's nothing much wrong with him, but there's no knowing what nasties there may have been in the water he swallowed, so you'd better keep an eye on him for a few days. And watch him in case he tries again, of course.'

'So, it was deliberate, but not premeditated?' Anna felt strangely detached from the incident. It felt more like one of her suspicious death cases than something that affected her personally. 'He didn't just spontaneously leap into the river, but he hadn't brought stuff with him to weigh him down; he improvised from what was there in the car?'

'Yes, ma'am. That's how it looks. But you can ask him yourself after I've gone.'

'Oh yes! Do you need a lift back to Sandford? I saw you'd brought Phil in his car.'

'No thanks. I've already radioed for someone to pick me up. I was trying to be discrete. I know how tongues wag whenever neighbours see a police car parked in the street.' He broke off as his radio crackled and a brief message came through. 'And that's my lift,' he added, moving towards the door. 'They're waiting in the next street – discrete, like I said. Your husband should be OK. Lucky your Marcus was in. He's been doing a great job of looking after him.'

'Oh! That's good. Well, thanks again, and ... maybe I'll see you around.'

Anna held the door open for the constable to leave. She watched him walking jauntily down the path and along the street until he disappeared round the corner. Then, with no further excuse for delay, she closed the door, taking in a deep breath as she did so and then letting it out in a long sigh. She could hear Donna's voice in the kitchen, explaining to her brother the finer points of her pasta dinosaur picture. She couldn't hear his answers, but it was clear that they were not the impatient dismissals that she would have expected from him. This was turning out to be a very strange day!

8. CHERCHEZ LA FEMME

The following day passed very slowly for Yakubu. Andy left the flat early, warning him that he would probably be late back. Apparently, the police force was very short of officers at present and those there were all had to work long hours. Or was that just an excuse to avoid spending time with his estranged father?

Yakubu washed up the breakfast dishes, drying them carefully and putting them neatly away in the cupboard. Then he wiped the table and swept up some crumbs from under it. He tidied his own bedroom and then crossed the living room to the smaller one at the back. Looking in, he saw that the covers had been pulled up neatly on the bed. The small table next to the bed was empty. There was no sign of Andy's rucksack or of the pile of aerogrammes. No sign, in fact, that anyone was occupying the room. Andy must have put everything away in the wardrobe, which was the only other piece of furniture in the tiny room.

Yakubu resisted the temptation to go in and look for that intriguing pile of letters, at least one of which he was convinced had had a Nigerian stamp on it. If the bedroom had been in disarray, then he could have excused his inquisitiveness under the guise of tidying it and he might have stumbled across the letters accidentally, but … no! He could not justify the intrusion and it would be certain to alienate his son even further, if he were to find out.

He backed out of the bedroom and closed the door. Then he put on his jacket, picked up his stick and left the flat. He would spend the day revisiting his old haunts from the time when he had been a student in Oxford. It would be interesting to see how things had changed after all these years.

The entrance to his old college had a board outside it announcing, *The College is Closed to Visitors*, but he walked boldly past it into the main quadrangle. A gardener clipping the edge of the lawn looked up but did not question his presence there. Yakubu gazed round. The buildings looked much as they were when he had been student – and probably much as they had been for the last four hundred years – but there were some changes. The entrance to the library now had a plaque outside it declaring that this was the way to *The Old Library Junior Common Room*. He remembered now, Jibrilu had told him that there was a new library, at the back of the college, and the old JCR, which had become far too small for the growing number of undergraduates, had become a seminar room.

He wandered through an archway into the next quadrangle and stood staring up at one of the first-floor windows. That was where he had lived for two years. It had been cold and dark, and he had been glad to move out into lodgings for his final year. But that was where he had met Mandy! She had had a Saturday job helping the Scouts with cleaning and other domestic chores. And they had got talking one day when she came in to empty his bin and hoover the threadbare carpet square in his room. She had been interested in hearing about Nigeria and flattered when he invited her to come with him to a concert of African music. And one thing had led to another …

The entrances to all the staircases had combination locks on them. He could not go up to see what his room looked like inside. How very different from the free-and-easy regime of forty years earlier! It would be more difficult now for a schoolgirl – which, after all, was all that Mandy had been – to slip up to a student's room without being observed or questioned.

Sighing, he turned round and walked back out into the street. Nostalgia was all very well, but you could never really go back. He wandered round the corner into Goose Lane, the narrow street that separated his own college, Lichfield, from the next one, Holy Cross. This was where Jibrilu had been killed. According to the police, he must have climbed out of the window of his ground-floor room to accost his killers as they tormented a young black boy whom they had come across on his way out of the back entrance of Holy Cross College. That was something to hold on to: his Jibrilu was a hero, albeit a dead one.

Yakubu ate lunch in a café in the covered market, another place that felt the same and yet strangely different. He had come here with Mandy many times to snatch some time together after the end of her Saturday morning job at the college before she went home to her parents who had not yet been told about her new boyfriend. And then later, when she became student herself, they would meet here after her lectures finished for the day and have lunch before spending whole afternoons together, walking along the river or through the botanical gardens, or on wet days, back in his digs.

He pushed away his empty plate and sat wondering where to go next. He still had five or six empty hours to fill before there was any chance of Andy finishing work and returning to their flat. Visiting his old haunts had been less rewarding than he had hoped, and his feet were starting to ache from walking. Perhaps he ought to spend the afternoon finishing his report on that doctoral thesis. It had to be done and that would at least give some rest to his old bones.

Coming out on to the High Street, he saw a bus sailing past and then slowing to pull up at a stop a short way off. Last time that he was here he had used a bus like that one to get to the mosque. The sun was high in the sky; it must be about time for the midday prayers. He had not liked to risk waking Andy by praying during the night, and with the strange long days in England, that had meant missing both the night-time and dawn prayer times.

It was difficult keeping to a strict routine of religious observances while sharing a home with a non-Muslim – especially when you didn't know what his attitude might be to religion. Andy had never expressed any opinion about his faith – but had he ever expressed an opinion to his father about anything? He was still being the conscientious police officer offering support to a victim of crime, and carefully avoiding any controversial issues. The only subject upon which he had allowed himself to show his feelings was his mother and Yakubu's treatment of her.

Mandy's family had expected her to go to church with them every Sunday, but she'd always said that she didn't think it mattered what faith you belonged to. Is that what she had told Andy when he was growing up? But, of course, everything was different now. Jibrilu had told him that many people in Britain thought that Islam was synonymous with terrorism. Could his Mandy have come round to that way of thinking too?

Back then, she'd been mildly interested in his beliefs, but never said much about her own. Perhaps she didn't really have any. Perhaps, when she said that all religions were equally valid, she meant that they were all equally untrue.

But then, let's be honest, he hadn't been particularly devout back then either. Not even when he was at home among other

Muslims. And as a student in Oxford, he had rarely got up to pray during the night or interrupted his studies to do so during the day. With nobody around to prompt him, he had failed to notice the approach of Ramadan and had made excuses to himself for omitting to observe the fast. It was only after tragedy had struck his family, killing his wives and daughter in a house fire, that he had started to make an effort to fulfil his religious obligations and raised Jibrilu to do the same.

So, now he would get a bus to the mosque and, if he was in time, join in with the communal prayers, or if not, at least make his own devotions. And he might meet some of the kind brothers who had taken care of Jibrilu's body while he had been waiting impatiently to get a visa to come to Britain to bury him.

An hour or so later, his conscience quieted, he got the bus back to the city centre and stood under Carfax tower pondering on what to do next. Of course, he really ought to get back to the flat and finish that PhD thesis, but the prospect had no appeal. Telling himself that he would do better justice to the student's efforts if he waited until he was in a better frame of mind, he made his way to the library where Amanda Lepage worked.

He lingered outside, hoping that she might come out and he could contrive an "accidental" meeting with her. Could he risk going in and looking for her? He still had the small piece of green card that he had been given when he was a student, which entitled him to use any of the university libraries for life. In front of her colleagues and in a place where raised voices were not allowed, she would have to receive him with politeness if nothing better. But putting her into such a position would almost certainly alienate her all the more. He must find some way of getting to speak to her alone.

He stood in the shade of a tree, leaning against a low wall. From this position he could see the entrance to the library without being conspicuous. He took out a leaflet that one of the brothers at the mosque had given him and pretended to be very interested in reading about the "Oxford Eid Extravaganza" that was taking place at the weekend. He planned in his mind what he would say to Mandy when he did manage to get to speak to her, trying out alternative opening lines and trying to guess what her reaction would be. He must make it clear to her that he knew that he had treated her badly and was sorry for it. But, if he had deceived her, so had she deceived him! Why did she never tell him about their son? Even if she did not know that she was pregnant until after he had left Oxford, she could have written to him to let him know. Why had she not replied to any of the letters that he had written to her?

But dwelling on her unfairness was not the way to make his peace with her now. He must put that out of his mind and allow her to continue to put all the blame on him. He must be contrite and humble. Perhaps he should begin by speaking about Andy? He would tell her what a fine son she had and what a good job she had done of bringing him up. And then he could work round gradually to saying how much he regretted not having been a part of that (emphasising, of course, that this was his own fault) and how much he wanted to get to know him properly now – and to re-kindle his relationship with Mandy too.

But it wasn't all his fault! If she had replied to his letters – if she had told him that she was carrying his child – he would have divorced his wives and come back to Oxford and married her. His father would have been angry at first, but when he knew that he had a grandson, he would have become reconciled to the situation. Mandy had told him that she loved him. How could she say that and then keep from him the news that he had a son?

After what seemed like hours, his patience was rewarded. Two women came out of the library: one a redhead wearing designer jeans and an open-necked shirt; the other older, dressed in a blue skirt and a matching short-sleeved jacket. It was Mandy! He recognised her from the brief video conversation that she had permitted him last year after he first discovered about their son, but he would have known her anyway. She was older and her hair had turned an attractive mixture of shades of grey, but still unmistakably the same woman that he had fallen in love with more than four decades ago.

Yakubu watched them as they walked together to a row of cycles chained up outside the building. The younger woman bent down to remove the padlock securing her bike. Mandy stood beside her waiting and chatting. Yakubu resisted the urge to step forward and greet them. It was frustrating to be so close to her and yet not able to approach for fear of rejection.

Instead, he watched as, still deep in conversation, they walked side-by-side, pushing the bike past his secluded spot and out to the road. For a moment, she was so close that he could have reached out and touched her. They stood on the pavement talking for a few minutes before the younger woman mounted her bicycle and pedalled away while Mandy set off down South Parks Road at a brisk pace.

Yakubu's first instinct was to hurry after her, calling her name. Surely out here, in a public place, she would stop and listen to him rather than make a scene in front of strangers? Or might that be just what she would like? An opportunity to claim that he was harassing her? What if she called the police and accused him of attacking her or paying her unwanted attention? They would be bound to believe her word against his! And, in an unfamiliar country, what laws might there be against chasing after women in the street?

He started to follow, keeping back so that she would not notice him – which was not difficult, since she set a faster pace than he was accustomed to, now that he had arthritis developing in his right knee. It was strange that the age difference between them seemed to have widened over the years. Apart from the grey hair, which made her looked distinguished rather than old, Mandy seemed hardly to have aged at all.

She was several hundred yards ahead of him now. It was lucky that the road was so straight or she would have been out of sight. She reached the crossroads at the end of the Broad just as Yakubu was approaching Wadham College. A lorry turning down Holywell Street kept her waiting to cross and allowed Yakubu to gain some ground. Then she was off again, heading down Catte Street. For a moment, he lost sight of her among a group of American tourists standing in the road admiring the bridge that spans New College Lane, linking two parts of Hertford College.

But he was confident that he knew where she was heading. Andy had let slip that they still lived in Headington. She must be planning to catch a bus from one of the stops along the High. He hurried on past the Bodleian Library and the Radcliffe Camera and stood at the end of Catte Street, looking to right and left. There she was! Just passing a red telephone box; still walking at a rapid pace. Not far now: She must be aiming for the row of bus stops outside Queen's.

A bus swept past Yakubu and then slowed as it approached the stops. It had a number 8 on the back. He quickened his pace as he saw that Mandy had joined a queue of people who had stepped forward ready to climb aboard when it stopped. A young man carrying a guitar ran past him and joined the line behind Mandy. If he hurried, Yakubu could probably get to the stop in time to board the bus without Mandy noticing him. Ignoring the protestations of his arthritic knee, he pushed himself to walk faster.

The driver had already closed the door and was preparing to move off, but she opened it again when she saw him there. He stepped forward and was about to mount the shallow step when his nerve failed him and he moved back again waving apologetically to the driver. 'My apologies! I mistook the number. This is not the bus I wanted.'

She nodded understandingly and close the door again. The bus glided away into the rush-hour traffic. Yakubu caught a glimpse of Mandy, sitting near the back of the bus, her head bowed as if she were looking at something on her lap. She did not see him staring after her.

Yakubu stood at the bus stop, undecided what to do next. Another bus drew up and waited at another of the five stops clustered outside The Queen's College. More people arrived at his stop and stood in line behind him. Only a few minutes had passed when another number 8 bus appeared. The doors opened and the driver looked out expectantly.

Yakubu climbed aboard and bought a ticket to Headington. He was still not sure what he hoped to achieve by following Mandy in this way. She would be well on her way up Headington Hill by now. The bus stopped several times in Headington, and he had no way of knowing which stop was hers or which direction she would walk in after alighting.

He got off at the stop that he remembered using when visiting Mandy at her parents' house all those years ago. Perhaps she and Andy lived close to that. As a single parent, she wouldn't have wanted to be far away from the support that they could offer. He made his way through the familiar, and yet strange, streets to the large semi-detached house where Mandy and her three sisters had grown up.

The green-painted front door had been replaced by a white plastic one and the drive had been re-laid and expanded to cover most of the front garden, but it was unmistakably the place where he had first met Mandy's mother and father; where her young sister, Jennifer, had asked all sorts of questions about what it was like to live in Nigeria; where her older sister, Clare, had made it quite clear, without actually saying anything, that she disapproved of Mandy's involvement with him. He had never met the oldest of the Lepage girls. What was her name now? Paula, was it? No, Pauline. She was already married and living in another city. Mandy had liked her best out of her sisters and said that she never tried to boss her about the way Clare did.

He marched up to the front door and raised his hand to knock. Then his nerve failed him and he turned abruptly and hurried back down the path and back out into the road. Glancing back over his shoulder, he saw an old man – presumably Mandy's father, although his face was so changed that Yakubu would not have known him – peering out of the bay window. He must have seen Yakubu coming up the path. Had he recognised him? Would he tell Mandy that he had been there?

Yakubu hurried away, back to the bus stop. This was not the way to get to speak to Mandy. It would be unfair to impose himself on her elderly parents and futile to wander the streets of Headington hoping for a chance meeting. She would be in her own home by now, busy getting a meal for herself – and probably angry with him that her son – their son – would not be eating there too!

Soon he was back in the city centre. He got off the bus outside University College and turned into a side street, planning to take one last look at the place where Jibrilu had died, before returning to the flat. There was a young woman coming out of Goose Lane as he rounded the corner from Lichfield Street.

'Mr Danjuma!' she greeted him. 'How are you?'

Yakubu stared at her. Her face was familiar, but he could not place it.

'I'm sorry. I don't suppose you remember me. I'm Esther Orugun. We met last year. Just Before Christmas. Andy was helping you to clear Jibrilu's room.'

'Of course! Forgive me; my memory is not what it was. You were kind enough to help too. You folded Jibrilu's clothes most expertly!'

'I'm glad you think so,' Esther smiled. 'Andy told me you were in Oxford. The trial begins tomorrow – is that right?'

'Yes.' Yakubu hesitated before adding, 'so you have spoken to Andy recently then?'

'Yes,' Esther smiled. 'I thought he might have told you. We've been "walking out together" as it says in Victorian romances, for a while now. Mind you,' she added mischievously, when he did not reply, 'I am beginning to wonder about his intentions. I don't think he's told his mother about me yet.'

'That could be difficult for him,' Yakubu said, nodding in understanding. 'I think she might have preferred an English girl.'

'Or no girl at all,' Esther sighed. 'Don't be too hard on him. It was a big deal for him telling her he was staying with you. She isn't used to sharing him with anyone.'

'I can see that my son has confided in you,' Yakubu murmured. 'I am very glad that he has found someone that he can trust. I wonder … I would like to get to know you better. Please, would you join us for dinner tonight?'

'Thank you, but no.' Esther continued to smile. 'I think you two need to spend some time alone together. Maybe later, when you've got to know each other better. I would only be in the way.'

'Perhaps you are right. But I would like to get to know you too. I will tell Andy that I must see you again before I return to Nigeria.'

'I'll look forward to it.'

9. PIECING TOGETHER A PICTURE

Andy left the flat before his father had finished breakfast, glad of the excuse that he had to meet with Anna for an early briefing before setting off for Coventry to visit a new witness that they had tracked down. He was in no mood for making small talk – and even less for feigning interest in the photographs and reminiscences of his Nigerian family, which Yakubu seemed intent on sharing with him. Up until last December, life had all seemed pretty simple. Now it had suddenly exploded in his face, with the father whom he had been brought up to despise turning out to be a man rather than a monster, and one who, based on all the evidence available, had really loved his mother. Or was he just very skilful at manipulating the feelings of people around him?

He was the first to arrive in the open plan office for the morning briefing, with Jennifer Moorhouse a close second. Usually, Anna was also among the early ones, but today, not only did she appear after everyone else but she seemed distracted and several times had to ask members of her team to repeat what they had said. She brought them up to date with Ruby's news on the fingerprints – or the lack of them – on the whisky bottle and pill box, and handed Rory's laptop over to Jennifer with instructions to see what she could find on it.

This was Jennifer's cue to feed back the results of her scrutiny of Rory's mobile phone data.

'There were lots of missed calls, voicemail messages, texts and WhatsApp messages from the same number during the days leading up to the day he died,' she reported. 'The caller's name is in his contacts list as "Jamie".'

'That'll be Jamie Mercer,' Andy put in. 'The friend from uni that Rory's girlfriend told us about. I managed to get his full name and home address from the registrar's office there and I was planning to go over to speak to him today.'

'That's right,' Jennifer nodded. 'The calls came from a phone registered in the name of Jamie Mercer, with an address in Coventry. I think they must have been close. A lot of the messages sounded a bit annoyed, but in the way that people get annoyed when they're actually worried about someone – you know: angry, but anxious at the same time.'

'You mean like when teenage kids won't pick up because they're out with their mates and don't want you checking up on them, but all you want is to know they're safe?' Anna suggested with a smile.

'Yes. Or when you've had a row with your other half and want to make up but they won't talk to you.'

'Hmm.' Anna looked towards Andy. 'It sounds as if this Jamie could hold the key to the whole business. If he and Rory were lovers, Rory's life was a whole lot more complicated than his parents knew – or at least than they're willing to admit to us. I could imagine he wouldn't exactly be looking forward to his grand birthday party where he was supposed to be announcing his engagement to the *good Catholic girl* of his parents' dreams! You'd better get off to Coventry and have a word with this Jamie Mercer.'

The drive to Coventry provided Andy with a welcome hour for reflection – not on Rory Quinn's death but on the letters that he had found in his grandparents' loft. He had brought them to the flat, concealed among his clothes, and had spent more than an hour, after Yakubu had retired to bed, studying them in the same painstaking way that he would have approached evidence in a murder enquiry.

First, he had gone through them all, checking the postmarks and arranging them in date order. The oldest had been sent in December 1981. That could not be long after Mum and Yakubu had met. She had only started working at the college that Autumn. Then there was nothing more until July of the following year. Perhaps Yakubu had stayed in Oxford over Easter, only going home when the long vac began. Across that summer, the letters came thick and fast. Yakubu was writing to her every two or three days. How had he kept the answering letters secret from his two wives? They would surely have been curious about the frequency with which he was receiving mail from England.

Then there was another gap until the following summer. It looked as if he had spent both the Christmas and Easter vacations in Oxford that year – to save on air fares? Or because he did not want to be separated from the love of his life? Andy reluctantly concluded that it looked as if there had been genuine feelings on Yakubu's side of the relationship. It could not simply be dismissed as the predatory behaviour of an older man taking advantage of a naïve teenage girl.

That was the end of the opened letters. After August 1983 there was a gap of three months – presumably Yakubu's final term in Oxford – and then the letters resumed, but they were all still sealed, unread.

But not thrown away. Why had she kept them if she was not interested enough to open them and see what he had to say? Or could it be that Mum had never seen them? Perhaps Nana and Gramps had intercepted them and hidden them from her?

Perhaps she had always believed that Yakubu had abandoned her without a second thought, and hadn't realised that he had been writing to her constantly! There were more than a dozen letters between January and March 1984, then fewer in the remaining months of that year, and then one each October until 1992. On the face of it, Yakubu's claims that he had never forgotten her and that he had always dreamed of them being reunited were borne out by the evidence!

Having completed his systematic sorting of the correspondence, Andy had begun an equally meticulous examination of the contents of each letter in turn, cross-referencing them with entries in his mother's five-year diary, which had been stored with them. The diary made it clear that she had fallen for Yakubu big-time almost as soon as they met. There were pages filled with descriptions of his magnificent physique and liquid brown eyes – and also a lot about his kindness and the wonderful stories he told about life in Nigeria. Her 17th birthday fell only a few weeks after their first meeting and there was an entry that waxed lyrical about the small leather shoulder bag in an authentic African design that he had given to her.

She was only just turned seventeen, and he was … what? … mid-twenties at least. And with two wives and a baby daughter. It was obscene the way he must have encouraged her infatuation!

The Mercer family home was a spacious between-the-wars semi-detached house: mock Tudor black and white frontage upstairs with red bricks to the ground floor. The roof was covered with solar panels and Andy recognised the rectangular bulk of an air-source heat pump attached to the side wall. The front garden was paved over with a pattern of red and grey setts on which he was pleased to see there were two cars parked. That suggested that someone would be in and his journey would not be wasted.

He rang the bell and stood gazing round as he waited for a reply. One of the cars was a brand-new e-Golf. The Mercers must be well-off as well as environmentally conscious to be able to afford that. It was plugged in at a charging point on the front wall of the house. Taking advantage of the sun beating down on the solar panels above, Andy supposed.

'Yes? Can I help you?' A woman in her fifties appeared at the door and looked out enquiringly at Andy, who held up his warrant card.

'I'm Detective Inspector Lepage from Thames Valley Police. I'd like to speak to Jamie Mercer. Is he here?'

'No. He's in Oxford. He's been there since last Friday. We got back from visiting family in North Wales that afternoon and he went off the same evening. He's going to be studying in Oxford next term and he was looking for somewhere to-.' She stopped abruptly and leaned forward, her expression becoming suddenly anxious. 'Look what *is* this? Why do you want Jamie. He's not in any trouble, is he?'

'No, no,' Andy hastened to reassure her. 'Not at all. We just want a word with him, that's all – about a friend of his who appears to have taken his own life. We were hoping he might have been able to give us some insight into his state of mind. I gather they were quite close. Do you know where-?'

'Not Rory?' Mrs Mercer exclaimed, the anxiety in her face now replaced by horror. 'It's not Rory who's killed himself, is it?'

'You know him?' Andy was taken aback. Everyone in Oxford was treating the friendship between Rory and Jamie as some great secret, making it a surprise that Jamie had apparently been completely open about it with his mother.

'Oh yes! Of course! He was always there when we went to see Jamie at uni, and he's been to stay here a couple of times.

He's the reason Jamie chose Oxford Brookes for his PGCE. Poor Rory's being forced into a solicitor's office there – a friend of his father returning a favour, I gather. They were planning to rent a flat there together. That's why ....' She tailed off into silence for a few moments then grasped Andy impulsively by the arm. 'So, when did this happen?'

'Last Saturday.'

Mrs Mercer dropped her hand back down to her side and stared at Andy in disbelief. 'Saturday? Three days ago? And Jamie hasn't rung to tell us? I don't understand!'

'We don't think he knows yet,' Andy told her. 'Did he leave you an address for where he was planning to stay while he was in Oxford – so that we can get in touch with him?'

'No. We just assumed he'd stay with Rory. Rory's parents have got a big enough house. His Dad owns Quinn's Superstores, so they must be loaded.'

'Has he stayed there before?'

'No, not that I know of.' Mrs Mercer thought for a moment, 'No, definitely not. I remember, Jamie said he'd never been to Oxford before. He did the interview for the course on Zoom.'

'I see.' Andy held out one of his business cards. 'OK. Thank you for talking to me. If you're speaking to Jamie, please ask him to ring me on that number.'

'I can ring him now for you if you like. Just let me get my phone.' Jamie's mother disappeared into the house, returning a minute or two later with a smartphone held to her ear. She frowned as the ringing tone clicked off and was replaced by an invitation to leave a message. 'Hi Jamie, it's Mum. Ring me back as soon as you get this, please.' She looked helplessly up at Andy. 'He's not picking up. Would you like me to give you his number, so you can have a go later?'

'No thanks. That's OK.' Andy decided against admitting that they already knew the number through Rory's call history. 'Just let him know we want to speak to him when he rings you.'

Finding Jamie Mercer proved easier than Andy had anticipated. On his return to the police station in Oxford he found a loud altercation going on at the front desk. A young man dressed in tee-shirt and jeans was loudly demanding to speak to the person in charge of investigating Rory Quinn's death. When the desk sergeant looked up at Andy's approach, he wheeled round and redirected his anger at the Detective Inspector.

'Get back, you!' he shouted, pushing back a lock of brown hair that had flopped down over his eyes. 'She hasn't finished with me yet!'

Andy silently got out his warrant card and held it up in the young man's face. 'I think perhaps I'm the person you're looking for,' he said calmly. 'And I suspect that *you* may well be the person that *I've* been looking for all morning. Would your name be Jamie Mercer, by any chance?'

'Yes. How did you know?'

'Intuition,' Andy told him, deadpan. 'Plus, your mother told me you were in Oxford and your face matches a photo that we found in your friend Rory's room. Now, let's go somewhere a bit quieter and we can have a little chat about you and Rory and what happened last Saturday.'

Jamie stood staring back for a moment or two. Then he gave a sheepish glance towards the desk sergeant, who gazed back impassively. She was used to angry young men sounding off with righteous indignation that soon turned to embarrassment when they sobered up or came to their senses for other reasons. She wouldn't hold it against him, but saw no reason to ameliorate his shame by acknowledging his feelings.

'Interview room three is free,' she told Andy.

'Perfect! Could you let DCI Davenport know. She'll probably want to be there too.' Andy turned back to Jamie. 'Well? How about it?'

Jamie continued to stare round as if confused by the turn of events.

'OK,' he said at last. Then, more combatively, 'just so long as you tell me what's happened to Rory and why nobody's doing anything about it.'

'We are, in fact, doing quite a lot to investigate your friend's death,' Andy told him, as he led the way to the interview room. 'Much more than you might expect in a relatively straightforward case of suicide.'

'You're sure that's what it was? You don't think …?'

'What?' asked Andy, then when Jamie did not reply, 'What else might we think?'

'That … well that someone else did it to him.'

'Is there anyone who might want to?'

'No, I don't think so … except …'

'Except what?' Andy stood holding open one of the fire doors on the long corridor leading to the interview rooms, waiting for Jamie to go through.

'Oh nothing! Only he had been getting a few weird comments on Instagram.'

'Death threats?'

'Sometimes – but not the sort you'd take seriously. Just trolls who get a kick out of frightening people.'

Anna was already there when they arrived in the interview room. She stood up and introduced herself, then gestured to Jamie to sit down.

'Don't worry,' she told him. 'This isn't a formal interview. It's just a friendly chat to give you a chance to ask us questions and so we can get a bit more background on what Rory Quinn's state of mind may have been last Saturday. I gather you were a friend of his?'

'Yes.' Jamie seemed about to say more. Andy and Anna waited patiently for him to continue. 'Er ....' The two officers continued to sit in silence, watching the young man expectantly. 'Well, we were more than just friends,' he said at last.

'You were lovers?' Anna suggested. 'Partners?'

Jamie nodded, looking from Anna to Andy and back, nervously gauging their reactions, before dropping his eyes and staring down at the table in front of him.

'It's OK,' Andy assured him. 'We're not here to judge you – or Rory.'

'And we already knew,' Anna added. 'About Rory being bisexual.'

'He's not!' Rory's head jerked up and he stared, wide-eyed at Anna. 'He's gay! He's not interested in girls. And how do you know about him, anyway? He said he couldn't tell anyone in Oxford. He said his mum and dad would go ballistic if they knew.'

'They still don't – or at least, I don't think so.' Anna spoke quietly, trying to calm the storm of emotions that her words had stirred up in her witness, knowing that what she was about to say would most likely hit him hard. 'Ellie told me – Rory's fiancée.'

'His fiancée? You mean he went ahead with all that, after all? He promised he wouldn't. He was going to end it all at that stupid party they were having on Saturday. He promised!'

Jamie's distress was clear to both police officers. His shoulders sagged and he sat with head lowered. Andy thought he saw him blinking back tears.

'The party never happened,' Anna told him gently. 'His dad went looking for him when the guests started to arrive, and he found him in the garden, hanging from one of the trees there. We're trying to find out how he got there, and why?'

'Why?' Jamie raged. 'It's obvious, isn't it? His parents! They're living in the Dark Ages! They've got a basin of holy water stuck to the wall in the hall, and a picture of the pope halfway up the stairs – not Francis, the one before him, the one who said being gay is a "moral disorder". Rory promised he was going to tell them about us on Saturday, at the party. He must've bottled it. It's that holiday in Italy did it! All those grandparents and great uncles and cousins and things, all saying how much they were looking forward to coming to England for the wedding, and how nice it was he'd found a nice Catholic girl to marry. He said it was going to break his mother's heart when he told her.'

Anna and Andy remained silent as Jamie gulped in breath to continue his outburst of rage and pain. 'But he *promised* me he'd do it! He said he wasn't going to live a lie any more. We'd got it all planned. That's why I was going to Oxford Brookes – so we could be together. His dad had got him this place in some law firm here. He didn't want to be a solicitor, but he said he couldn't not take the job. He said it would be enough of a shock for them when he told them he wasn't going to live at home with them, without letting them down over his career too. They'd got his life all mapped out for him and he didn't have any say in it!' His voice dropped to a whisper as he repeated, 'but he *promised*! He *did* promise he was going to tell them about us.'

Andy got up without speaking and left the room. Anna sat looking at Jamie who seemed completely enveloped in his misery, oblivious to her presence and Andy's disappearance.

'I'm sorry,' she said at last. 'I know this is difficult for you, but I do need to know. When did you last speak to Rory?'

Jamie's shoulders shook with silent sobs. Anna waited, but he did not reply.

'We know that you tried to call him on his mobile last week,' she pressed him gently.

Still no reply.

'Your mum said you were here in Oxford to find somewhere to live. Did you meet up to look for places together?'

Jamie shook his head without looking up.

Anna pondered what to do next. She needed him to open up, to tell them what Rory's state of mind had been that Saturday morning. Had Rory perhaps gone out to meet Jamie after all? The texts and messages on his phone all suggested that he had refused Jamie's appeals, but he could have given in in the end. Could a confrontation between the two have turned nasty? Jamie did not look like a killer, but scorned lovers were notoriously unpredictable.

Her thoughts were interrupted by the reappearance of Andy, carrying a box of tissues and three paper cups of coffee. He put them down on the table and pushed the tissues, one of the cups and a sachet of sugar towards Jamie. Anna picked up another of the cups, looking gratefully towards Andy. This was shaping up for becoming a long session.

Jamie put out his hand, hesitated for a moment and then pulled out a tissue and blew his nose, raising his head as he did so just enough for Andy to glimpse moisture on his cheeks. He dabbed his eyes and then dropped the tissue down on to the table and grasped the coffee in both hands.

'You haven't answered my question,' Anna said quietly. 'When was it you last spoke to Rory? We know you tried to phone him on Friday.'

'Yes.' At last Jamie looked up and made eye-contact with Anna. 'I rang him to tell him I'd got to Oxford.'

'But he didn't pick up,' Anna pointed out. 'We've heard the voicemail you left – and seen the texts, lots of them.'

'No. He'd left his phone charging. He didn't have it with him. After a bit, I rang his landline and we arranged to go flat-hunting together.'

'When?' asked Andy. 'I mean when were you planning to go looking for flats?'

'Monday. But he never turned up. And his phone was turned off. And then there was this stuff on the news about ....' Jamie reached for another tissue and covered his face with his hands.

'So, the last time you spoke to Rory was on Friday night on the landline to his house?' Anna persisted. 'How did he seem?'

Jamie blew his nose again and shrugged his shoulders. 'Fed up about this big party they were putting on for him. That's why we couldn't meet till Monday.'

'He didn't invite you to go to it then?' asked Andy.

'No. He said it was going to be bad enough trying to explain to everyone about .... He was going to have to .... Everyone thought he and Ellie were going to ....' He wiped his eyes and nose and then looked round at them both defiantly. 'He didn't want me there when he came out to his family, because he didn't want them thinking about what we might have been getting up to in bed together!'

'How did that make you feel?' asked Anna.

'How do you think?' There was a bitterness in Jamie's voice, which changed to misery as he went on, 'but I understood. It was those dinosaurs of parents that he had. It was like they were still living in the Dark Ages. And he was his mum's favourite, 'cos he was the baby of the family. And all those brothers and sisters he had – all married with kids. And good jobs – the respectable kind: doctors and accountants and teachers. Rory didn't want to be a solicitor! He wanted to draw cartoons for the newspapers and write graphic novels. But that wouldn't be good enough for his dad. He wanted him sat in some stuffy office all day, bored to death but bringing in a steady income so that *he* could have loads of kids with that *good Catholic girl* they were all so pleased he was getting married to!'

Jamie's voice rose to a howl as he poured out his anguish. Then, suddenly he ran out of steam and collapsed into open sobbing. He leaned forward and hid his head in his arms as they rested there on the table in front of him. Anna and Andy exchanged looks. His distress appeared genuine, but that did not exclude the possibility that he could have had a hand in Rory's death.

Eventually the sobs subsided. Jamie reached for another tissue and wiped his face. Andy placed his hand gently on the young man's shoulder.

'Thank you for coming here and telling us about Rory,' he said kindly. 'Now, I think it'll be best if you go back home to Coventry. Your mum will be worried about you.'

Jamie nodded. 'I'm sorry. I don't usually ....'

'That's alright,' Andy assured him. 'Now, tell me where you're staying and we'll go and pick up your things, and then I'll drop you off at the train station.

While Andy saw the still tearful Jamie on to the train home, Anna paid a visit to Rory's family. Their reactions on being informed about his relationship with Jamie were predictable. Patrick was clearly shocked at the suggestion that any son of his could be *queer* as he insisted on putting it.

'This Jamie?' he asked. 'He won't make trouble, will he? Is there anything you can do to keep him away from the funeral, for example? He won't expect to …?'

'He's given an undertaking not to come to this house or harass any of you,' Anna assured him. 'But he *does* want to be told when the funeral is. And don't you think Rory would have wanted him to be there?'

'Of course he would!' Martina, who had collapsed into tears on hearing the news, now leapt to her feet to confront her husband. 'Poor Rory! What have we done to him? He should have known that we would still love him just the same! We should have made sure that he did! The least we can do for him now is to welcome his – his – his boyfriend into the family.'

'*Welcome* him?' Patrick sounded incredulous. 'Can you hear yourself? Why should we have anything to do with this – this *pervert* who's corrupted our son? *Think*, can't you? What are you going to tell your mother? The shock could kill her!'

Emma remained calm. Anna wondered what kind of bombshell would have to be dropped in order to prompt this cool customer into displaying emotion. Out of her parents' hearing, as she showed Anna to the door, she confided that Rory's sexuality had been obvious to her for a long time.

'Of course, Mamma and Dad could never see it. And some of the things they said made it impossible for him to tell them.'

'Him having a steady girlfriend must have made it harder for them to guess,' Anna suggested. 'What do *you* think was going on there?'

'Mutual support,' Emma replied confidently. 'It kept both lots of parents off their backs. Ellie was grateful to Rory because he was about the only person who didn't laugh at her stammer, and he went along with it because it made Mamma happy. Plus, he was in denial. He probably convinced himself that he *was* in love with Ellie. I expect he'd have gone through with marrying her, if this Jamie hadn't turned up.'

'Was that what drove him to kill himself, do you think?'

'So, you don't go along with Dad's murderous intruder theory then?'

'We're keeping an open mind on that,' Anna said quickly. 'But the picture I'm getting from you is of a young man in emotional turmoil, who feels he's being pushed into marrying a girl that he doesn't want to hurt, when he really wants to be with his gay lover, whom he can't admit to his family even exists. And

I'm wondering if you think that he took his own life because he couldn't see any other way out of that mess.'

'Well, you're the detective,' Emma smiled, 'but that all sounds fairly plausible to me.'

She opened the door to let Anna out.

'Don't judge Dad too harshly. He's spent his whole working life selling people the past, which makes living in the twenty-first century hard for him sometimes.' Then, seeing Anna's puzzled expression, she went on, 'He came over here to find his roots, and then he built his business on the back of helping other people find theirs: tours of historic sites with an emphasis on discovering where your ancestors lived and what they did, then hotels for people to stay in while they're doing it. The grocery business is just a side-line. As far as Dad's concerned, its main function is to provide a steady income to support the rest – and a toy for me to play with while he manages the important stuff.'

Anna was still pondering upon the inner workings of the Quinn family as she turned into the drive and parked her car alongside Philip's. Could anyone – especially a business man as successful as Patrick Quinn – really be as out of touch with modern life as he had appeared to be, and as his daughter had portrayed him? Did he really believe that Jamie was responsible for turning his son into a homosexual? Martina, on the other hand, had taken the news far better than anyone else seemed to have expected. Ellie, in particular, had singled her out as the person who would have been most shocked and upset. Had she perhaps had some intuition about Rory's sexuality, so that it came as less of a bombshell to her than to her husband?

Emma was a cool customer. You wouldn't think she was part of the family at all, the way she seemed to be observing them all so dispassionately. Or maybe not ...? Was that just a façade that

163

she put on to conceal her real feelings? What did she mean by that final remark about the grocery business being a toy for her to play with? Was her detachment caused by her feeling excluded in some way, despite her being the one who was there at the centre of things helping to run the family business? Would Patrick have preferred to keep it entirely within his own control? Would Martina have preferred her to marry and have children?

'Hello everyone, I'm home!' Anna called out as she opened the front door and let herself in. There was no reply, so she headed through the kitchen into the back garden expecting to find Donna outside enjoying the warm, sunny weather.

Sure enough, there she was, sitting in her paddling pool with a small flotilla of plastic ducks. To Anna's astonishment, Marcus was there too, dressed in red swimming shorts, sitting on the grass watching over his little sister. Philip was notably absent.

'Hi Mum.' Marcus turned his head to look up at her, squinting in the bright sunlight. 'You're early!'

Anna looked at her watch. 'I make it bang on the time I said I'd be back.'

'That's what I meant,' Marcus grinned. 'Really early!'

'Where's Dad?'

'Upstairs.'

'Thanks. I'd better go and let him know I'm back.' Anna turned to go, wondering at Philip's failure to respond to her call, but not yet alarmed. 'Are you OK to keep an eye on Donna for a bit longer?'

'Sure. We've been having a good time, haven't we Don?'

'Thanks. I won't be long.'

She had not got far when Marcus caught up with her. He spoke urgently, keeping his voice low. 'He's been up there most of the afternoon. He *said* he'd got some plans to finish, but ....'

'But what?'

'You know that bottle of wine that was in the fridge? Well, it's gone. And there's two more empties in the recycling.'

'OK.' Anna struggled to digest this information. 'Thanks. Maybe we need to talk later – after Donna's in bed. And thanks for looking after her. I know it's not exactly …. I know you've got lots of things you'd rather be doing.'

'Actually, it really wasn't so bad,' Marcus admitted, giving a sheepish grin. 'And I think maybe it's you and Dad who need to talk.'

Anna nodded. 'Yes, well, thanks anyway.'

'Oh! And by the way, there's a shepherd's pie in the oven,' Marcus called after her. 'Donna helped me make it, didn't you Donna?'

'Yes!' shouted his sister. 'I made the potato! It was fun.'

'Only instant mash,' Marcus explained. 'She stirred it up and then made the ridges on the top with a fork, the way Dad always does.'

'Well done, both of you. Now I'd better go and see how Dad's getting on.' Anna started off for the house again. Philip had never drunk to excess before. But then, he'd never tried to kill himself before either. What had happened to him? Was it all her fault?

10. TEENAGE DIARY

After they had eaten that evening, Andy retreated to his bedroom, telling Yakubu that he had work to do. The older man was clearly disappointed, but Andy could not face more reminiscences of his father's time in Oxford or photographs of his home and family in Nigeria. And he didn't want to encourage Yakubu in his belief that some sort of reconciliation was possible with his mother or that Andy would ever be able to forgive him fully for the way he had deserted her.

He sat down on the narrow bed and powered up his laptop. He set it down next to him so that he would appear to be busy if Yakubu were to come in, and then hoisted his rucksack onto his lap. He rummaged under a bundle of clothes and drew out the package of letters, which he had hidden there after the scare when his father had walked in on him the previous evening. Delving in again, he located his mother's diary and laid it down on the bed with the letters. Then he got up and put the rucksack away in the wardrobe.

He sat down again, but his eyes kept being drawn to the bedroom door. Yakubu might decide to come in at any time offering refreshments or begging Andy to join him in the living area. Looking round the room, he spotted a chair standing against the wall between the bed and the window. He picked it up and wedged it under the door handle. If that didn't prevent

Yakubu from getting in, it would at least make a noise that would give Andy time to hide the diary and letters.

He sat for several minutes holding the pile of letters on his lap. He had already studied all the ones that had been unsealed. To read further would involve opening letters that his mother had never seen. Was that fair? Was it a betrayal of her trust?

But they had been delivered to her house. She must have known about them or she could not have put them away with the opened letters and her private diary. She had *chosen* not to open them, she could have read them if she wanted, and surely he had a right to know what his father had written to her during the first years of his life? What if he had known – or suspected – about the existence of his son? Wouldn't that make a difference to how Andy should view him now?

On the other hand, ...

He decided to leave the letters for the time being and to start with the diary. He opened it at the book-mark that he had left in it after his previous examination of the entries up to the summer of 1983, when Yakubu had gone home to Nigeria for a holiday while awaiting a date for the examination of his thesis.

15th August Yakubu's viva has been fixed for 8th September. He's coming to Oxford the week before to prepare for it! I'm so happy I could cry! He'll be here for at least a month, maybe more if he has corrections to do. He hasn't said anything about all my suggestions for jobs that he could get here, so that he doesn't have to go back at all. Maybe he's frightened that it'll be too big a disappointment if none of them come off.

16th August I've decided that I won't go back on the pill. I don't care if I get pregnant with Yakubu's baby. In fact, I'd quite like that. He'd have to stay in England then! And they'd have to let him, too. Our baby would be British and they couldn't throw its father out, could they? Once he's got his DPhil, he'll be able to get a job at the university and then we can be a family and we'll get married and then Clare will have to stop saying all those awful things about what a mistake it is getting involved with a black man.

Andy's mouth dropped open. This was quite different from the story his mother had given him. She'd led him to believe that his conception had all been a big mistake – or that it had been Yakubu's fault. Maybe he had refused to wear a condom or he had forced himself on her when she wasn't prepared. Now it looked as if it had been deliberate calculation on his mother's part! Because she thought that if she had a baby it would force Yakubu to stay in England and marry her – and because she wanted to get back at her sister for warning her against him.

He turned the pages, reading about her preparations for starting her degree course (buying books, choosing posters and a rug for her college room, receiving presents of mugs, a kettle and a toaster from kind aunts and uncles) and her excitement at the prospect of living away from home for the first time. Then, as August was about to give way to September, delighted anticipation of Yakubu's imminent arrival, and finally:

*1st **September** Yakubu landed at Heathrow this morning. I went to meet him at the bus station and we walked back to his room together. He's renting a ground-floor room in a student house up Banbury Road. The other students are all postgrads like him. He gave me a long piece of cloth with traditional patterns on it and showed me how to wind it round my head to make a sort of turban, the way his mother and aunts do. In his part of Nigeria, all the women cover their hair because of being Muslims. He told me he'd missed me terribly while he was there and I told him how much I'd missed him. We made love twice, we were so pleased to see each other again. Then I had to come home because Aunty Muriel was coming to tea and I'd promised Mum I'd be back.*

There were a few more entries in a similar vein. It appeared that the lovers had met daily during the period leading up to the start of the Oxford undergraduate term. The diary described romantic punting expeditions on the Cherwell, walking hand-in-hand along the canal or across Christchurch Meadow, visits to the theatre and cinema, and usually the meetings ended with a return to Yakubu's room. It was hardly surprising then to read,

*15ᵗʰ **September** I'm starting to think it could have happened! I'm 3 days late now. It's so exciting to think that by this summer we could be parents! I won't tell Yakubu yet, in case it's a false alarm, but I've got this funny feeling that it's for real.*

*16ᵗʰ **September** I should have known it was all too easy! I'm glad I didn't say anything to Yakubu. He doesn't know I haven't been taking precautions and he might insist if he knew. I know he'd love us to have kids together, but he'd probably think it was too soon. He's very responsible like that. I suppose it comes of being older and having to take care of his mum and sisters while his dad's ill. I hope he gets better or Yakubu will probably think he has to go back to live in Nigeria to look after them.*

Andy put down the diary and made some rapid calculations on his fingers. Then he flicked forwards four weeks. Mum was living in college now. There were accounts of Freshers Week events and societies that she considered joining. Her first tutorial was described in detail, with particular attention paid to some idiosyncrasies of her tutorial partner. Yakubu passed his viva with, as Mum had hoped, minor modifications to his thesis, which would keep him in Oxford for another month or so. Then,

*28ᵗʰ **October** I'm almost certain now! I've never been as late as this before. And I feel different somehow. I won't say anything to Yakubu until I'm sure. We couldn't see each other today anyway.*

He's shut himself away to work on his corrections. His dad's taken a turn for the worse and he wants to get it finished so he can go home and see him. He's booked to fly out on Wednesday. Only 5 days! I can hardly bear to think about it.

29th October *I felt really nauseous waiting in the queue for breakfast this morning. I managed to eat it without being sick and then it was OK until dinner when the smell of the liver and bacon set me off again. It isn't very nice, but I'm happy that it means I probably really am pregnant this time!*

Andy dropped the diary into his lap, and sat staring at the wall. This was not at all as he had imagined it! He had always pictured his mother as a scared eighteen-year-old finding herself unexpectedly pregnant by an older man who had taken advantage of her and then deserted her. Now, by her own admission, she had been scheming to force him into fatherhood without his knowledge or consent. She might have been deluded and he had certainly not been honest with her about his wives and baby, but …. He picked up the book again and continued to read.

1st November *Our last day together! I went round to his place before breakfast and we made love before eating toast cooked on the electric fire in his room. I brought it all up again in his toilet right afterwards and I was on the verge of telling him why, but then he sat me down on the bed and said he had something important to say to me, and anyway, I'm still not sure and I'd promised myself I wouldn't tell him until I was. I said I'd got a lecture at 10 so maybe this should wait until after that. I was hoping we'd be able to spend the afternoon together. But he insisted he had to do it there and then.*

The first part was great. He asked me to marry him and go to Nigeria to live with him. He said we couldn't live here in England because he had to look after his family in Nigeria, especially now that his father was ill and might not recover. I could finish my degree first and I wouldn't need to decide properly until after I'd been for a few visits, but he couldn't bear to think of not seeing me again, so would I at least consider it? It all sounded so exciting and I wanted to be with him so much! I started to say "Yes, of course," but he put his hand over my mouth and said there was something I needed to know before I answered.

I couldn't believe it at first! Yakubu is already married!! He's been married for 6 years! In fact, he's got 2 wives!!!! And he's got a little girl who's going to be five in two weeks. That's another reason why he wanted to get back to Nigeria right away after his viva, so he'd be there for her birthday. And he still had the nerve to ask me to marry him! I told him that I didn't want to be wife number 3, thank you very much! And then I walked out and came back to my room in college and just cried and cried.

Andy sat there reading the entry over and over. The sympathy that he had been beginning to feel towards his father had evaporated. How cowardly he had been, leaving it until their last day together to break it to his English girlfriend that he already had two wives! And what a callous way of doing it – building her up with a proposal of marriage, and then dashing her dreams by telling her that she would be just one of three. Having deceived her for two years, it would have been kinder to have left her in ignorance and written or phoned from Nigeria saying that his feelings for her had changed or that he had found someone else or even that his family had forced him into marriage with a Nigerian girl and he couldn't refuse his dying father's wish. Poor Mum! She'd invested so much in this relationship and it had all been built on lies!

2nd November *I found a letter from Yakubu in my pigeonhole this morning. It was a grovelling note asking for forgiveness. He says that he can't live without me and he'll marry me here in*

Britain and that will mean that I'm his real wife and the others won't count here, only in Nigeria. But he won't divorce them because it would break his mother's heart and one of them is mentally unstable and might kill herself if he did. He should have thought of all that before he started going out with me.

5th November *Mum and Dad had a bonfire and fireworks in the garden and insisted that I came. I didn't really want to, because I knew they'd ask about Yakubu, but in the end I was glad I could tell Mum about what he'd done. She was great about it and so was Dad, but Clare was there too and she really crowed about it. Talk about "I told you so"!*

10th November *I went shopping for new bras today. All my old ones are too small now. I never knew that was something that happens when you're pregnant, but I got a book about it out of the Westgate library and it says it's one of the early signs. The nausea has been worse this week too but so far I haven't actually been sick again. I keep worrying in case I have to run out in the middle of a tutorial or a lecture but so far it's been OK.*

11th November *A letter arrived today from Yakubu. I was going to tear it up without reading it. Then I thought, "What if my scout gets it out of the bin and puts it together and reads it?" So then I thought of burning it, but I don't have anywhere I could do it. In books, there are always open fires where people can burn documents, but there's only an electric heater here and central heating at home. So I locked it in the bottom drawer of my desk with my cheque book and purse.*

Andy thumbed through the pile of letters, which lay on the bed beside him bound together with an elastic band. Sure enough, there was one postmarked 9th November 1983. The next one was dated 5th December. Andy flicked through the pages of the diary to the next month.

8th December another letter came today from Yakubu. It was addressed to our house this time, instead of to college. I don't know if that's because he knew I'd be living back here once term ended or if he thinks I'm more likely to reply from here. I was in my bedroom trying to write the essay that Dr Pennington set for us to do over Christmas. Mum brought it up to me and then hung around talking. I think she was curious to know what was in it. But I'm not! I don't care what he has to say to me now. I wouldn't believe a word of it anyway, the lying creep.

9th December My shameful secret is out!!! Mum came to my room this afternoon while Dad was at work and came right out with it. "Are you pregnant?" she said. I said yes, I thought so. Then I asked her how she knew, because I was sure it wasn't showing yet, and she laughed and said that after having had four babies, she knew the signs. She said, "Presumably Yakubu's the father?" and I said, "Yes, of course, I've never been unfaithful!" I'd been dreading them finding out, but Mum was very good about everything. She asked how many weeks it was since my last period, and I counted up and we worked out it was 12. She asked if I wanted to have an abortion, and I said "No, definitely not!" but she left me a leaflet about the British Pregnancy Advisory Service anyway. I asked if we could keep quiet about it until after Christmas, because I didn't want Grandma and Grandpa and all the aunts and uncles fussing about it when we see them. She said, yes, but we had to let Dad know. She offered to tell him, which was a relief.

10th December Dad came to my room this morning. Mum must have told him about me last night. He said that, whatever I decided, they'd stick by me, but I needed to think seriously about how having a baby was going to affect my degree and my future job prospects. I said I couldn't even consider having an abortion and he said he admired me for that, but he really did think I ought to have *the baby adopted. I said, no, I wanted to keep it. It was the only good thing that had come out of my relationship with Yakubu. He started to argue and then backed down and said I ought to talk it over with Mum. Typical man! Wanting everyone to dance to his tune and then expecting his wife to fix it all for him!*

***12th December** Mum came with me to the doctor. He felt around inside me, which wasn't very nice, and he felt all over my stomach and listened to it with his stethoscope, and then said he was 99.99% certain I was pregnant, but I'd better have a test to make sure because there was such a thing as a phantom pregnancy. He sent me into the toilets with a little bottle to collect a sample. The receptionist will phone in a few days with the results. On the way home, Mum talked about how worried Dad was about me wanting to keep the baby. She said if that's what I want, she'll help me to look after it, but even so it was bound to get in the way of me finishing my degree. That's why they wanted me to consider adoption. There were loads of couples out there who couldn't have children of their own who would love to give mine a good home with two parents. I could see she was trying her best, but she did keep on and on about how young I was and how much better it would be to make a clean start and how I'd be sure to find someone else and be able to have children later, when I was in a better position to look after them. I just switched off in the end and let her talk. Whatever they say isn't going to make any difference. It's my baby and I'm going to keep it.*

Andy found tears welling up in his eyes. At least that part was true. Mum had always said that he was a wanted baby – not that he had ever believed her about that! He'd always assumed it was just something she said to make him feel better, so that he wouldn't blame himself for ruining her life. It was good to know, but at the same time it was a bit anxiety-provoking. Had he lived up to her expectations? Should he be back at home with her, instead of here in Yakubu's flat, spying on her private diary? He was all she had, and now she must think he was deserting her!

He got to his feet and began pacing the floor, his mind in turmoil. It would have been so easy for Mum to have got rid of him one way or another and she'd *chosen* to keep him. Chosen! It wasn't the only option. He owed her everything!

But didn't he have a right to choose his own life too? Nana and Gramps – or Gramps at least – had wanted her to go for adoption; but then, after she made her choice, they'd bent over backwards to support her even though she didn't go along with their advice. Mum had to understand that she couldn't be the only person in his life for ever. Whether she liked it or not, Yakubu was part of it too now – and so was Esther. Esther! It felt like years since they'd been together, although it was only last Saturday. But so much had happened since. He needed to see her, to talk to her. She would know what he ought to do.

He reached for his phone. It rang out twice before he cancelled the call and stuffed the phone back in his pocket. He couldn't do it! It wouldn't be fair on Mum. It was a big enough intrusion to have him reading her diary, and letters intended for her eyes alone, without him sharing them with a stranger.

Except that Esther wasn't going to be a stranger for much longer. She might even become part of the family. It was time he took her home to meet Mum. Esther expected it, and Mum had been getting suspicious that there must be something – or someone – apart from work that was taking up his time and keeping him out of the house more than usual. How would she react when he told her he was seeing Esther? A lot of women her age would be pleased that he'd got a steady girlfriend at last and be looking forward to the prospect of grandchildren. But Mum had never dropped hints in that direction the way that the mothers of some of his contemporaries had. And she had always seemed pleased that he still lived at home with her instead of finding a place of his own. She depended on him, and looking after him gave purpose to her life.

His phone started ringing. It was Esther.

'Andy? Were you trying to ring me just now?'

'Yes. I'm sorry. I wanted to talk to you about something, and then I wasn't sure if I ought to.'

'Was it something to do with your work then?'

'No. It's … well, it's about my mum – something new I've found out about her and Yakubu. I don't know quite what to make of it all and I wanted to share it with you. And then I thought maybe I shouldn't because it's rather private and she might not like it – well, I'm sure she wouldn't like it; I don't suppose she'd be exactly pleased that *I* know, although it does confirm what she always said about how I wasn't a mistake and …. I'm sorry, I'm not making a lot of sense, am I?'

'Not totally coherent,' Esther laughed, 'but I think I get the general picture. And it's good to hear your voice anyway. How is your father doing? Did he tell you we met today?

'Yes. He was very pleased about it. He kept saying *alhamdulillah*, which seems to mean praise be to God or something like that, as if God was behind you bumping into him.'

'Maybe He was,' laughed Esther.

'Apparently you told him we were going out together.'

'Aren't we?'

'Well yes, of course we are, but …. Well, I haven't even told Mum about it yet, so I'm not sure about Yakubu knowing. I mean … Mum wouldn't like him finding out before she did.'

'There's an easy solution to that,' Esther said brightly. 'Don't you think it's about time you did tell your mum? And I'd like to meet her. You've told me so much about her but you don't seem to want us to get to know each other.'

'It's not a good time,' Andy hedged, 'what with her already being upset about Yakubu being here. She thinks he's trying to steal me away from her. She'd just see you as another threat – another person who's coming between her and me.'

'And what about me?' Esther's voice suddenly took on a sharper tone. 'I know she's your mother and I know she's dedicated her life to you, but don't you ever think about the way *she's* always coming between *us*? Is that what it's always going to be like? Am I always going to come second to your perfect mother?'

'I never said she was perfect!' Andy protested, taken aback by this outburst from the usually accommodating Esther and grasping at this last accusation as the easiest to defend. 'She drives me up the wall sometimes. You know that – I've complained about her often enough. But you have to understand that I just can't do anything to hurt her. I'm all she's got!'

'Then isn't it about time to change that?' challenged Esther. 'Do you really think she wouldn't be pleased to have a daughter-in-law and grandchildren – if ever you were to find someone you loved enough to risk stepping away from her a little bit for?'

'Is that how you see us?' Andy stammered, astonished at what seemed to him to be an enormous leap from what he had kept telling himself was just a casual relationship to the prospect of marriage and children.

'Don't you? Or is it a case of *like father like son*, and you're hoping I'll disappear off back to Nigeria at the end of my course and you won't have to be troubled with me again?'

'No, of course not! I just hadn't realised …. I mean I thought we were still ….' Andy took a deep breath. 'I suppose I'm not very good at looking into the future – not further than a few weeks, anyway. I know things can't go on the way they are forever, but I just can't seem to take the plunge and do anything to rock the boat with Mum. Her whole life revolves around me. I know you're right that that's not healthy for either of us, but that's how it is! And it makes it hard for me to admit that there could be someone else who's more important to me than she is.'

'And is there?'

'Yes, of course there is!' declared Andy, realising this fact himself for the first time. 'I love you, Esther, and I want to be with you forever. And I *will* tell Mum and take you to see her – but not quite yet, not while she's so upset about Yakubu being here. She'd probably see you as part of a plot to whip me off to Nigeria so she'd never see me again.'

'Yes, I'm sorry.' Esther's tone changed abruptly. 'I didn't mean to complain. I just sometimes feel ....'

'No, I'm the one who should be sorry,' Andy cut in quickly. 'I know how it must seem to you. But really, I'm not just stringing you along – honestly! It's just ....' He sighed. 'Everything is just so complicated at the moment!'

'Yes. I understand.' Esther's resentment appeared to have evaporated. 'I wasn't trying to make you feel bad. Now, you said you wanted to talk to me about something – before I took us off on a tangent. What was it?'

'It was ....' Andy paused. 'I was going to ask you ... no, forget it. I think I need to work this one out for myself. Sorry for bothering y- – no! I'm not sorry. It was great hearing your voice. Let's talk again soon – and meet too! Just as soon as all this stuff is over – the trial and everything.'

'Yes.' Esther sounded a little disappointed, but she quickly continued. 'It was nice hearing your voice too.'

'Good. Well ... I'd better go now. I'll ring you again tomorrow,' Andy promised. He moved his thumb across the screen to cancel the call, and then added hurriedly, 'I love you!'

'I love you too, Andy. Bye!'

Andy sat staring down at his phone with a bewildering mixture of emotions churning inside him. This was the first time that they had declared their love out loud in words. And it was certainly the first time that he had considered the prospect of marriage and children. Would Mum really be pleased to have grandchildren? Probably she would. And it would give her someone else to focus her devotion on so that her life didn't simply revolve around him! Of course, Esther would have to agree to come to live here. There could be no question of them setting up home in Nigeria. Mum would be devastated. But they would go on visits to Esther's family, and maybe call in on Yakubu while they were there – which would mean that he would never need to come to Oxford again. That would certainly please Mum!'

He put the phone back in his pocket and turned back to the diary lying on his lap. Pushing to the back of his mind the guilt that he couldn't help feeling over intruding on his mother's privacy, he read on … and on …

He read about the awkwardness of Christmas, with relatives coming round, eager to hear about Mandy's first term. Had she made lots of new friends in college? How was the course? Did she have a boyfriend – there must be lots of eligible young men at the university? Her oldest sister, Pauline, married for a year and now back from Birmingham with her husband for a visit of several days, talked endlessly – or so it seemed to poor Mandy – about how much they were looking forward to having children. Now that her probationary year as a teacher was over, they were trying for a baby, but so far without success.

He read about visits to Mothercare, accompanied by her mother to give advice on choosing maternity clothes that would hide her expanding bump; about lectures missed to attend ante-natal appointments at the hospital; and about morning sickness receding and being replaced by swollen ankles. There was no mention of the usual student activities: parties, pub crawls, sports, societies … not even long evenings with friends *setting the world to rights*! Did she have any friends? She didn't mention any. Her whole life seemed to revolve around preparing for her baby, while slogging away for hours on end to keep up with demands from her tutors for essays.

The six-week Easter vacation meant a let-up in the pressure of work – just a long reading list to get through and revision for the upcoming Prelim exams – but brought sister Clare back from her own studies at Exeter University. Clare who had predicted that dating an African would cause trouble. Clare who had said that it was cruel to bring mixed-race children into the world because they would never fit in anywhere. Clare who – or so it seemed to Mandy – was smugly gloating over her sister's situation.

Then back to college for the next term. Andy turned the pages, rapidly scanning past descriptions of arriving back there – a new kettle for her room, the re-furbished JCR, Cadbury's creme eggs on sale in the buttery at reduced price – anxiety over whether her essays were well-enough researched, and a long diatribe about Clare's behaviour towards her during the holiday. He was considering whether to skip forward to June and his own arrival into the world when an entry caught his eye.

20th April We all went to Dr Pennington's pre-term meeting for First Years this afternoon. She told us all about the lectures she expected us to go to this term and when our tutorials were going to be. Then she launched into a spiel about how Trinity Term had lots of distractions for undergraduates, but we weren't to allow ourselves to be so obsessed with Eights Week and punt parties that we neglected our studies, because the main thing for us was to pass our Prelims. She talked as if we were two-year-olds, not adults who were perfectly capable of managing our own lives!

Then, just as we were all filing out of her room, she called me back and said she wanted a word with me on my own. She got up and closed the door and then stood there staring at me.

'I think you've been a silly girl,' she said eventually, staring pointedly down at my stomach.

I didn't know what to say! I just stood there feeling awful. I could feel my face getting hot. I must have been blushing as red as a beetroot. So she went on. 'I suppose it must be too late to get rid of it?'

That made me really angry, but I still couldn't think of anything to say, so I just carried on standing there like a lemon, while she went on and on. Hadn't I read the booklet about contraception that I'd been given when I came up? Didn't I go to the meeting for freshers with the college nurse in Michaelmas Term? She asked when I was due. When I said June, she sort of snorted and said, "Well, you'll have to hope it doesn't decide to make its appearance in the middle of your Prelims!'

I said I thought it would most likely be after they were over, which she seemed pleased about. She nodded as if she was thinking, and then said, 'Let's hope so, and then you'll have the long vac to get over it all. Have you got the adoption sorted yet? The college nurse will be able to put you in touch with a good agency if you haven't.'

She was so patronising and so sure that she knew best! I told her that I was keeping my baby and she said, 'so that's the end of your career then! You might as well go down now and stop wasting rate-payers money on your education.' Very final as if that was my fate sealed for all eternity. I told her that Mum's happy to babysit while I'm at lectures and tutorials and so on, at which she pursed her lips and said, 'I suppose your family being in Oxford will make it easier, but mark my words, I've seen it all before and

JUST ANOTHER SUICIDE

I've never known a girl in your predicament to finish her degree. You just give it some thought my girl. You'll soon see that adoption will be better for you and the baby, mark my word!'

I was furious, but I didn't dare to say all the things I thought of saying, so I just mumbled, 'Yes Dr Pennington.' And made my escape as soon as I could. It was so humiliating!

Sally was waiting outside for me and she asked what it was all about, so I told her. She was almost as indignant about it as I was.

Andy paused in his reading. Who was this Sally? He flicked back to the entries from the start of Michaelmas Term and discovered that Sally Coe and Amanda Lepage were tutorial partners. Stretching his memory back to his early childhood, he now remembered vaguely someone he called *Aunty Sally* who had been a friend of his mother's. Good! At least Mum wasn't quite as alone as she had begun to appear.

Diary entries from Trinity Term reflected increasing anxiety over both her academic performance and the approaching birth. A few days in hospital due to high blood pressure shortly before the Prelim exams marked a particularly low point. The examinations themselves were dealt with only cursorily, but Andy got the impression that they had not gone well. Antibiotics to treat a water infection were mentioned and also the embarrassment of having to ask to be escorted from the examination room to visit the toilet several times. Once again, Andy felt that he was intruding on matters that his mother would not have wanted him to be privy to. He skipped passed the next few pages without reading them, hunting for one significant date.

Yes, here it was!

30th June 1984 It's really happened! I'm a mother! I went into labour during the night and Andrew Wilfred Lepage was born at two thirty-two this afternoon. "Wilfred" is after Dad. I hope

Andrew doesn't get teased for having a funny middle name, but I wanted to do something for Dad because he's been so good about everything. Unlike a certain sister I could mention! Jenny has been great. I can see she's excited about being an aunty and is looking forward to helping with looking after little Andrew. I feel a bit sorry for Pauline, because she's desperate for a baby of her own and it must be awful for her seeing me with mine when she did what everyone says is the right thing and waited until she was married. Mum rang her to tell her the news and she says Pauline put a brave face on it and sent congratulations. Clare, fortunately, is still in Exeter. Her term doesn't end for another week. Mum rang her too and she told me that Clare also sends congratulations, but I don't believe her. I can just imagine her voice when she sees Andrew's lovely frizzy black hair! "He'll stick out like a sore thumb," she'll say. "It's cruel bringing mixed race kids into the world. They can never fit in anywhere.'

Andy sighed. So that was why they never had anything to do with Aunty Clare and her family! Had she really been so cruel to Mum? Or was she in fact just saying out loud what other members of the family were thinking? And there was, after all, some truth in what she'd said about him not fitting in. If he had a pound for every time someone had assumed that he must be an expert on reggae music or feel the cold particularly badly in the winter or …!

He closed the diary and pushed it back down to the bottom of his rucksack. So, Mum really had wanted to have a baby and had gone out of her way to conceive him! Although that was what she had told him his whole life, he had never really believed it before. And that put a completely different complexion on Yakubu's role. Yes, he had deceived her by not telling her about his wives and daughter, but she had tricked him into fathering a child and then kept him from knowing of that child's existence. And, far from disappearing back to Nigeria without a care in the world, he had written to her repeatedly over a period of months – even years – letters which she did not even deign to open!

He reached out for the first of the unopened letters and slid his finger under the flap with the intention of unsealing it. Then his nerve suddenly went and he slid it back under the elastic band that bound the letters together. He stuffed the whole pile back into his rucksack and pulled its drawstring tight just as there came a knock at the door and Yakubu's voice offering to make them both some supper.

11. FATHERS AND SONS

'So, on the face of it, we've found the motive for Rory's suicide,' Anna concluded, as she described her visit to the Quinn family home at the morning team briefing. 'He couldn't face coming out to his parents, knowing that his father would be horrified – and probably assuming that his mother would be too – and couldn't see any other way out of an impossible situation.'

'So, is that it?' asked Alice. 'It's definitely suicide and we can close the file?'

'It's certainly looking that way,' Anna began. Then she saw Jennifer Moorhouse raising her hand and trying to catch her eye. 'Yes Jen. Did you want to say something?'

'It's these social media posts,' Jennifer replied. 'There are a lot of quite threatening ones – death threats even. They've been posted to look as if they're from lots of different people, but an awful lot of them have names that are variations on "Ollie" or "Oliver" or related to that name in some way – "The Twister" for example is most likely a reference to Oliver Twist. I thought it might be worth finding out what this guy's real name is. Whoever he is, he seems to have taken offence at Rory's political cartoons. And he seems to have brought them to the attention of a lot of right-wing trolls, who've joined in posting some quite vicious comments about them.'

'OK. Keep digging and see if you can identify this "Ollie" character.' Anna spotted a look of dissatisfaction on Alice's face and added, 'even if we accept that Rory killed himself, we need to find out if it was the trolling that drove him to it.'

'Of course we do!' Alice commented to Joshua Pitchfork, who happened to be sitting next to her, in a voice low enough to be clearly not addressed to the room but just loud enough that Anna would be sure to hear. 'After all, we can't allow a rich American businessman and his wife to feel guilty that their homophobic attitudes may have been responsible!'

'And who knows how many other vulnerable young people *Ollie* and his friends could be targeting,' Anna continued, pointedly staring towards Alice, who looked back rebelliously. 'So, let's see what we can find out about him and any other people who've threatened Rory online. I'll leave that to you Jen. And Alice! You can do some more digging into Rory's background. I want to know more about his political views and affiliations. Was his activism restricted to drawing satirical cartoons or has he been involved in anything more hands-on?'

'OK.' Alice still looked sulky. 'But I have to say that this all seems a bit OTT for a death that we're all agreed is ninety-five percent certainly a suicide. I've got a string of burglaries I could be looking into – one where a little old lady's lost all her husband's World War II medals – if we weren't all chasing our tails over this case. Are you sure we'd still be devoting so much time and energy to it if Rory Quinn's father wasn't a multi-millionaire and a friend of the PCC[2]?'

'Yes, I am,' Anna said firmly. 'You may find this hard to believe, but even rich and influential people have feelings. Mr and Mrs Quinn have lost their son. No parent ought to have to bury their child. And suicide is the worst possible way to lose anyone you care about. I'm sure that I can trust you to be just as

---

[2] Police and Crime Commissioner: an elected official responsible for overseeing the local police service.

thorough about investigating Rory Quinn's death as if he were a down-and-out living on the streets! I'm leaving you in charge of this investigation: Andy and I are going to be tied up with the Jibrilu Danjuma murder trial today. Find out what you can and we'll catch up again tomorrow.'

She walked out of the room, followed closely by Andy.

'Are you really going to court this morning?' he asked as they descended the stairs. 'Nothing much is going to happen on the first day.'

'I've had a tip-off that Logan Wyatt could be planning to plead guilty to manslaughter. If he does, and the prosecution decide not to hold out for murder, things could be over almost before they start.'

'Hardly worth Jibrilu's father coming all this way to see the show,' Andy commented, thinking how much simpler things would have been if the youth who stabbed his half-brother to death in the street last year had admitted to his guilt at once.

'He'll still be able to see the sentencing,' Anna pointed out, 'and look the killers in the eyes. I don't imagine he'd have wanted to miss that.'

Coming out to the street, they parted company. Anna headed straight for the Crown Court, hoping to speak with the prosecution team before the trial began, while Andy hurried back to the flat, where he found Yakubu anxiously peering out of the bedroom window waiting for his return.

'Ready for the off?' Andy called out cheerfully, glad that his father would at last have something to keep his mind occupied other than dreams of re-kindling his relationship with "my Mandy" and getting to know the son they had produced together.

It was only a ten-minute walk down Abingdon Road to the court building in St Aldate's, but to Andy it seemed far longer. Yakubu, very tense and nervous, chattered away apparently at random, interspersing inconsequential remarks with demands for information about court procedure and likely sentences for his son's killers.

'I understand that there is no death penalty in the UK,' he said as they entered the court building, 'but you say that even a life sentence does not mean prison for life. That seems strange to me.'

'I suppose we like to think that prison reforms people,' Andy replied. 'And it's expensive keeping someone in jail if they're no longer a threat.'

'Under Shariah Law, the family of the victim is permitted to choose whether a murderer should be executed,' Yakubu observed.

'And would you choose for the man who stabbed Jibrilu to be killed?'

'It would be the just thing to happen,' Yakubu answered without hesitation. 'A life for a life. That is what it says in the Holy Qur'an.'

They joined the long queue to be allowed into the court. Yakubu was surprised to see the level of scrutiny that every visitor to the building was put through. Following Andy's example, he handed over his bag to be scanned and then walked through the metal detector arch. The large buckle on his belt set off an alarm, and he was sent back. Andy, who had known what to expect and had dressed accordingly, waited patiently for him to remove it and return for a second, successful, attempt.

'This way.' Andy set off purposefully, with Yakubu hurrying to keep up. 'DCI Davenport reliably informs me that we're in court number two.'

The entrance to the public gallery was blocked by an enormous man whose body appeared about to burst out of the dark suit, which he had presumably bought at a time when he was several stones lighter. He was engaged in an argument with a woman of indeterminate age in a figure-hugging dress and a large hat. They seemed to be finding it difficult to agree about where they should sit. When Andy asked politely to be allowed through, he turned round with a look of thunder on his face and seemed about to let rip with expletives, but evidently thought better of it when he caught the eye of the court official who was supervising the gallery. He turned back to his companion, grunting at her irritably, 'make your mind up, there are people waiting.'

They took seats next to the aisle because Andy wanted to be able to leave once the proceedings were underway, pleading an urgent need to be back at work. That there was plenty of work for him to do was true enough, but if he was honest with himself, his motivation was more a desire to avoid an inevitable meal with his father were he to stay around until the court adjourned for lunch. He was finding it increasingly difficult to work out what his feelings towards Yakubu were, now that he had discovered the degree of his mother's deceit towards her lover, and he could not face a lengthy conversation with him.

While they waited for the proceedings to begin, Yakubu gazed round at the other occupants of the public gallery. The couple who had been blocking the door when they arrived were now sitting in the front row. The woman was touching up her makeup with the aid of a small mirror. The man had taken off his jacket to reveal muscular arms generously tattooed with images of demons, dragons and a snarling wolf. As Yakubu watched, another couple approached them, accompanied by a boy in his late teens. The boy and his father both had flaming red hair and towered above the diminutive woman accompanying them. The first couple moved up to make room for the trio of newcomers. Yakubu observed that the two families appeared to know one another. Who were they? Relatives of the defendants perhaps?

He was about to ask Andy whether he recognised them when a new arrival caught his attention. She was a flamboyant woman with a mass of blond hair and a big bust. She clattered to the front of the gallery in shoes with implausibly high heels, calling out a greeting in a voice designed to attract attention from everyone present.

'Terry! Sharon! You made it then?'

The large man turned and waved a hand in acknowledgement of her arrival. Across his knuckles Yakubu could read the word LOVE spelled out, a letter on each finger. 'Hi Hayley. Come to see the show?'

'I could hardly miss it, could I?' the woman replied, still speaking in an unnecessarily loud voice. 'My one and only daughter in the dock, fitted up for something she never done!'

'Don't you come acting all innocent with us, Hayley Middleton!' Yakubu stared as the tiny woman who had arrived just before her got to her feet and stepped out into the path of the woman called Hayley. 'It's your Courtney caused all of this! Showing off, egging them on! None of this would have happened if she hadn't been there!'

'You bitch!' Hayley took a step forward, but Andy was too quick for her. Leaping to his feet he placed himself between the two women. The large man was also on his feet by now levering himself up with a hand on the back of his seat. Absently, Yakubu read the letters H A T E across the knuckles, his main attention focused on the drama that was unfolding in the aisle.

It was all over in seconds. The court official stepped forward and ushered Hayley into a seat at the other side of the gallery. The tall red-headed man put his hand on his wife's shoulder, urging her in a low voice to sit down.

'Don't let that cow get to you, Natalie. Tyler's lawyer will soon set the jury straight on her Courtney.'

So those were indeed relatives of the defendants – the parents of one of them by the sound of it. There had been two young men and a woman, Yakubu remembered. Two young men showing off in front of a girl by tormenting a young black boy who had the audacity to be taking organ lessons from the music tutor at an Oxford college. Jibrilu had intervened and received a fatal knife wound in return.

'Be upstanding!' The abrupt command from a court official interrupted Yakubu's thoughts. Andy was on his feet already, standing to attention, his eyes forward watching as the judge entered the court and took her place. Leaning heavily on his stick, Yakubu pulled himself laboriously into a standing position. The public gallery fell silent.

It seemed a long time before the trial began. The swearing-in of the jury alone appeared interminable to Yakubu. Then there seemed to be a lot of whispered conversations and to-ing and fro-ing among the various lawyers and officials, while the watchers in the public gallery began to become restless. The red-headed youth took out his phone and became engrossed in a game on it. His mother whispered angrily to her husband, too low for Yakubu to pick up the words. The big man, whom Hayley had called Terry, got out a copy of the Daily Mail.

'I've heard a whisper that he may be going to plead guilty to manslaughter,' Andy murmured low in Yakubu's ear. 'That may be what the conflab is about.'

At last, the judge called the court to order and the trial got underway. Whatever negotiations there may have been had evidently come to nothing, since all three defendants pleaded not guilty on all counts. As the prosecuting council got to his feet to set out the case against the defendants, Andy got silently up and walked briskly to the door. Yakubu turned his head to watch him leave and then focused his attention once more on the scene below.

He had not expected the judge to be a woman. She looked distinctly odd wearing the strangely curled grey and white wig on top of luxuriant black hair, tied back in a long plait which was clearly visible whenever she turned her head to one side. Her face looked very brown in contrast to the pale wig, almost as dark as Andy's. Not at all his idea of what an English judge should look like.

The prosecuting barrister was more what he had anticipated: a middle-aged man, rather portly with reading glasses that he took on and off strategically to emphasis points in his argument. There were several other people in wigs, presumably lawyers engaged to represent the three defendants.

The defendants! Yakubu studied them, trying to divine something of their characters from their appearance. The woman – Courtney – was dressed more soberly than her mother, presumably on the advice of her lawyers, in a long-sleeved white blouse and a navy-blue skirt. Yakubu found it difficult to assess her age under the heavy makeup that covered her face making her look rather like a china doll. The two men both looked very uncomfortable in dark suits over collar and tie. It was not difficult to guess whose offspring they were, since one was tall and lanky with vivid red hair and the other was heavily-built with a shaved head adorned with tattoos. They all looked so young! How terrible it must be for their parents to see them there, accused of such serious crimes.

The judge addressed them each by names which Yakubu carefully committed to memory: Courtney Middleton, Tyler Briggs and Logan Wyatt. They were all charged with murder and with various lesser offences relating to their abusive behaviour towards Gabriel Sibanda, aged thirteen, which had been the catalyst for the killing of his rescuer. They all looked sombrely back at the judge as they solemnly declared their innocence, but Courtney could not resist a glance up at the public gallery and a little smile in response to a wave from her mother. Could it be that she still did not realise the seriousness of her situation? Or perhaps bravado was her way of covering up her fear?

Yakubu was disappointed that nothing much seemed to have been achieved by the time that the judge declared a lunchtime adjournment. He had imagined that by now the prosecution would have outlined the sequence of events leading up to his son's death and perhaps called at least one witness. As it was, the time had been frittered away with arcane legal processes that were surely unnecessarily time-consuming. He got up from his seat and made his slow way out of the building into the dazzling light of the July day. Andy had warned him that the trial could last several weeks, but he had not really believed him until now.

***

As he made his way back to the office, Andy pondered on the little scene that he had witnessed in the public gallery. Two fathers had come to see their sons accused of heinous crimes. Did they believe them to be innocent in the face of the evidence, with which they must by now be familiar? Mrs Briggs seemed to blame it all on the young woman, Courtney Middleton, but Courtney had not been the one wielding the knife that killed Jibrilu. That had been Logan, the oldest of the three, the son of the tattooed colossus who had one hand dedicated to love and the other to hate. What sort of role model did he offer to his son?

Or was that just prejudice? Perhaps Mr Wyatt senior was merely a fan of fantasy fiction, where dragons and wolves abounded – think *Lord of the Rings* or *Discworld*. For all he knew, Terence Wyatt could be a model husband and father. He had at least been present when his son was growing up – unlike so many fathers these days!

In fact, of the five parents present, it was Natalie Briggs who had appeared the most aggressive – a mother tiger fighting to protect her young! Was it she who had sown the seeds of racial hatred in her son's heart? Or was she right, and there was no real animosity between the young men and their victims – just a

193

desire to look big in front of a girl they wanted to impress? What a mess! What a reason for Jibrilu to lose his life!

When he got back to the office, Jennifer greeted him with the news that she had traced the elusive *Ollie*, whose full name was Oliver Cash. He had been a student at Nottingham University on the same course as Jamie Mercer.

"The university won't give us his home address without a warrant,' she told Andy, 'but I thought you might be able to find out something about him from Jamie, seeing as you've already spoken to him.'

'They've obviously tightened up on their GDPR procedures since I contacted them,' Andy smiled. 'The person I spoke to handed Jamie Mercer's address over right away.'

'Or else, *Detective Inspector* makes more impact than, "Jennifer Moorhouse from Thames Valley Police",' Jennifer grinned back.

'Either way, it looks like I'd better have another word with Jamie. I'll give him a ring.'

'I've also been looking into the other trolls that have been attacking Rory on social media. The most persistent one calls himself "Archie the Avenger" and gives his location as *Oxford*, which could make it easy for him to move from online attacks to real-life ones.'

'Great. See if you can find out what his real name is and where he lives. He may not have physically attacked Rory, but knowing that someone who hates your guts lives in the same town would be pretty frightening. My money's still on Rory having killed himself and Archie's social media attacks may have been part of the reason.'

Jamie received Andy's phone call eagerly, clearly hoping for news, but when he realised that Andy was asking questions rather than imparting information, he became guarded, if not exactly hostile.

'Yes,' he admitted reluctantly, 'I knew Ollie Cash.'

'Were you mates?'

'Yes, I suppose you could say that. We were on the same course. We sometimes compared notes about the work we were doing.'

'But you don't keep in touch now? You said you *knew* him in the past tense?'

'No. We fell out.'

'Did Rory know him too? Were they friends?'

'Hardly!' Jamie gave a bitter laugh.

'So, did you know Ollie was trolling Rory on Instagram? Were you thinking of him when you said Rory had had death threats made against him?'

'I … OK,' Jamie sighed. 'Ollie and I were an item. Then I met Rory and I told Ollie it was over between us. Ollie didn't take it well. He played some really silly practical jokes on Rory and said all sorts of stupid things to him. But I know he'd never go through with any of it. He wasn't a violent type. It was all … It was just words, that's all.'

'OK. But you can see that we have to speak to him about it, can't you? Do you know his home address?'

After some ineffectual prevarication, Jamie supplied an address in Newbury. Andy thanked him and rang off. Newbury! Only half an hour's drive from Headington! He looked at his watch. Time for a quick lunch in the canteen and then a trip down the A34 to seek out Oliver Cash.

'I'm sorry, Ollie's not back from work yet,' apologised the teenage boy who answered Andy's knock at the door of the Cash family home in Newbury. 'I'm his brother – Charlie.'

'I'm DI Lepage from Thames Valley Police. I was hoping to have a word with Ollie. Are either of your parents in?'

'No. It's just me.' Charlie hesitated then added helpfully, 'Mum'll be back soon – and Ollie's usually home by half five.'

'Where does he work?'

'Harwell – the Rutherford Appleton Lab.'

'A good job then?'

'Oh yes! He was over the moon when he got it. So was Mum. Things have been a bit tight, what with the cost-of-living crisis and Dad-.' He broke off suddenly, then resumed in more measured tones. 'Our Dad's maintenance payments haven't been coming through every month – not since he got married again.'

'I see,' Andy murmured, wondering what to do now. He did not want to return without having seen Ollie, but he did not like to ask to come in and wait. That might get the obliging Charlie into trouble with his mother, who could quite reasonably be worried at her son inviting complete strangers – albeit bearing a police warrant card – into her home.

Thankfully, at that moment, Mrs Cash herself arrived. She parked an elderly blue Vauxhall Corsa on the road outside and walked briskly up the path to join them.

'Can I help you?' she asked when Andy turned to face her.

He introduced himself and showed her his warrant card. She scrutinized it carefully with pale blue eyes surrounded by almost invisible blond lashes. Andy got the feeling that she was struggling to match up the rank of Detective Inspector with the brown face in front of her.

'I was hoping to have a word with Ollie,' he explained. 'Charlie here tells me he should be back from work soon.'

'You'd better come in.'

Charlie stepped back and they both followed his mother into the house and down a short passage to the kitchen.

'Ollie's not in trouble, is he?' she asked anxiously, pulling out a chair and gesturing to Andy to sit down at the table.

'No, no,' Andy said quickly. 'It's just that someone he knew at uni died at the weekend in suspicious circumstances and we're talking to everyone who knew him to find out more about his background to try to piece together why it happened.'

'Suicide, you mean?' Mrs Cash asked abruptly, turning back from the sink where she had started filling a kettle.

'It's looking like that,' Andy confirmed. 'His family can't throw any light on why he might have wanted to take his own life, so we're wondering if it was because of something that happened in Nottingham. That's why we're talking to people who knew him there.'

'Was he gay?' Charlie blurted out.

'Why do you ask that?' Andy fixed his eyes on the boy, interested in this reaction to the news.

'Well because, if he was, I don't see why you need to ask why he killed himself. That'd be enough, wouldn't it?'

'I don't follow you,' Andy said mildly. 'Would you care to elaborate?'

'Well, he'd be feeling everyone was against him, wouldn't he? Like Ollie does.'

'Does he?' Andy began.

'And why's tha-'

'Charlie!' his mother broke in. 'Don't exaggerate.' She turned to Andy, speaking apologetically. 'You mustn't take any notice of Charlie. He tends to see everything very black-and-white. Ollie used to get a bit of stick from kids at school – the usual name-calling and stuff – but he's been fine since he went to uni.'

'That's all you know,' Charlie muttered, just loud enough for Andy to hear, but when Andy looked at him enquiringly, he turned away, declining to elucidate.

'Cup of tea?' enquired Mrs Cash, flicking on the kettle. 'I'm having one.'

'Thank you. Yes, that would be very nice.'

'Ollie won't be long,' she went on, getting out a packet of custard creams and shaking half a dozen out on to a plate, which she set down on the table in front of Andy. 'Help yourself.'

An awkward silence descended on the room. Charlie sat down opposite Andy and stared at him across the table. His mother busied herself getting out mugs and a bag of sugar.

'Charlie was telling me that Ollie works at the Rutherford Appleton Lab,' Andy said, trying to make conversation. 'He's done well to land a job there.'

'He got a first-class degree,' Mrs Cash replied proudly. 'Maths. I've no idea where he got it from, I could never do maths at school and his dad wasn't any better. But, right from Infant School he was interested in numbers. In the art lessons, he used to make up sums for himself instead of painting pictures.'

'You must be proud of him.'

'I'm proud of both of my boys. Charlie here's got a place at Bristol for September.'

'Congratulations!' Andy looked across at the young man. 'What will you be doing there?'

'English.'

'Charlie wants to be a teacher.'

'Well, maybe,' Charlie blushed. 'I haven't decided for definite.'

'And what about you, Mrs Cash?' Andy intervened, conscious of Charlie's embarrassment. 'What do you do?'

'I'm a community pharmacist.' She poured boiling water on to teabags in three mugs. Just as she was retrieving the last one with a teaspoon, there was the sound of a car reversing on to the drive. 'That'll be Ollie. I'll go and tell him you're here.'

Andy did not know what he expected the vicious troll *Oliver Outrider* AKA *Ollie Hardfists* AKA *The Twister* to look like, but he certainly wasn't expecting the slim, smartly-dressed young man with tidy brown hair and an oval face marred by acne who walked through the door a few minutes later. Entering the kitchen, he put down a small briefcase on the floor and held out his hand.

'Hi. I'm Ollie. Mum says you want to speak to me about someone from uni.'

'That's right.' Andy stood up and shook hands. 'I'm DI Andy Lepage from Thames Valley Police. We're investigating the death of Rory Quinn. I believe you knew him when you were both studying at Nottingham University?'

'I knew him,' Ollie answered guardedly, 'but we weren't exactly best mates. He was doing a different course, we only met through mutual acquaintances.'

'Such as Jamie Mercer?'

'Yeah. Jamie was one of them.' Ollie was definitely on the defensive now.

Andy turned to Mrs Cash. 'Do you think Ollie and I could talk on our own now? Is there somewhere we could …?'

She stared at him for a few seconds then turned to address Ollie. 'Here's my tea. I haven't touched it. Take the inspector in the front room. You can take the biscuits with you.' Then, to Andy, 'You'll be private in there, though I don't see-'

'It's OK, Mum. I can handle it.' Ollie picked up the mug and the plate of biscuits and led the way into a small sitting room dominated by a large television screen, which almost filled one wall. They sat down and Andy resumed his questioning.

'Why were you trolling Rory on TikTok and Instagram?'

'What do you mean?'

'Commenting on his posts; accusing him of anything from poor dress sense to bestiality; issuing threats to maim him; mocking his cartoons and his political opinions. It's no good hiding behind all those different user names; we know it was you.'

'Oh.' Ollie sat staring down at his feet.

'Well,' Andy prompted. 'I'm waiting.'

After five minutes, which felt like five hours, Andy decided that he would have to give Ollie some help.

'We know about you and Jamie, and how Rory came between you. That must have hurt. I can understand you being mad at Rory. Is that how it started?'

Ollie took a deep breath. 'You're right. I wanted to get back at Rory and I could see he was no good for Jamie. He needed to sort himself out first before …. Underneath, he was still under the thumb of his church and its homophobic attitudes. He hated himself for being gay.'

'So, you posted messages on social media to make him hate himself even more?'

'No! I just … I was mad with him about losing Jamie and I couldn't say anything because that would have made Jamie mad at me. So, I posted some things about him on social media – nothing really bad, just saying his cartoons were crap and that sort of thing. And then people started liking my posts and replying to my comments and I started thinking up worse things to say about Rory to get more likes and …. I never meant any of it – the death threats and stuff. It all just snowballed and I couldn't stop.'

'So, when *The Twister* says, "you'd better keep looking over your shoulder Cartoon Boy, because one day I'll be right there with my corkscrew at the ready," you weren't intending to intimidate him?'

'No! It was all just fantasy. Nobody would really attack someone with a corkscrew, would they?'

'You'd be surprised the things people use as weapons,' Andy observed. 'If my grandfather had seen you waving a corkscrew around, he'd have said, "put that thing down; you'll have someone's eye out with that!" How was Rory supposed to know you weren't being serious?'

Ollie stared back at Andy in silence. It seemed that this was the first time that it had occurred to him that Rory could have believed that there was someone out to get him in real life.

'You don't think I killed him?' he asked at last. 'I couldn't have. I don't even know where he lives!'

'So you say, but you could easily have found out. Maybe Jamie told you or you sneaked a look at the contacts on his phone. Where were you last Saturday afternoon?'

'I was walking the Ridgeway with some guys from work. You can ask them – they'll tell you I was there.'

'Whereabouts?'

'We met up in the car park at West Ilsley and headed west.'

'What time was that?'

'I left here about one and got to the car park about at about twenty past. We were aiming to set out at half one, but a couple of the guys were late, so we didn't get going until about quarter to two.'

'Which way did you go?'

'West. We walked to the Lord Wantage Monument and back.'

'Arriving back at the car park at …?'

'I'm not sure – four thirty, quarter to five, something like that.'

'And you came straight home?'

'We went for a drink at the Harrow in West Ilsley. I came home after that.'

Andy wrote all this information down in his notebook. On the face of it, Ollie had an alibi for the time when Rory Quinn met his death, but West Ilsley could not be more than half an hour's drive away from the Quinn family home. It might be worth checking with those work colleagues whether Ollie was really there and if he might have been one of the ones who turned up late.

'Thank you, Mr Cash. That's all for now.' Andy drained his mug and got to his feet.

'Hang on!' Ollie stood up to and stepped into Andy's path. 'You haven't even told me how Rory died. What happened? Why are the police involved?'

'He was found hanging from a tree in the garden of his family home,' Andy told him. 'We're investigating how he got there and why.'

Ollie's mouth fell open. 'He killed himself?'

'It looks like it, but that's not the only possibility.'

'And you think it was my Instagram posts that made him do it?' The distress in Ollie's voice was palpable. 'I never meant for that to happen. You've got to believe me! It was all just a joke – a bit of fun.'

'Not so funny for Rory, though, was it?'

'No. I just didn't think.' Ollie looked genuinely contrite, but Andy was reluctant to relent.

'We've downloaded all those posts you put up, so we've got all the evidence we need for a charge of harassment; and we will be checking out your alibi for last Saturday. Thank your mother for the tea and biscuits. I'll see myself out.'

Back at the flat, while Yakubu warmed up two supermarket ready-meals, Andy scrolled through a stream of texts from his mother, asking in increasingly peremptory tones how he was, what he was doing and why he hadn't rung her or been back home. Sighing, he deleted them all and sent a brief message assuring her that he was well, apologising for the lack of contact and pleading pressure of work as the excuse for his negligence in this respect.

Yakubu seemed disappointed at the lack of progress in the trial. How could it be that the bureaucratic preliminaries took so long? Why did court proceedings start so late and finish so early? Andy tried to explain that the assumption of innocence, unless and until proved guilty, meant that a prosecution could collapse if any shortcuts were taken. For example, defendants had to be told the names of the jurors and to be given an opportunity to object to any whom they had reason to believe would not view them fairly.

'And you wouldn't want to have someone on the jury who was a great friend of one of the defendants, would you?' he challenged Yakubu. 'There have to be procedures to make sure they're all impartial. Don't worry, I'm sure things will get going tomorrow. The DCI is expecting to be called to give evidence.'

Andy helped Yakubu to wash up the dishes and then, when his father fetched a photograph album from his room and seemed intent on sharing pictures from his time in Oxford, he pleaded a need to go home to reassure his mother that he had not deserted her. He could not face more of Yakubu's sentimental reminiscences, with their subtext of entreaty to be allowed a larger part in Andy's life.

At the suggestion of a visit to Amanda Lepage's home, Yakubu begged to come too. There was no need for Andy to worry. He would not force himself on her. If she refused to let him in, he would sit in the car until Andy was ready to go. What harm could there be in simply asking her to see him?

Andy, who could imagine a lot of harm coming out of permitting Yakubu to know their home address, stood firm. He told Yakubu a little about the texts that his mother had sent him, emphasising the need to reduce her fears that his father's unexpected reappearance was driving a wedge between them. Yakubu's answer to this was to offer to give her his personal assurances of his good intentions towards both mother and son, but Andy refused to be moved.

He collected his jacket from his room and, on impulse, stuffed the package of unopened letters into the pocket.

His route home took him past the police station. Deep in thought, he discovered too late that he had absent-mindedly turned into the staff car park. He backed into a space, intending to turn round. It was quiet and peaceful there. He turned off the engine and sat for several minutes wondering what to do.

Eventually, he telephoned his mother and apologised for his lack of communication. He had been out on a case all day, he told her. In fact, he was on his way back to the office now to catch up on some paperwork. She seemed pleased to hear that he was not spending the evening with Yakubu, and contented herself with urging him not to work too hard before allowing him to end the call, in order to get back to typing up his notes.

Andy, feeling only a little guilty for deceiving his mother – after all he had not told any actual lies – locked the car and headed up to the open-plan office where Anna's team worked. He turned on the light and stared round at the empty chairs and deserted desks. Then he walked over to his own workstation and laid down his "paperwork" on his desk.

He had fleetingly thought of taking the letters home with him and asking his mother if they could open them together. But what if Mum said *no*? She might insist on taking them from him, and then he would never know what his father had written to her during those years when Andy had been led to believe he had taken no interest in the girl he had left behind him.

FATHERS AND SONS

The first letter was postmarked November 1983. Andy opened it carefully, trying not to damage the thin paper.

'Dearest Mandy,' he read, 'I cannot tell you how much I miss you! You told me that you never want to hear from me again, but I hope that you still at least have enough interest in me to wish to know that I landed safely in Lagos and I am now travelling north to Kaduna. I will post this letter as soon as I arrive there.'

There followed a declaration that she was the only love of his life and that his marriages were mere business arrangements between two families, which he had entered into to please his parents. His wives' family – they were sisters – was not wealthy enough to support them, so it would be cruel for him to divorce them, but really they meant nothing to him compared with her. He would never forget her and would dream of a day when he might be able to return to England to see her again.

Andy shook his head. The arrogance of the man! He clearly assumed that, despite his outrageous behaviour, she was still besotted with him and would throw herself into his arms were he to come back to claim her!

At the tail end of the letter there was a half-hearted apology, defending his decision not to tell her about his wives by claiming that, at the time, he thought that this was the best way of protecting all three women from distress.

It beggared belief! How could an intelligent man not have considered what was going to occur when the inevitable happened and he had to come clean about his relationships? Perhaps he had planned to live a double-life long-term, with jobs and homes in Britain and Nigeria – like the proverbial sailor with a wife in every port.

The next letter was brief. It conveyed the news that Yakubu's father had died and he was now the head of the family, with responsibility for supporting his mother and sisters as well as his wives and daughter. It ended with another declaration of undying love and a promise to return to Oxford once his family affairs were more settled.

What egotism! What hubris! How could he still be assuming that the woman – only a girl really – whom he had deceived and deserted would welcome him back with open arms merely because he deigned to return to her?

The next letter, dated January 1984, showed a greater degree of contrition. Yakubu had confided in his mother, and she had evidently told him a few home-truths about his behaviour. For the first time, he admitted to the selfishness of his motives for concealing the truth, and the damage that he had done to all three of the women by his dishonesty. He went through a lot of metaphorical beating of the breast and begging for forgiveness. Then he spoiled it all at the end of the letter by declaring, 'I only did it because I was afraid of losing you. I could not bear the thought of being alone in Oxford without you.'

What was he saying? He made it sound as if Mum were just a convenient temporary companion to warm his bed while he was thousands of miles away from his wives back home! Why had he not considered what was going to happen at the end of his course when the inevitable time came for him to return to Nigeria?

Andy stuffed the letter back into its envelope and tore open the next … and the next … and the next. As the opening months of 1984 passed, the tone of the letters became more remorseful and less arrogant. The one dated 31st March ended with something approaching despair. 'Mandy, my Mandy, why don't you reply to my letters? Even words of reproach – and please believe me when I say that I know how much I deserve them – would be welcome, because I need more than anything to know that you have not forgotten me. I can never forget you or cease to love you.'

FATHERS AND SONS

Andy put the letter to the bottom of the pile and sat staring down at the next envelope. The postmark was October 1984, a gap of more than six months and, although Yakubu did not know it, the first letter after he had become a father. Or rather, after his second child had been born. His little daughter must have been five or six by then. How strange for Andy to think that he had had an older sister!

A weird fantasy crept into his head. Suppose that Mum had agreed to Yakubu's proposal that she marry him and live with his family in Nigeria! He would eventually have been the middle child of three instead of an only child. Would his big sister – what was her name? Samirah, that was it! – have bossed him around? Or would his status as the firstborn son have given him some authority over her? How would the three women have got on together? There would probably have been resentment between the two sisters and their new, younger rival. Understandably so. And what about Mum? She had spoken in her diary about her excitement at the prospect of going to Africa and learning to fit into a different culture, but he had a feeling that in practice it would have been very difficult for her to abandon all the norms and habits that she had grown up with.

He opened the letter. It was a short one, hardly more than a note. It reminded "dearest Mandy" that this was the anniversary of the day that they first met and implored her to write back to let him know that she was safe and still remembered him. The same message, in slightly varying words, was repeated in letters each October until 1992, when there was an addendum containing news of the death of his whole family, apart from the new baby, Jibrilu, and a despairing plea for a response.

That was the last letter. Presumably, having heard nothing back after breaking such devastating news, Yakubu had at last accepted the bitter truth that Mandy was lost to him. Or maybe he was too busy in the aftermath of his family tragedy to think about her any more. The fact that he did not re-marry perhaps gave credence to his repeated claims that she was the only woman with which he had ever been truly in love. His regret about his deception did seem to be real. And yet … and yet …

12. CROSS EXAMINATION

Yakubu spent the following day in court, sitting alone in the public gallery. Andy had told him that he was too busy to accompany him, but he suspected that this was just an excuse. He tried to concentrate on the detailed questioning to which counsel for the prosecution was subjecting DCI Davenport on the conduct of the investigation into the assault on Gabriel Sibanda and the subsequent killing of Jibrilu Danjuma, but his mind kept wandering off. Why was Andy less delighted in having found his father than he was about discovering his new son? Why did Mandy still refuse to meet him? What harm could it do to her simply to talk? Why had she not answered his letters? And why, why, why had she never written to tell him that they had a son?

The prosecuting barrister sat down and the judge invited the defence to examine the witness. There were three barristers, one representing each of the defendants. One of them stood up and thanked the judge before beginning her cross-examination.

Yakubu leaned forward and studied her face. He had hardly noticed her up until now. She was tall and moved with elegance and confidence. She looked older than the judge, but probably a little younger than the prosecuting counsel. She questioned Anna with decisiveness.

'I understand that, during the course of your investigation, you had some shoes belonging to one of the defendants taken away for forensic examination. Is this correct?'

'Yes,' Anna confirmed. 'We had all the clothes that the defendants were wearing that day examined.'

'And traces of blood were found on the laces of a pair of training shoes belonging to my client, Logan Wyatt?'

'Yes.'

'Did you tell the defendants about this discovery?'

'Yes.'

Yakubu wondered why Anna was looking uncomfortable. Surely this was cast iron evidence against the young man? Why had Andy not told him about it before?

'And then they made their "confessions"?' The inverted commas around the final word of that sentence were clearly discernible.

'It was after they were told, yes.'

'You told them that the victim's blood had been found on Mr Wyatt's shoes, and then they confessed to having attacked the victim?'

'No.' Anna's voice was calm and firm. 'We told them that blood had been found on his shoe laces.'

'Blood. And you did not tell them what sort of blood?'

'No.'

'And why was this?'

'Because it had not been DNA-tested at that point.'

'So, at that point you had no reason to believe that the blood belonged to the victim?'

Anna made no reply.

'DCI Davenport. I repeat my question: at the point at which you told the defendants that blood had been found on their clothing, you had no evidence that it belonged to the victim – yes or no?'

'We were waiting for further tests to confirm the nature of the blood.'

'And when the results of those *further tests* came through, what did they tell you?'

'That the blood was non-human.'

The defence barrister looked meaningfully towards the jury, waiting for this statement to sink in before continuing with her questions.

'So, can we be quite clear – the defendants made their "confessions" while under the impression that you had found blood from the victim on one of them?'

'No.' Anna returned the barrister's stare with a look of calm determination. 'They confessed after they realised that we had a witness who could place them at the scene of the crime shortly before it took place and that their clothes were being examined forensically.'

Yakubu glanced anxiously across at the jury. What effect had this exchange had on them? Had the barrister convinced them that the defendants' confessions were false and had been forced out of them by the police?

'You were not the first Senior Investigating Officer leading the investigation into this incident, were you, DCI Davenport?' Miss Stephanie Bulloch QC asked next. 'Why did you take over part way through the case?'

'The original SIO became aware of a conflict of interest.'

'A conflict of interest,' Miss Bulloch repeated. 'Perhaps you could explain to the jury the nature of this *conflict of interest?*'

'It came to light that the deceased was a relative of the SIO.'

'A close relative?'

'A half-brother,' Anna admitted. 'A half-brother who he had been unaware existed,' she added quickly. 'His parents had been estranged since before he was born. As soon as he discovered the relationship, he declared the conflict of interest and was removed from the investigation.'

'As soon as he discovered the relationship?' Miss Bulloch's raised eyebrow and sceptical tone were designed to raise questions in the minds of the jury as to the accuracy of this assertion. 'Or, when he realised that the relationship could not be concealed any longer?'

'As soon as he discovered the relationship,' Anna repeated firmly.

The barrister turned to the judge. 'I have no more questions, Your Honour.'

The judge then invited the other defending barristers to examine the witness, but they each declined politely. They probably thought that it was better not to give the jury anything new to think about at this stage. Let their final memories of the police witness be a vague impression that the investigation might have been tainted in some way by a relationship between a senior officer and the victim.

The judge consulted her watch. 'In that case, I think that this would be an opportune moment to adjourn for lunch. We will resume at one forty-five.'

She got up and started walking to the door. A voice from somewhere called out abruptly, 'Be upstanding!' and Yakubu reached for his stick to haul himself painfully into an upright position as the strange procession of lawyers in wigs and gowns trooped out.

Over lunch in a café in the covered market, he tried to ring Andy, but the call went straight through to voicemail. Surely, if he had asked, he would have been given time off to attend the trial of his own brother's killers! Was he really as unconcerned about the outcome as he appeared to be? Or was his absence a strategic one, to avoid giving more ammunition to the defence case? Would his presence make their allegations of police bias more plausible to the jury?

The afternoon session was given over to testimony from the other victim. Thirteen-year-old Gabriel Sibanda looked nervous as he answered questions via a video link. Gentle probing from the prosecuting council extracted a hesitant but lucid account of the assault that he had suffered at the hands of the defendants.

As his tale unfolded, Yakubu studied the faces of the jurors. A middle-aged motherly woman looked shocked at the racist language used against the boy. That was promising. However, at the other extreme, the young-looking man sitting next to her was smiling as if he found taunts about bananas and bongo drums highly amusing. His sympathies appeared to lie more with the perpetrators than with the victim. There was only one non-white face in the jury box: a man of African heritage dressed in a smart navy-blue suit. He was listening attentively and taking notes on a small pad. There would at least be one member of the jury who could speak from experience in favour of Gabriel and Jibrilu.

After Gabriel had finished relating his story and the prosecuting counsel had stated that he had no further questions, the judge declared a short adjournment to give the witness a breather before being cross-examined. Yakubu decided to stay in the public gallery, waiting for the trial to recommence. Most of the other spectators remained there too, including the friends and relatives of the accused.

Yakubu listened in on their conversations, which they made no attempt to keep private.

'I can't see what all the fuss is about,' declared the boy whom Yakubu had identified as the brother of Tyler Briggs. 'They were only having a laugh. I've been called a lot worse than that at school, because of my hair.'

'That's right!' his mother agreed. 'Nobody cares about redheads getting bullied.'

'And they was only asking him what he was doing there,' Sharon Wyatt added in an aggrieved tone. 'Why hasn't anyone said about that? They was told to watch out for anyone acting suspicious around the college.'

'Hold on there, Shar,' her husband remonstrated. 'Our brief hasn't cross-examined the kid yet. She'll set the jury straight about that, I expect. The main thing is the kid hasn't said anything about Logan having a knife. If they find him guilty of harassment, he'll just get community service, seeing as it's a first offence. If they manage to stick murder on him, that means life.'

Yakubu looked across the aisle to where Hayley Middleton was sitting. She had got out a small mirror from her handbag and was engrossed in touching up her face. Suddenly she paused and moved the mirror slightly to one side. Then she put down the powder sponge, snapped the mirror closed and turned her head round so that she could look directly at Yakubu. She must have caught sight of him watching her in the mirror.

Fortunately, she did not appear to bear him any animosity. She smiled coquettishly and gave him a little wave. Taken aback, it took him a second or two to force a smile in return. Did she know who he was? Did she care? He had a feeling that she was the sort of woman who couldn't resist flirting with every man she came across.

'Be upstanding!'

The judge was back, walking briskly across the court to take her place at the bench. The video link was restored and cross-examination began.

Each of the three defence barristers took a turn in questioning young Gabriel Sibanda who looked increasingly anxious and flustered as the examination proceeded. It seemed that each lawyer was intent on getting him to say that their client had taken a smaller part in tormenting him than the others had done. He stammered and contradicted himself and finally, close to tears, declared, 'I don't know! I can't remember!'

At this point, the judge intervened. 'I think that we have heard enough,' she said firmly, directing a steely stare towards Mr Anthony Fawcett, counsel for Tyler Briggs, who was the current questioner. 'I am satisfied that this witness has already told the court everything that he can about this incident. I see no good purpose in continuing in further examination that is unlikely to produce any additional evidence, but will clearly cause him additional distress.'

'If it please you honour,' Logan Wyatt's counsel was on her feet at once, 'I have just one further question, which it is important that I put to this witness.'

'Very well.' The judge motioned to her to continue.

The lawyer turned towards the video screen and spoke in a quiet, kindly voice. 'Now Gabriel, I want you to think very carefully before you answer, because this is very important. My client, Mr Wyatt, admits that he said things to you that upset you, and he's very sorry about that. But he has also been accused of something much more serious, something that happened afterwards. Now, you've told us that a big black man ran across the road and shouted at Mr Wyatt and Mr Briggs and Miss Middleton to leave you alone. Did you see what happened next? Did you see any of them take hold of him or strike him, for example?'

'No.' Gabriel shook his head. 'I ran away.'

'Thank you.' The QC looked up at the judge. 'That is all, your honour. I have no more questions.'

'And counsel for the other defendants?' enquired the judge in a discouraging tone, 'Do you have any final questions for this witness?'

Both lawyers indicated that they were satisfied, so the judge turned to address the witness.

'Thank you, Gabriel. I know that this has been difficult for you. You've done very well.' Then, turning back to the court, 'I think that's enough for today. The court is adjourned to tomorrow at ten-thirty.'

Yakubu walked slowly back to his flat with a feeling of discouragement nagging at him. So little seemed to have been achieved after two days in court. And the defence lawyers were so clever at sowing seeds of doubt in the jurors' minds about the evidence of the witnesses and the integrity of the police investigation! Should he be preparing himself for the prospect of them all walking free with just a rap over the knuckles for intimidating Gabriel with their taunts?

His disappointment was increased when he arrived back to find the flat deserted. Of course, it was unreasonable to have expected Andy to be there so early, but it came as a blow nevertheless. He would have liked to have let off steam about the aggressive cross-examination to which Gabriel had been subjected. Could a complaint be made to the judge? Or was this just normal behaviour by lawyers intent on winning their case regardless of the consequences?

He tried ringing Andy's mobile, but it was switched off or out of signal range. He paced the room impatiently and then fired off a sequence of angry texts … and then an apology and a request that they talk about the conduct of the trial when Andy got back.

Receiving no immediate response, he began wandering around the flat opening drawers and cupboards in search of something to do to distract his mind. Previous occupants of the flat had left a shelf full of paperback books, but none of them appealed to him. A drawer in the living room yielded a pile of leaflets and brochures advertising tourist attractions in the

Oxford area. Shelves inside the wardrobe in Andy's room held boxes of board games and a chess set. And in a small drawer above them … what was this? It looked like an old diary! It must have been left behind by the owner of the flat.

Yakubu picked it up and opened it at random. He read an entry dated 1982. Then, in wonderment, he turned back to the first page. There it was! *This diary belongs to Amanda Lepage.* He sat down on the bed and began to read from the beginning.

So, she did really love him! He had begun to wonder if her youthful declarations had been mere artifice with no substance behind them. His heart soared as he read the entries up to the end of Trinity Term 1983. The entries from that long vacation were full of anticipation of his return to Oxford in September. Then came the surprise.

> *I've decided that I won't go back on the pill. I don't care if I get pregnant with Yakubu's baby. In fact, I'd quite like that. He'd have to stay in England then! And they'd have to let him, too.*

He let the diary drop on to his lap and sat staring into space, trying to make sense of this new information. He wasn't the only one in their relationship who had been less than totally honest! Mandy had deceived him, too! She had tricked him into fathering a child and then kept that child's existence secret from him.

He put the diary away and began an urgent search of Andy's possessions. Eventually, he found what he was looking for: an envelope with his home address on it. He quickly noted it down and then replaced everything as he had found it. Fearful that Andy might return any moment, he went into his own bedroom to consider what to do next.

Dare he go round to see Mandy at home? Surely, she wouldn't refuse to speak to him if he were there on the doorstep? He must somehow find an opportunity to make peace with her! But not right away. Not while he was still indignant about her subterfuge. And not when Andy could return any minute. He must wait for an evening when his son was working late and he would not have to explain where he was going.

His phone buzzed, announcing the arrival of a text. It was from Andy: just a brief note saying that he would be late back and that Yakubu should have dinner without him. He would get a takeaway and eat it in the office.

Yakubu stepped off the bus outside a row of small shops in Headington. He waited to cross the road and then headed down a side street, consulting the map on his phone every so often to check that he was going the right way. Before long, he was standing there, outside the house, a modest semi-detached among many similar dwellings. The front garden had been laid to gravel and almost half of it was occupied by a small silver hatchback. That must be Mandy's car. Andy's was blue, and was presumably parked at the police station.

He leaned on his stick, wondering if he dared to go up and knock on the door. A large ginger cat came up to him and wound itself around his legs. Then, when he looked down, it walked sedately along a line of stepping stones set into the gravel, glancing round occasionally to see if he was following, and sat on the front step, looking up expectantly at the door.

'Alright,' Yakubu smiled. 'I'll ring the bell for you.'

At his summons, there was a sound of footsteps inside the house followed by some jangling of keys. Then the door opened, and there she was!

'I hope this is your cat,' Yakubu smiled, pointing down as the animal pushed past Mandy and trotted down the hall. 'He was asking to come in.'

'And you just happened to be passing?'

'No exactly.' Yakubu held out the diary. 'I found this. I believe it is your property, so I came to return it to you.'

Mandy stared at the book with eyes and mouth wide open.

'What ...? Where ...? You'd better come in.'

13. ASSEMBLING THE EVIDENCE

Meanwhile, Andy was having a busy day. With Anna taken up with preparing for her court appearance and then giving evidence, he was left in charge of the team investigating Rory Quinn's death. This kept him occupied from the early morning briefing through until late in the evening, giving him little time to brood on the revelations in his mother's diary and his father's letters.

He started the morning meeting – such as it was, the team having been reduced by circumstances to himself, Alice and Jennifer – with an account of his visit to Oliver Cash.

'I don't think he's a killer,' he concluded, 'but I'm going to check out his alibi with his colleagues, just in case he could have had time to fit in a return trip to Oxford on Saturday. Now, how're we doing with our other lines of enquiry? Anything from the house-to-house, Alice?'

'Yes.' Alice got to her feet. 'There's a corner shop not far from the Quinn house – a sort of general stores and off-licence. You remember that Rory went out for a run that morning?'

Andy nodded.

'Well, the shop woman knows Rory. He used to buy sweets there with his pocket money when he was a kid. Apparently, he called in on Saturday morning and bought a bottle of whisky – a large one. The woman said she was surprised, because Rory had never bought alcohol there before. She asked if it was for something special and Rory got a bit flustered and said that he supposed it was in a way. Then he said actually he was buying it for a friend. After that, he paid with a credit card and went off as if he was glad to get away in case she asked any more questions. She said it wasn't like him. Usually, they'd have a bit of a chat when he came in.'

'It looks as if the whisky bottle they found in the garden *was* Rory's,' Andy commented. 'And we now have evidence that he was behaving oddly that morning, perhaps as if he had something on his mind. OK, anyone else got something to report?'

'I've got a name and address for *Archie the Avenger*,' Jennifer called out in the silence that followed. 'His name's Archie Fisher. He's seventeen and lives in Littlemore with his Mum and Stepdad. I ran him through the computer. He's been cautioned for threatening behaviour while he was taking part in a demonstration against asylum-seekers being housed in a hostel down there somewhere. That was about a year ago.'

'Good work.' Andy reflected that some of his warranted officers could do well to emulate Jennifer's dedication and attention to detail.

'His social media attacks on Rory are all based on his political cartoons,' Jennifer went on. 'He disapproves, shall we say, of the way that Rory expressed support for refugees and immigrants and attacked the right-wing press and government policy. I'd class *Archie the Avenger* as a radical right-wing fantasist. He appears to imagine himself leading some sort of white supremacist revolution.'

'OK,' Andy nodded. 'We'd better check him out. 'It's probably all talk, but you never know, he may have had a go at turning his fantasies into reality. Alice – can you call on him and find out where he was last Saturday?'

JUST ANOTHER SUICIDE

'I was planning to go to see Jack Lampard this morning,' Alice answered. 'He's the guy who tried to take Patrick Quinn to court for unfair dismissal. I've found out where he's working now. It's a DIY store on that trading estate out along the Botley Road.'

'You can probably catch Archie on the way,' Jennifer told her. 'He's working at a supermarket down there. I'll write down the details for you.'

She copied Archie's details from her computer screen on to a small pad, tore off the top sheet and handed it to Alice.

'Good.' Andy looked at the board where he and Anna had listed the key individuals in this case. Those three are the only suspects we have outside of Rory's circle of family and friends. If we can check out all of their alibis today, maybe the Quinns will accept that the most likely scenario is that Rory killed himself. I'll-'

He was interrupted by his phone. It was Ruby Mann with some news.

'We've found some prints on that love spoon you gave us,' she told him. 'They don't match Rory or any of his family and they're not on the database either. The chances are they just belong to whoever sold it to him, but I thought you'd want to know, just in case.'

'Thanks Ruby.' Andy turned to look at Alice and Jennifer. 'Did you get that? I'd forgotten all about that love spoon thing. It was the one thing in his room that the family said they'd never seen before. What if Rory had a visitor that day and they gave it to him?'

'Or maybe he met someone while he was out for his morning run?' suggested Alice.

'Either way, they'd be valuable witnesses,' Andy nodded. 'Of course, Rory may have bought it himself. Maybe he was going to give it to Ellie at the party or to – hey! I've just remembered something! Jamie Mercer's mother said they'd come back from visiting relatives just before Jamie came to Oxford last week. I'm sure she said they'd been to Wales. Isn't that the most likely place for someone to buy a Welsh love spoon?'

He looked round at Alice and Jennifer. 'Good work, both of you. Now, Alice, you get off to Botley Road and see if you can talk to Archie Fisher and James Lampard. Jennifer, have a look at the photos of that love spoon and see if you can find out where you can buy them. They're supposed to all be hand carved and unique, so you never know there could be some identifying feature that people who know about these things would recognise. Ring me if you find out anything. I'll be doing the rounds of Rory's nearest and dearest asking them about it – once I've rung Ollie Cash's work mates to check his alibi.'

'No, I've ne-ne- never s-seen that before,' Ellie told Andy, when he showed her a photograph of the love spoon. 'I d-d-don't know who c-c-c- who could've given it to Rory. I d-d-don't think he knows any W-w-w- anyone from Wales.'

'I wondered if he might have got if for you?'

'I su-su-suppose he m-might have, but I don't s-s-see why he would. It's n-n-not like it's a f-family tradition for either of us or anything.'

'OK. Thank you for your time.' Andy got up to leave, but her mother, who had insisted on remaining in the room while Andy talked to her, called him back.

'Inspector! Is it true what people are saying?'

'I don't know. Which people? And what *are* they saying?'

'That Rory was planning to jilt Ellie and go off with some young man he met at university. It's all nonsense, isn't it? Just people trying to make trouble.'

'We have no evidence that Rory Quinn had decided against marrying your daughter,' Andy told her, picking his words carefully. 'But we would be interested to know who started this rumour. How did you hear of it?'

'It was all anyone was talking about at my flower arranging group yesterday. I'd mentioned last week that we were hoping we'd soon be able to fix the date after Rory's birthday party, and they were all interested in volunteering to help with the flowers.'

'And you don't know where they heard it from?'

'No. I expect it's just spite from someone who's jealous that Patrick Quinn's son chose Ellie. I'm so glad it's not true. I can tell them all that this has got nothing to do with him getting cold feet about the wedding. And that it's all nonsense that he had a-a-a *boyfriend* – I mean to say: how ridiculous! They all know he's a good Catholic boy.'

Andy said nothing. It was likely that Mrs Unwin's illusions would be shattered before long, but he had no intention of being the one to do it. Instead, he held out the love-spoon photograph for her inspection.

'Presumably Rory didn't show this to you?' he asked. 'We think he may have been intending to give it to Ellie at the party.'

'No. I've never seen it before.' She shook her head. 'But it's a love token, isn't it? The *proves* he wasn't planning to leave her, doesn't it?'

'Well, not exactly,' Andy said cautiously. 'We don't have any proof that it was intended for Ellie. It could even have been a present that someone else gave to Rory. That's why I'm asking people if they've seen it before. Anyway,' he added, moving towards the door, 'that's all for now. Thank you for answering my questions, Ellie, Mrs Unwin.'

He hurried back to his car, keen to get away before Ellie's mother thought of anything more that she wanted to ask him. This was someone else who would be seriously upset if the final verdict was that Rory Quinn had taken his own life. He didn't want to find himself backed into a corner where he either had to lie or to admit this as a real possibility.

He drove slowly through quiet residential streets and then along the ring-road to Headington, pondering as he went on the best strategy for finding out the origin of the love spoon. It was only a little thing, but it was unexplained and also, in some way, symbolic – a declaration of passion directed either to or by Rory. Either way, it must be relevant to his state of mind on the day he died.

Most of the family were out when Andy pressed the buzzer at the gates to the Quinn family home. A young black man in clean white overalls let him in and led him into the office, where Emma was working alone. She greeted Andy politely and invited him to sit down.

'Bring us some coffee and biscuits, please, Paulo.'

The young man retreated, closing the door quietly as he left the room. Emma turned back to Andy.

'I don't think you've met Paulo. He's over here from Brazil on a business studies course. He helps out round the house twice a week.'

'Was he here last Saturday? We don't have him down on our list.'

'No. His days are Monday and Thursday – just three hours in the morning.'

'And he has access to all the rooms – including Rory's bedroom?'

'That's right. Why? Does it matter?'

'Only that we've got some fingerprints that we can't identify from there and it could be that they're his. Do you think he'd mind giving them, for the purposes of elimination?'

'I'm sure he wouldn't. But you can ask him when he brings the coffee. Was it those fingerprints that you came here about?'

'Yes. And this.' Andy showed her a picture of the love spoon. 'It was lying on Rory's bed when DCI Davenport looked at his room the day he died. Your father said he'd never seen it before. Do you recognise it?'

'No, but they must be common enough. Standard gift shop stuff – alongside the boxes of fudge and dolls in Welsh national dress. Probably some friend of Rory's brought it back from a holiday in Wales.'

'But we're interested in knowing who that friend might have been and why this spoon was left out on Rory's bed. Is it at all possible that he had a visitor that day? Could he have let anyone into the house without you knowing – maybe in the morning or early afternoon, before the party guests started arriving?'

Emma leaned back in her chair and appeared to be concentrating hard.

'I was working in the office all day,' she said slowly, 'trying to get things done before the party started. I answered the door to the postman at about nine-thirty. He had a parcel for Dad that had to be signed for. Rory was out on his run. I heard him come back in some time between ten and half past. I'm sure nobody called between then and lunchtime – unless they happened to turn up when Mum was leaving and she let them in without them having to ring.'

'What about later – when you and Rory were alone in the house?'

'I don't think so.' Emma shook her head. Then she suddenly froze for a second or two and creased her forehead in a frown of concentration. 'Come to think of it, I heard the door open and close about ten or fifteen minutes after Dad went out. I thought he must've forgotten something and come back for it.'

'Could it have been Rory letting someone in?' Andy asked eagerly. 'Maybe someone who rang him on a mobile to let him know he was there without buzzing the intercom?'

'Yes, I suppose it could.'

14. CONFESSION

Father Damien was also finding it hard to fit all his duties into the twenty-four hours allotted for that day by a creator who, he sometimes thought, had not taken fully into account the human ability to waste that most precious of commodities: time. He got up early, completing his morning devotions before six, with the intention of putting in a couple of hours researching and writing his Sunday homily before his first appointment of the day, which was a meeting with the headteacher of the local Catholic Primary School to discuss the upcoming Summer Fête.

He put on the radio news while he ate a frugal breakfast of cereal and strong coffee. Depressing reports on the war in Ukraine gave way to depressing speculation about further rises in energy prices and increases in inflation generally. The Conservative Party leadership election dragged on, with Suella Braverman being eliminated. An in-depth interview about the spread of monkeypox had just started when the telephone rang.

Damien turned off the radio and hurried through to his study to take the call. It was Kathleen Powell, a keystone of St Cyprian's congregation whose voluntary duties included editing the weekly newsletter.

'I'm sorry to disturb you so early, Father, but my mother has just rung. My father has been taken to hospital with a suspected stroke. I'm on my way over there now, could you meet us there, in case...?'

'Yes, of course. I'll come right away.'

Kathleen's concerns for her ninety-year-old father were justified. By the time Damien arrived at the hospital, Jude O'Driscoll was lying in a small side-room, with his wife and daughter sitting on either side of his bed watching anxiously. He was not expected to regain consciousness and further efforts to prolong life had been declared useless.

'The doctor says that he's not in any pain,' Kathleen told him. 'She said he'll most likely just slip away peacefully. I suppose that's the best we could have hoped for at his age – a quiet death, as they say. Can you give him the last rites before he…?'

'Of course.' Damien looked round the room for a clear surface on which to set out his small bottles of holy oil and water and the laminated card on which he had printed the words of the prayers for the anointing of the sick. The small locker at the bedside seemed to be the only option. He cleared a space by carrying a box of tissues and an empty water jug over to the windowsill. Kathleen got up and moved her chair to make more room for him to approach her father.

He performed the prescribed ritual, first praying with the two women, then blessing the old man and pronouncing absolution over him. Finally, using his fingers, he placed a small smear of holy oil first on the dying man's forehead and then on each of his hands. 'Through this holy anointing, may the Lord in his love and mercy help you with the grace of the Holy Spirit.'

'Amen,' Kathleen and her mother joined in.

'May the Lord who frees you from sin save you and raise you up.'

'Amen.'

After the last prayers were completed, he sat in silence, sharing in the women's sad vigil, listening to the wheezy breathing of the sick man. He surreptitiously pushed up his sleeve to check his watch. He was late for his appointment at the school, but …

'He's stopped breathing!' Suddenly Kathleen was on her feet and shaking her father gently by the shoulder. Mrs O'Driscoll pressed the buzzer to call a nurse. There was a flurry of activity, but the outcome was inevitable. Jude O'Driscoll had departed this life, peacefully and in a state of grace.

While Kathleen and her mother were occupied with the hospital staff, Damien phoned the school and made his apologies. He re-scheduled his meeting for the lunch hour and then turned his attention back to the grief-stricken women. Kathleen wanted to begin discussing the funeral, while her mother needed reassurance that the absolution that Damien had given to her husband would be valid without his having been conscious and able to confess his sins and express contrition. He did his best to answer their questions and allay their fears, conscious that he was by now missing the toddler group, which met in the Parish Centre every Thursday morning. He usually tried to call in to meet the young mothers – and sometime fathers – and to say a few prayers with them. And there was now no way that his homily would get written that morning!

Arrangements for the School Fête turned out to be more complex than he had imagined, and consequently, Damien's meeting with the Headteacher was only drawn to a close by the need for her to take the Year Four music class.

'I'll ring you tomorrow to finalise everything,' she promised as she showed Damien to the door.

'Thank you. I'll look forward to it,' he lied. 'And I'll see that the fête is in the Newsletter this Sunday,' he added, making a mental note to ring Kathleen with an offer to type and print it himself. He could not expect her to do it in the current circumstances, but neither did he want her to feel that she was being excluded from the role that she had performed faithfully for more than thirty years.

Looking at his watch as he emerged through the school gates, he realised that he was already late for his appointment with the Quinn family to discuss funeral arrangements for Rory, whose body had been released for burial by the coroner the day before. He mounted his bicycle and set off, pedalling at full speed in an effort to make up time, conscious that they would be waiting for him, anxious to begin the process of saying goodbye to their son, grandson and brother.

Breathing heavily, he pressed the buzzer on the gatepost and was admitted by Emma, who led him into the large living room at the back of the house, overlooking the garden. As he entered, Patrick Quinn got up from a bulky easy chair near the open patio doors and came forward to shake his hand. Martina and Giovanna remained seated on a matching sofa. They were both wearing black dresses, which contrasted starkly with the cheerful floral print design of the upholstery. Giovanna was knitting stoically, while her daughter had a magazine lying upside-down on her lap. She set it aside at the sound of Damien's voice and looked up at him with red eyes.

'I am so sorry for being late,' he said, repeating the apology that he had already given to Emma over the intercom and then again at the front door. 'It's just been one thing after another today. Poor Kathleen's father passed away this morning.'

'Jude O'Driscoll?' Martina's eyes opened wide in dismay. 'But he was so fit for his age! He walked here only yesterday to pay his respects. I hope it wasn't overdoing himself that caused it.'

'No, no. He had a stroke during the night. The ambulance came and took him to the John Radcliffe, but there was nothing they could do except make him comfortable. I was there when he died, and so were Kathleen and Mary. It was all very peaceful.'

'That's a blessing, I suppose,' Martina nodded, 'but poor Kathleen! And poor Mary! She'll be lost without him. They'd just celebrated their diamond wedding anniversary. Sixty years! And now …'

Sit down, Father,' Patrick urged, indicating another of the floral print chairs. 'No need to stand on ceremony. And it's very good of you to make time for us. After all, we only rang you last night. We wanted to talk to you about the arrangements before we got the funeral director involved.'

Damien settled into his seat and took out a small notebook, ready to take notes of the family's requirements. As he did so, the door opened silently and Emma entered pushing a trolley laden with a teapot, a glass jug of aromatic coffee and five bone china cups, saucers and plates. She must have slipped out for them while Damien was talking to Martina.

'What would you like, Father?' she asked. 'We have tea and coffee, and I hope I can tempt you to some of this cake.' She bent down and picked up a large sponge sandwich from the lower shelf of the trolley. 'Deirdre brought it round this morning. It must be the third this week. It's very kind of her, but we've none of us had much appetite since Rory died, and we still have lots of the party food to eat up.'

'Dear Deirdre!' Damien smiled. 'She is so generous with her baking talents. I'll have a piece of cake – just a small one! I know how difficult it can be to stem the flow, once she has you marked down as being in need of her bounty.'

'Perhaps you would like to take some food home with you, Father,' suggested Martina. 'It would save you cooking. Maybe you'd like some cold meat and salad for your supper?' We've plenty in the fridge, and it'll only go to waste.'

It took a few minutes for the efficient Emma to serve everyone with their chosen beverage and a slice of cake. Then she pushed the trolley to the side of the room and sat down opposite Damien. 'Now, we'd better get started. We know how busy you are, Father.'

'I try never to be too busy to take time over something like this.' The priest turned to Martina. 'Have you made any plans, or shall I talk you through the possible alternatives?'

'First of all, Father,' Patrick interjected, 'tell me — what if the police, and the coroner, insist that Rory killed himself? Can he still have a Catholic burial? Can you give him absolution?'

'Yes, of course,' Damien said firmly. 'The church is very clear that, although suicide is a grave matter, it is far from being unforgiveable, and God is able to provide the opportunity for salutary repentance for everyone, regardless of how they die.'

'My dear Patrick,' Giovanna intervened. 'How can you be so ignorant? The Father has already told you that there will be no problem. Things are so different now. His Holiness, dear John Paul, changed everything years ago. If poor Rory did take his own life, it must have been because he was not in his right mind. He was always such a dutiful boy. He would never do anything to upset his mother unless he was quite out of his mind!'

'You are absolutely right,' Damien confirmed, grateful to receive support from this unexpected quarter and glad that he had taken the trouble to bone up on the matter the evening before. 'Pope John Paul II approved a new catechism in 1992, which makes it clear that grave psychological disturbances diminish the responsibility of someone who commits suicide. You need have no fear that the Church will deny Rory any of the comforts that it can offer to the faithful departed.'

'And what about us?' Martina asked in a low voice. 'What about *our* responsibility? I'm his mother. I should have realised that he was depressed. I should have helped him.'

'No, Marty.' Patrick reached out his arm and took his wife's hand in his. 'You mustn't blame yourself. We none of us realised what he was going through. We were all seeing things through rose-tinted glasses. If anyone is to blame, it's me for pushing him into Law, when he really wanted to be an artist.'

'No Patrick,' Martina insisted, 'I don't think that's what it was.' She lowered her voice again and leaned towards her husband to prevent her mother overhearing. 'I'm sure it was because he was afraid of what we'd say if he came out to us.'

'Came out?' Giovanna asked sharply. Her deafness was unpredictable and it had been risky for Martina to attempt to keep her out of this conversation. 'Came out where?'

An uneasy silence ensued, then Emma explained. 'Rory was gay, Nonna. You do know what that means?'

'Yes, yes, of course.' Giovanna waved her hand to indicate her exasperation with the younger generation, who seemed intent on assuming that she was out of touch with modern life. 'Did you think I didn't know about that? You've all been whispering behind my back, but I'm not stupid, you know.'

'My dear children,' Damien intervened. 'No-one is to blame here. You must put all thoughts of guilt out of your minds – or if that is impossible, come to me in private and I will hear your confession and grant you absolution. Whatever Rory's mental anguish may have been in life, he is now at peace, safe in the infinite care of God.'

'Exactly,' agreed Emma. 'And besides,' she added, staring pointedly at her father, 'how could Rory have hanged himself and then put the ladder away in the shed?'

Damien finished the pork pie and salad, which Martina had insisted on him taking home with him and put the plate in the dishwasher. This was a new appliance, which he was still a little nervous of, but he felt obliged to use it, knowing that it was symbolic of the affection in which his parishioners held him. A group of the ladies had clubbed together to buy it out of concern that he must struggle with housework, living alone as he did. They did not realise that he did some of his best thinking over mundane household chores such as washing up or ironing!

He was just pondering on whether or not to try a slice of the large piece of Rory's birthday cake that he had been obliged to accept, knowing that the family would be keen to remove all reminders of that occasion from their home as soon as they could, when there was a ring at the door. He closed the dishwasher, without turning it on, thus putting off, for the time being, the bewildering decisions as to what programme to set it on and whether he needed to replenish the dishwasher salt or rinse aid (whatever they were for) and went to answer the summons.

He found Patrick Quinn on the doorstep, standing with his hands in his pocket and his head down as if contemplating some problem with his shoes. He looked up when Damien spoke.

'Patrick! What can I do for you?'

'I er …,' Patrick mumbled, looking up nervously into Damien's face. 'I'm afraid I've done something – or rather not done something – rather stupid. In fact, I may have committed a criminal offence. I … I need your advice, and then … Will you hear my confession?'

'Of course, of course! Come in.' Damien led the way to his study and sat Patrick down in one of the chairs that were arranged around a small table in the centre of the room. 'I was just about to make myself some coffee. Will you join me?'

Without waiting for an answer, he left the room and hurried to the kitchen, where the coffee maker – another gift from his parishioners, but this one more welcome – was already keeping a large jug of coffee warm on its hotplate. He transferred the jug to a tray together with two mugs and a jug of milk. Then, after a moment's hesitation, he added a plate of Deirdre's biscuits, of which he always had an ample supply. The birthday cake would have to wait for another day.

Patrick continued to look nervous throughout the coffee-pouring and biscuit-distribution process. His eyes darted round the room, as if he were worried that the figures in the icons on the wall were staring at him and passing judgement. His left hand was in his jacket pocket and he seemed to be fiddling with something there. At last, he pulled out an envelope and put it down on the table.

'I found this in Rory's room the day he died.'

Damien looked down at it. It had been torn open and he could see a piece of lined paper inside.

'Go on! Read it!'

The priest picked up the envelope and carefully extracted the paper. He unfolded it and read the brief paragraph written on it. Then he read it through again, reluctant to raise his eyes from the page and meet Patrick's gaze.

But he could not put off the moment for ever. He looked up and their eyes met.

'And you haven't shown this to the police?'

'No. I let them think … They searched Rory's room. I knew they were looking for a suicide note, but I just … I didn't want his mom to know he killed himself. I knew she'd blame herself!' Patrick's eyes filled with tears, as he thought of his wife's distress. 'And I was afraid it was a mortal sin and he wouldn't be able to have a proper funeral. And that would have devastated her. And then there was her mother! I never thought she'd be so calm about it all! I thought she'd die of shame if she knew her grandson killed himself. But I got it all wrong, didn't I? And now …'

'No, no.' Damien got up and came round the table to lay his hand gently on Patrick's shoulder. 'You were trying to spare your

family some of their distress. That's an admirable aim. But ...
you should have given that note to the police.'

'I know,' Patrick nodded. 'And there's more!'

He put his hand back in his pocket and pulled out another
envelope. Damien looked down on it as it lay on the table
between their two coffee mugs. This one was unopened and had
a first-class stamp in the corner.

'He must have wanted us to post this for him,' Patrick said
dismally. 'See the name? That's his boyfriend – the one he
hooked up with in Nottingham. The detective who's in charge of
things says he wants to come to the funeral.'

'That's natural enough,' Damien nodded.

'I suppose I'll have to give this to the police too?'

'Yes. Or ....' An idea was forming in Damien's mind. 'Or I
might be able to .... I could ask Peter Johns to deal with it. You
know he's a retired police officer? – Yes of course you do! And
you've met his friend Jonah too, haven't you? They might be able
to .... You see, the thing I'm concerned about is ... This is
probably a very private letter. I think this Jamie ought to be
allowed to read it first – before the police do. Do you see what
I'm getting at?'

'Yes,' Patrick said thoughtfully. 'Yes, I do. My first thought
was to destroy it. I didn't want him coming anywhere near our
family. And I didn't see why he should have anything from Rory,
when Rory only wrote us that little note that doesn't tell us
anything about *why* he did it!'

'Leave it with me. I'll see what Peter says.' Damien took the
envelope and put it in his pocket before Patrick could change his
mind.

'Thanks. And could you ask him ...? Do the police really
need to see this letter? Or can you make sure they don't let it get
out into the media? I don't want people ...'

Damien took a deep breath while he considered how to answer. 'Well, I think the police do have to see the letter. It's evidence, isn't it? But we can ask them to keep it confidential – unless it throws light on what happened. Then it might need to go to the coroner, I suppose.'

'So, people are bound to find out? They'll know that Rory was gay? They won't want you burying him or giving him a requiem mass. They'll say he died in mortal sin.'

'And if any of them say such things to me, I will tell them that they are wrong,' the priest answered firmly. 'The Holy Father himself has said so. It was in the Vatican news only a few weeks ago. I can show you.'

He got up and walked over to his desk. It did not take him long to find the computer printout, which he had made in anticipation of the need to reassure Rory's family that his sexuality did not present a barrier to acceptance by the church.

'Here! See! God is Father and he does not disown any of his children. And "the style" of God is "closeness, mercy and tenderness." Along this path you will find God. And here: What do you say to an LGBT Catholic who has experienced rejection from the Church? And the Holy Father answers: I would have them recognize it not as "the rejection of the church," but instead of "people in the church." The church is a mother and calls together all her children.'

Patrick sat staring down at the page, reading and re-reading the words. 'So, what they did together is not a sin?' He asked at last.

'That is not for you or me to say,' Damien told him. 'That is between Rory – and his boyfriend – and God. After all, we don't even know what went on in their relationship, do we? And it is not our business to ask. I suggest that you try to think of Jamie as Rory's best friend from uni. You have male friends, don't you?

At the golf club, for instance? Imagine Rory and Jamie playing a round together or going fishing or …'

'OK. I'll try,' Patrick nodded. He got to his feet and held up the open envelope containing Rory's suicide note. 'I'd better go now. I'll show this to Martina tonight and take it to the police tomorrow. And you'll … deal with the other letter?'

'I'll take it over to Peter's this evening,' Damien promised. 'And I'll let you know how it all turns out. Why don't you come to the church on Saturday and I can fill you in? I'll be hearing confessions from four-thirty, as usual. Come along a few minutes before that – four fifteen, say – and we can have a chat.'

'And then you can hear *my* confession,' Patrick smiled back sheepishly, 'after I've been to the police.'

'That's right.' Damien got up and opened the door. 'And mind you do! Don't go getting cold feet about it – it's too late for that now.'

15. CASE CLOSED?

Arriving early the next morning, Andy nodded towards the desk sergeant, who looked up briefly and waved a half-eaten slice of toast in his direction by way of greeting. As he walked briskly up the stairs, his phone started ringing. He took it out of his pocket, anticipating that it would be Anna asking him to stand in for her at the morning briefing. Too late, he swiped up to answer the call and then saw that it was from his mother.

He listened in silence as she berated him for failing to answer her previous calls, recognising that any pleas that he might make of being on duty and unable to take private calls would be ignored. It was better to let her go on until she ran out of steam and then make an abject, if not wholly sincere, apology. His feelings of resignation turned to dismay, however, when she finally got to the nub of her complaint.

'How *could* you give that man our address?' she demanded. 'Now I'm going to have him stalking me forever. You promised you wouldn't-'

'Hang on!' Andy broke his unspoken vow and interrupted her flow. 'What are you talking about? What man?'

'Yakubu of course! He must have got it from you. How else could he have found out? We're not in the phone book. You might at least have come with him, instead of letting him come round when I was in on my own.'

'Really Mum, I don't know how he got it. I certainly didn't give it to him. Are you saying he's been to see you?'

'Last night. I suppose you'll say you were working late and didn't know what he was up to.'

'Well, actually-,' Andy began. Then he broke off, debating rapidly in his head how best to answer without telling a direct lie. The truth was that, after ringing Yakubu to say that he would be staying at the office to catch up on paperwork, he had called Esther, who had put it to him that dinner as her guest at Lichfield College would be pleasanter than a lonely takeaway. The paperwork having been more of a ploy to avoid spending time with Yakubu than a necessary duty, Andy had not needed much persuasion to accept the invitation. Dinner was followed by coffee in Esther's college room, and one thing leading to another resulted in Andy not arriving back at the flat until after Yakubu had retired to bed. How much of this it would be wise to tell his mother was at best debatable.

'Actually,' he repeated, 'I *was* late back last night, so I didn't know he'd been to see you. He didn't say anything about it at breakfast either. I'm really sorry, but I promise you he didn't get the address from me.'

'Well, I don't see how else he could have found out,' she retorted, refusing to give way; but Andy could tell that she was tiring of the argument. 'But don't let's keep bickering. What are we going to do now?'

'About Yakubu? Nothing. What do you want us to do? Look, it'll all be over in a few days – or a few weeks at the most – and he'll be off back to Nigeria and you'll never see him again – if that's what you want.'

'And what about you? Is that what *you* want?'

'Look Mum, I'm at work. I've got to go now. I'll ring you this evening.'

The kettle was boiling when he reached the big office. Jennifer poured him a reviving mug of coffee.

'Late night, last night?' she enquired, 'or is the responsibility of high office getting to you?'

'Just a phone call from my mum,' Andy grinned back. 'Do I look that bad?'

'Ah!' Jennifer nodded sympathetically.

'Hi, Andy, Jen!' Alice came up behind them brandishing her own mug. They made way for her to pour hot water on to a teabag. 'I've followed up on both of those "suspects" that you wanted me to look into. I don't rate either of them – not for murder. Bullying, maybe – stalking even, but not killing. They don't have the guts. I reckon the kid did it himself. I don't see why Anna won't just close the case, tell the coroner it was suicide and let us get on with more important things – like the little old lady I went to see the other day, who's scared to sleep at night after someone broke into her house and turned her whole downstairs upside down looking for things worth stealing. They didn't take anything, but it was knowing they'd been there, while she was upstairs in bed. That's what got to her. Those are the people we ought to be prioritising – not multi-millionaires who don't want to believe any son of theirs could've topped himself.'

'Right! Let's get cracking!' Anna walked briskly up to the front of the room and clapped her hands for silence. 'I want to get this over as soon as possible so that I can sit in on the Jibrilu Danjuma trial. Ruby's going to be giving evidence today and I want to see how the jury take it.'

Alice hurried back to her desk while Andy stepped forward.

'I've been investigating those unidentified fingerprints on the love spoon,' he told Anna. 'They're from Jamie Mercer. I went over to Coventry again and spoke to him. He admits to having visited Rory the day he died, but he insists he was alive when he left, and, to be honest, I believe him.'

'Still,' Anna sounded more doubtful, 'he did lie to us about it, didn't he? We asked him when he last saw Rory and he didn't say anything about calling on him the day he died. What if Rory told him he was going through with the wedding to Ellie after all? That would have made him pretty angry, I'd have thought.'

'Oh yes, he admits to being angry,' Andy conceded. 'He didn't mention the wedding, but he agreed that he was angry at the way Rory begged him to leave before his father got back. He'd been assuming that he could stay there and come to the party and they'd have got everything out in the open once and for all. But Rory insisted he had to go. If we'd found Rory battered to death in his bedroom, maybe I'd buy the idea that Jamie just lost it when Rory told him things were all over between them – he didn't, by the way, according to Jamie. He just said he needed more time to explain everything to his family. But this murder – if it was murder – was planned. The whisky, the sleeping tablets, the rope. They're none of them spur-of-the-moment stuff.'

'And we now know that both the whisky and the sleeping tablets belonged to Rory himself,' Alice chimed in. 'It's suicide. That's the only thing that makes sense.'

'Apart from the problem of the ladder,' Anna pointed out. 'If Rory climbed up it to get to the branch to tie the rope, who put it away again after he hanged himself? I'm sorry Andy, I know you like this Jamie, and I feel sorry for him too, but he's definitely the suspect with the strongest motive and now we know he had opportunity too.'

'OK, so he was there, but how do you suggest he persuaded Rory to take all those tablets and drink so much whisky?' Andy challenged.

'And it was Rory who bought the whisky,' Alice added. 'And the woman in the shop said he'd never bought anything like that before. Why are we running round chasing our tails trying to prove this was murder when it's obvious he was planning to top himself? He saved up his sleeping pills and bought a bottle of whisky – two ways of numbing the pain – and then he took them out to the bottom of the garden and strung himself up from the big apple tree.'

'And then used magic to take the ladder down and put it tidily away in the shed?' asked Anna drily.

'Someone else must've moved it.' Alice refused to be convinced.

'But who? And why?'

'Could Emma have done it?' Andy suggested, the thought just having occurred to him. 'She's got a cool head and doesn't seem to be fazed by anything. What if she came across Rory hanging there, already dead, and was worried about the effect that his suicide would have on her parents? She knows they'll think he's committed a mortal sin and is on his way to hell as a result, so she moves the ladder to make it look as if he couldn't have done it himself.'

'There you are!' crowed Alice. 'I bet Andy's right. Emma likes organising things. You can tell she's there behind everything, pulling the strings. And she didn't seem very upset about her brother's death. She's only interested in the business. And she knows that bad headlines are bad for business. She wouldn't want the tabloids running with "Tycoon drives gay son to suicide" instead of "Quinn family in shock after brutal murder of their son."!'

'And, unlike her father, she hasn't been going over the top with theories about who might have killed him,' Andy added. 'I'm sure she'd make a much better liar than he would. She wouldn't overdo it.'

'Hmm.' Anna sounded unconvinced. 'Alright, we'll keep that in mind as a hypothesis. 'Now, what did I hear you saying to Andy about you checking out some other suspects?'

'OK.' Alice got out her notebook. 'First up, there's Archie Fisher. He's a radical right-wing fantasist. He made repeated attacks on Rory on social media for his cartoons supporting refugees and immigrants against the right-wing press and government policy. He likes to imagine that he'll be part of a white supremacist revolution, but it's all in his head, I reckon. He's seventeen. He failed his GCSEs last year and spent this year collecting trolleys and filling shelves in a supermarket alongside studying part-time to re-take them this summer. He'd probably like to have killed Rory, but he doesn't have the bottle to do it or the brains to work out all that stuff with the whisky and the sleeping tablets.'

'And where was he when Rory died?' Anna asked.

'In a supermarket car park on the other side of town, collecting trolleys,' Alice answered promptly. 'His supervisor confirms that he clocked in that morning. I suppose it's the sort of job you might be able to skive off from, but it would be a long way for him to go without any transport, and we've no evidence he even knew where Rory lived.'

'I've got similar news as far as Oliver Cash is concerned,' Andy reported. 'His colleagues back his story about hiking on the Ridgeway, but technically there's probably just enough latitude in the times that they gave me for him to have visited Oxford before meeting them at the car park in West Ilsley. I don't reckon he did it. I agree with Alice, the whisky and the sleeping tablets definitely mean suicide to my mind.'

'Mmm,' Anna nodded. 'I take your point, but we must keep an open mind until we find an explanation for the ladder. When I send in my report to the coroner, I want to be able to show that we've looked into every possibility. Alice! Weren't you checking out that disaffected employee that Emma told us about?'

'Jack Lampard? Yes, I interviewed him. He says he was working on Saturday. He said he works most Saturdays to keep out of the house while his teenage kids are at home. He's not exactly the perfect family man. He complained all the time at the way the kids spend all their time winding him up. And then he went on to say their mother was just as bad. He can't think why he doesn't up and leave them. I thought, if I was the wife, I'd have left him long ago! Anyway, his alibi checks out. His supervisor said he was at work all day, and one of his colleagues told me they had their lunch together in a caff round the corner. There's no way he could have got to Headington and back.'

'So it looks as if we can rule him out complete-' Andy began, but he broke off as a young uniformed officer entered the room.

'I'm sorry,' she apologised, looking towards Anna, but we've got a Mr Patrick Quinn down at the front desk wanting to speak to DCI Davenport urgently. I tried ringing your office, but there was no answer. He seems quite distressed, so I thought I'd better …'

'Yes. Thank you.' Anna hurried towards the door. 'I'll come at once. Take over here, Andy. I'll go straight on to court after I've seen to this.'

As she hurried down the corridor to the reception area, Anna wondered what could have happened to further distress Rory's father. Had threats been made against another member of the family, perhaps? Or was the failure of the police to come to an instant conclusion fuelling speculation that the family were somehow implicated in it?

'Inspector Davenport!' Patrick Quinn jumped up out of one of the plastic seats in the waiting area and advanced towards her. He certainly did appear considerably agitated. 'I must speak with you – in private!'

'Yes, of course. Come through to my office.'

Anna glanced up at the coffee-maker as she entered the small room that was her private domain. Good! There was still enough here keeping warm on the hotplate to offer Mr Quinn a cup.

And there was one clean mug left on the shelf above it. She pulled out a chair and urged him to sit down. Within a few minutes they were eyeing each other warily across the desk on which Anna had placed an open packet of bourbon biscuits.

'Now, Mr Quinn, what can I do for you?'

'It's – I'm – That is …,' Patrick swallowed nervously and moistened dry lips with his tongue. 'I'm afraid I've been very foolish. I – I am so sorry! I've wasted your time and ….' He thrust his hand into his pocket and pulled out a crumpled envelope. He put it down on the desk and pushed it towards Anna. 'Here! You need to see this.'

She picked it up and studied it. On the outside it was addressed "Mamma and Dad" in a simple style of handwriting that reminded her of her own son's scrawl. It had been torn open and she could see a sheet of lined paper inside.

'This was from Rory?'

'Yes. I know I ought to have given it to you before. I realise that now. I don't know what came over me. Go on! Read it.'

Anna carefully extracted the letter and unfolded it. It was brief and to the point – a declaration of the intention to end his own life, which he said had become unbearable, but no hint as to any specific causes for that state of affairs. No mention of social media trolls. No suggestion that he feared rejection over his sexuality or anxiety about going through with a marriage that he did not want or starting a career that he disliked. Anna re-folded the paper and put it back in the envelope.

'When did you find this?'

'Saturday afternoon. It was lying on Rory's desk when I went up to his bedroom to look for him to tell him Róisín and Bianca were there. I know I ought to have given it to you then and there, but I just wasn't thinking straight. My main concern was the thought that Martina and her mother might be back any moment and I had to protect them. Giovanna's over eighty you

247

know and not in the best of health. We keep trying to persuade her to come and live with us, but she insists that she wants to stay in London where all her friends are.'

'OK,' Anna said slowly, giving herself time to think. 'We'll need you to sign a new statement to replace the one you gave us in which you said that you saw nothing unusual or different about his room. Is there anything else that you didn't tell us when you wrote that statement?

'Er – yes. A few things, I'm sorry to say.'

'Go on.'

'For starters, there's the whisky bottle.'

'Yes?'

'On the desk, next to the suicide note, there was an empty whisky bottle and a couple of those blister packs that medications come in these days. I picked them up and stuffed them in my pocket. I didn't want his mom to know that Rory had been drinking. It wasn't like him at all – just a glass or two of wine with meals, the way Italians do, not spirits.'

'And these were the same bottle and blister packs that our forensics team later found among the leaves at the bottom of your garden?'

'Yes,' Quinn nodded miserably. 'I wiped them so there wouldn't be any fingerprints on them and hid them in the leaves, hoping nobody would find them – or if they did they would think ....'

'Was that before or after you found Rory?'

'Oh after! Well after. After I'd got him down and rung for the ambulance.'

'Using the ladder that you fetched from the shed.'

'Yes. Well, er, no.'

'Oh?' Anna stared hard at Quinn across the desk.

'No. That's the other thing I need to tell you.' Quinn's hands shook as he lifted his mug to his lips and took a sip of coffee.

'The ladder was there when I got there – lying on the ground where Rory must've kicked it away when he – he – jumped.'

'But you told PC Hughes tha-'

'That it was the ladder that we kept in the shed,' Quinn interrupted. 'I never said that I got it out of there after I found Rory. I said I got the ladder and put it up against the branch to get Rory down. He asked me if it was our ladder, and I said yes, it was the one we kept in our shed.'

'I see,' Anna nodded. 'But you didn't see fit to correct this misapprehension in your statement. Surely you must have realised how misleading it was.'

'I know. I know,' Quinn muttered miserably, 'but I just didn't – I didn't want to admit that Rory could have been so – so – so unhappy that he wanted to …. I *wanted* to believe that someone else killed him. And I wanted Martina and Giovanna to believe it too. And I was afraid ….'

'Afraid of what?'

'It all seems so stupid now – now that I've talked to Father Damien – but I had this idea that the Church would reject him. I had visions of them refusing to give him a Catholic funeral and Martina never being able to face her friends at St Cyprian's again and …. And the stupidest thing of all is that Giovanna knows far more about all that than I did! She quoted me chapter and verse from Pope John Paul and Pope Francis. And there was I thinking I had to protect her from thinking her grandson could have taken his own life!'

Anna sat contemplating what she had just heard for several minutes, while Quinn watched her anxiously. 'Oh well! She said at last. 'At least you've told us now. But you do realise that we've expended a lot of time and effort trying to find someone who could have killed your son, when you could have told us at once that he had done it himself?'

'Yes. Oh yes, I understand that. And I'm quite prepared to pay whatever you need to cover the cost.'

'It's not as simple as that, I'm afraid, Mr Quinn. Wasting Police time is a criminal offence and it can involve a jail sentence of up to six months. And the fact that you had several opportunities to show us that note and to clarify the business of the ladder but didn't do so means that this could even be Perverting the Course of Justice, which has a maximum penalty of life imprisonment.'

'But surely it won't come to that?' Quinn gasped. It seemed that the full implications of his action – or rather his inaction – had only just hit home. 'You haven't charged anyone or anything. Nobody has been hurt, have they? And I've said I'll pay.'

'Money can't fix everything,' Anna replied coldly. 'And it's not all just about police time. What about the people that we interviewed as potential suspects? Why should they have had to account for their time last Saturday when there was no question of them having harmed your son? Why should they have been subjected to the speculation of their neighbours and work colleagues about the police going round questioning them?'

'I – I never thought of all that,' Quinn said weakly. 'I suppose I hoped that you'd think it was just a random attack by an intruder and that nobody would ever be charged. You hear so much about how many crimes are never solved. So, I suppose I assumed this would just be one of them. It won't really have to go to court, will it?'

'I'm afraid that decision is above my pay grade.' Anna was determined not to let him off the hook too easily. This was a man who was used to being able to control everything and everybody around him because of his wealth and influence. It would do him good to squirm a little! 'There *is* the option of a fixed penalty notice – providing that we're only talking Wasting Police Time and not anything more serious. I'll take you down to a room where one of my officers will help you to write a new statement, retracting your previous one and filling in all the blanks, and then that will go to a more senior officer who will decide what to do next.'

'Thank you. And you will keep all this out of the media – to protect Martina? She'd die of shame if it all came out, and I was only doing it all for her!'

'That also is above my pay grade,' Anna told him. 'But provided that you are completely honest with us from now on … I'll see what I can do.'

'Yes. Oh yes! Thank you. I'll make that new statement right away.' Quinn got to his feet, ready to go. Then suddenly he sat back down again. 'But there is one more thing I need to tell you.'

'Yes?' Anna raised her eyebrows questioningly.

'There was another note – or at least I assume that's what it was – on Rory's desk. It was an envelope addressed to someone called Jamie at an address in Coventry. It had a first-class stamp on it, so I suppose he wanted us to post it for him.'

'And did you?'

'No, I kept it.'

'Right. So, let's see it.'

'No, you can't. I mean. I don't have it any longer.'

'But you said-'

'I know. I kept it until yesterday, but then, when I told Father Damien about … everything, I gave it to him. We – we agreed it wasn't fair on this Jamie for the police to see what was in it before he did. And Father Damien – he's our parish priest – at St Cyprian's, not far from where we live. He said he knew a retired police officer – Peter something – who would be able to deal with it. He was going to give it to him.'

'Peter Johns?'

'Yes. That's the name. Do you know him?'

'Oh yes! I used to work with him. I know him well. OK. I'll get on to him and find out where this letter's got to.' Anna got to her feet. 'Right! Let's get that new statement done and then you can go home while I untangle this mess you've made for us.'

After handing Patrick Quinn over to a junior officer, Anna returned to her room and summoned Andy to join her there. He listened in silence as she recounted everything that Quinn had just told her.

'So, he knew it was suicide all along?' he exclaimed when she had finished. 'And he kept going on and on about intruders and death threats and all that stuff, leading us up the garden path, sending us off on wild goose chases! And what for? Why did it matter so much if his son did kill himself?'

'Lots of reasons,' Anna answered. 'He's a Catholic, and Catholics believe that suicide is a sin. He was probably in denial – determined that there must be some other explanation. And he was afraid of the effect that knowing Rory killed himself would have on his wife and mother-in-law. But mostly, I expect it was ….' She took a deep breath and let it out in a long sigh as she fought to dismiss the vision that came unbidden before her eyes of Philip stepping off the landing stage into the Thames, his pockets weighed down with heavy tools to prevent himself from floating. 'When someone close to you takes their own life, you're bound to wonder whether it was your fault. Was it something you said – or didn't say – or something you did, or ….'

'Yes, I suppose so. I'll go and brief the team then, shall I? Stop the investigation?'

'Yes. Go ahead. Tell them everything. I've got to get off to court or I'll miss Ruby's evidence. But don't just pull the plug on everything. There are lots of loose ends need tidying up and we've unearthed quite a few unsavoury characters who could do with watching. The coroner ought to be told about the online persecution Rory was being subjected to. We may even have enough evidence to hand them on to the CPS. Suicide may not be a sin, but driving someone to do it certainly is, in my book.'

'OK. I'll get all that sorted.' Andy got up to go. 'Alice'll be pleased. She's been itching to wrap this case up and get on to other things. And she never believed it was anything other than suicide all along. Poor Gavin, though! He'll be mortified when he hears about the ladder.'

'What d'you mean?'

'Don't you remember? He was the one who told us that Patrick Quinn had to get the ladder out of the shed to get Rory down from the tree. Assuming Quinn's telling the truth when he says that he never said that explicitly, we built our whole case for someone else being involved around Gavin jumping to conclusions and then passing them on to us.'

'Mmmm.' Anna nodded. 'It just goes to show, doesn't it? You'd better have a quiet word with Gavin – before he hears about it through the grapevine.'

When she entered the public gallery a few minutes later, Anna saw that Yakubu was already there, sitting near the front, watching anxiously for the proceedings to start. She slipped in beside him.

'Professor Danjuma? How are you?'

'Inspector!' Yakubu turned and presented her with a brief smile, his teeth appearing very white against his dark skin, before fixing his eyes back on the scene below. 'I am very well, thank you. And you?'

'Oh, I'm fine.' Anna paused, unsure whether Yakubu would welcome more conversation. 'I wanted to see how things go. They're going to look at the forensic evidence today.'

'Good, good,' Yakubu murmured absently. Then louder and more vehemently, 'but why is there so much delay? It should have started by now! Where is the judge?'

Anna looked down at her watch. He was right: the trial should have resumed by now.

'I shouldn't think it's anything to worry about. Probably the van bringing the prisoners got stuck in traffic or something simple like that.'

'Be uprising!' The judge swept into the court and everyone scrambled to their feet. The murmur of conversation in the public gallery stopped suddenly and Anna became aware of her own breathing, which seemed unexpectedly loud in the silence. The judge took her place and everyone sat down again.

Anna watched intently as the proceedings got underway, expecting the prosecuting counsel to call his next witness. But it was Miss Stephanie Bulloch QC, counsel for Logan Wyatt who got up to speak.

'Your Honour, my client has instructed me to tell you that he wishes to change his plea. He wishes to plead guilty to the use of threatening behaviour towards Gabriel Sibanda and Jibrilu Danjuma. He also pleads guilty to the manslaughter of Jibrilu Danjuma, but not guilty to his murder. My client admits that he was holding the knife that severed the victim's artery and led to the loss of his life, but the injury was inflicted by accident and my client was unaware at the time that the knife had come into contact with the victim's person. Nevertheless, he is willing to plead guilty to manslaughter on the grounds that he did wield a weapon against the victim, albeit with no intention to cause him physical harm.'

'I see.' The judge turned to address the other defending barristers. 'And what about the other defendants? Do either of them wish to change their pleas?'

Mr Samuel Molyneux got ponderously to his feet. 'My client also wishes to plead guilty to the charges of threatening behaviour towards both victims, while continuing to deny strongly any involvement in the assault on Jibrilu Danjuma.'

'And your client?' The judge turned to the third barrister.

'He also wished to change his plea to guilty on the charges of threatening behaviour.'

'I see.' The judge paused and looked intently at each of the defendants in turn. 'I think that I need to discuss those changes with the learned counsel for the prosecution. The court is adjourned.'

The spontaneous gasp that went up from the public gallery at this announcement was instantly silenced by a sharp instruction from one of the court officials as the judge got to her feet and walked out, followed closely by the prosecuting barrister. As soon as the door closed behind them, a murmur of conversation broke out as the watchers tried to make out what was happening.

'What was all that about?' asked the red-headed boy, whom Anna recognised as Dale, younger brother of Tyler Briggs.

'It means Tyler's come to his senses at last,' his father told him. 'Threatening Behaviour, first offence, he'll most likely get away with a fine or a community order. No point arguing the toss and risking being sent down as an accessory to murder.'

'So, does that mean it's all over now?'

'Does it heck?' his mother answered scornfully. 'The lawyers'll be at it for hours – days maybe – arguing over whether to go ahead with pushing for murder anyway. They get paid by the hour you know. It won't suit them to cut all this short.'

'What happens now?' Anna realised that Yakubu was speaking to her. She turned and looked into his anxious eyes.

'The judge will discuss with the prosecution in private whether or not it would make sense to accept these new guilty pleas and drop the murder charges.'

'How long will that take?'

'How long is a piece of string?' Anna shrugged. She looked down at her watch. 'But I'll be surprised if the trial resumes before lunch. I'm heading back to the office. I suggest you go and get a bit of fresh air and a coffee or something.'

Arriving back in the open plan office, she found Andy in discussion with Alice, Joshua and Jennifer.

'I always *knew* he'd done it himself!' Alice declared as she walked in. 'I don't know why we wasted so much time pretending it could've been murder. Do I really need to type up these interviews I did with Lampard and Fisher – now we know they didn't do anything?'

'Yes,' Anna said firmly, walking briskly to the front of the room and standing there next to Andy. 'One: if they are a hundred percent innocent of anything then we need a proper record in case either of them get it into their heads to accuse us of police harassment. Two: who says they didn't do anything? Just because neither of them strung Rory up by the neck that doesn't mean they didn't contribute to him deciding to take his own life. His note doesn't say *why* he did it, only that life was unbearable and he couldn't see any other way out. People like Fisher, who post lies and death threats on social media need stopping. So, I want a clear record of everything we've found out about him – OK? And three: Rory's family have a right to know that we did our best to find out what drove him to it. They'll all be carrying the guilt that it could've been their fault – for not stopping him if not for making him unhappy. If we can get a conviction for online abuse then just *maybe* that'll help them believe they couldn't have prevented it.'

'Yes, ma'am,' Alice answered in a voice that was clearly intended to be contrite, but in which Anna detected a hint of sulky defiance. She turned to speak to Jennifer.

'I want you to collect together as much stuff as you can off *Archie the Avenger*'s social media postings. Not just things aimed at Rory Quinn – anything that shows he was systematically attacking people whose views he disagreed with. Some of the stuff you showed me is vile and needs to be stopped.'

'Yes, ma'am.' Jennifer nodded. Then, after a short pause, 'You do know he's only seventeen?'

'So he's young enough that we may be in time to turn him around – make him realise that all the issues he's getting himself het up about are more complicated than he thinks. He's obviously been radicalised by right-wing extremists. So, when you've got your dossier together, pass it on to the Prevent team.' She turned back to Alice. 'Did you see his parents at all when you went round to talk to Fisher?'

'No, I caught him at work – chasing trolleys in a supermarket car park.'

'He lives with his mum and stepdad,' Jennifer volunteered. 'And there's no father listed on his birth certificate.'

'OK.' Anna thought for a few moments. She probably ought simply to pass on everything they had about Archie Fisher to the Prevent[3] team, and leave them to investigate how likely it was that his extreme political views were causing – or likely to cause – him to commit crimes. But the memory of Patrick Quinn's look of desperation as he tried to explain why he had attempted to cover up his son's suicide made her want to see this thing

---

[3] *Prevent* is a government strategy aimed at countering terrorist ideology and preventing vulnerable people, especially young people, from becoming radicalised.

through herself. 'I think I'll pop round this evening, when they're all at home, and have a quiet word.'

She looked round the room, finishing with Andy, who looked back enquiringly. 'I'll sit down and let you get on with it, shall I, Ma'am?'

'No, no,' Anna said quickly, shaking her head. 'I'm sorry. This is your meeting. I shouldn't have gate-crashed. I'll sit down. You carry on.'

'Right!' Andy surveyed the room. Who would have thought that Alice Ray had that mutinous streak? Jennifer, as usual, was doing sterling work in the background, every bit as useful as the warranted officers. Josh Pitchfork? He was a steady worker too – reliable – but often overlooked because he kept his head down and got on with the job instead of always having an opinion of his own to share. They ought to be making more use of him. 'Josh! Could you just run through the list of suspects for us?'

'Suspects?' The DC looked up, his forehead creased in a frown. 'I thought we'd agreed that there wasn't any crime committed – or at least …'

'That's right. But, until we knew that it was suicide, we were keeping a list of people who might have wanted to kill Rory Quinn. I want us to go through that and make sure we've tied up all the loose ends.' He looked towards Anna, who had taken an unobtrusive seat near the back of the room. 'If you knew the police had been investigating you for murder, you'd want to be sure that you weren't still on their files, wouldn't you?'

'Yes, sir. If you can just give me a minute, I'll get the list up for you.'

'That's fine. Take your time.' Andy silently cursed himself for having put the young officer on the spot without prior warning.

'Here we are!' Joshua looked up from his computer. 'We've already talked about Archie Fisher and Jack Lampard. The other person with a clear motive is Oliver Cash, because Jamie Mercer threw him over in favour of Rory. And he also carried out a social media hate campaign against Rory using multiple identities. Then there was Jamie Mercer himself, who may have been angry with Rory for agreeing to go through with his marriage to Ellie.'

'We could do with seeing that letter Rory wrote to him,' Alice called out. 'Though, I suppose it doesn't matter now what he was planning to do about that love triangle he'd got himself into.'

'Yes. Thank you, Alice.' Andy said coldly. 'Carry on Josh.'

'The only other people we'd got on our radar were members of the Quinn family. They had the best opportunity, because they were there on the day and they knew the house and garden and may have known about Rory's sleeping tablets. But they don't really have a motive. We thought his siblings might have resented him being the favourite youngest son, but ...'

'I know,' Andy agreed. 'It was never very convincing, was it. Although, that Emma ... She was so cool about it all. So ...'

'Probably just her way of dealing with the horror of it all,' Anna suggested. 'Concentrating on organising things, which was what she knew she was good at, as a way of shutting out the picture of her brother hanging himself in their back garden on his birthday.'

'And then, there was the wild card of an unknown intruder,' Joshua resumed, 'which again never seemed likely. And that's it.'

'Right. Thanks.' Andy nodded towards Joshua, who leaned back in his chair with patent relief. 'OK. The only one of those who may conceivably have committed an offence is Ollie Cash, who at very least needs a talking to about the way he was persecuting Rory online. However, unlike Archie Fisher, I can't see him doing it to anyone else. This was personal, not down to some warped ideology. So, I think we'll drop any idea of charging him and I'll just give him a call and explain to him how lucky he is that we're too busy to take this any further.'

'The chances are he's already suffering enough thinking he may have driven Rory to kill himself,' Anna observed. 'But I agree, he needs to have it brought home to him how serious that sort of behaviour is.'

'OK.' Andy looked round the room. 'Let's get all this written up ready for the coroner and the CPS. And then-'

He broke off as the door opened and an electric wheelchair glided silently into the room.

'Jonah! What are you doing here? Oh, Peter!' Light dawned as Andy remembered that Patrick Quinn had handed the envelope addressed to Jamie over to Peter Johns. Inevitably that would have meant Jonah getting involved and ultimately taking over.

'Andy! Anna!' Jonah greeted them genially. 'We thought you might welcome a bit of help with this suicide case you've been wrestling with.'

'I suppose by now you probably know about the note Rory Quinn wrote to Jamie Mercer,' Peter cut in apologetically, holding up an envelope in his hand. 'We made a mad dash over to Coventry this morning to show it to him before bringing it to you.'

'It had already been handled by so many people that forensically it was worthless,' Jonah added. 'So we allowed Father Damien to persuade us that Jamie ought to be the one to unseal the envelope.'

'Under our supervision,' Peter assured them. 'He read it and then we took it back, but he'd like to have it to keep once the coroner's finished with it.'

'Of course, by now he must've known the sort of thing that would be in it,' Jonah went on eagerly before Anna had time to extract the note from the envelope. 'So he can't have been surprised by what it said, but he was visibly moved. I'd say there definitely was a real bond between the two of them. And he's a

Catholic too. That's how they met. But he'd been brought up in a more liberal atmosphere. His parents are both academics and not above criticising the Church when they think it's got things wrong. You'll see all that in the note.'

'Yes. Well, perhaps you could let me read it for myself?'

Anna unfolded the piece of lined paper and began to read.

Dear Jamie,

Please believe me when I say that I am so, so sorry! For everything. And specially for being so off with you just now. I wanted the last time we met to be that day in Nottingham when we exchanged rings. But then you turned up at home and all I could think about was getting you out before Emma saw you or Dad got back! I know I said some terrible things, but I didn't mean any of them. I just wanted to make you go.

By then I knew it would never have worked and I'd already decided that there was only one way out for me. I know it's the coward's way, but I just can't see how I can fix things any other way. I've let everyone down. You, Ellie, Mamma and Dad. I can't marry Ellie and live a lie all my life. I can't not marry her because I promised and she really wants it and my parents like her so much. I thought I could marry her and still carry on seeing you, but that wouldn't be fair on either of you. You see what a fix I'm in?

I know what I'm about to do will hurt you all, but not as much as if I was still here, turning the knife in the wound. Just try to forget I ever existed. I wish I hadn't.

If you can't forget then just remember that you were the best thing that ever happened to me.

Love

Rory

Anna passed the paper silently across to Andy, who studied it carefully before re-folding it and putting it back in the envelope. He handed it to Joshua Pitchfork.

'Process this and then get started on the report for the coroner.'

'Well, that's that then.' Anna looked round the room. 'I'm going to get a bite to eat and then go back to court to see if the prosecution has accepted Logan Wyatt's manslaughter plea.'

16. FORGIVE AND FORGET?

'Phil?' Anna put the tray down on the small chest of drawers that separated the twin beds, which she – or more accurately, their daughter, Jessica – had insisted they installed in their room to replace the marital double when her errant husband returned after his three-year sojourn in Devon. 'Wake up. It's nearly eight.'

Philip rolled on to his back and opened bleary eyes. 'I'll get up in a minute.' He closed his eyes again and rolled back on to his side. 'Don't worry; I'll be up in time to take Donna to pre-school. Just you get off to work and let me have a few more minutes.'

'I'm not going to work.' Anna sat down on the bed and rested her hand on his shoulder. 'I've taken the day off. And Marcus has volunteered to take Donna.'

'Marcus?' Philip opened his eyes again and raised himself on one elbow. 'Marcus volunteered?'

'Yes,' Anna smiled back. 'it's suddenly dawned on him that there's more to life than playing loud music and kicking a ball around. And don't let on to him that I said this, I think he quite enjoys the admiring looks he gets from the mums at the school gate for looking after his little sister!'

She stood up and helped her husband into a sitting position, piling up pillows at his back to make him comfortable. Then she set the tray down across his knees. 'Now, eat your breakfast before the bacon gets cold.'

Philip stared down at it in amazement. 'Bacon? But we never have a fry-up for breakfast. There's never time.'

'We've got all the time in the world today,' Anna told him firmly. 'You can stay in bed all day, if that's what you want. Or we can go out somewhere tog-'

'No, we can't. I've got to be in Islip at ten to measure up for an extension.'

'No, you don't. I rang your client last night and told her you weren't well. I've re-booked the appointment for Monday. She was fine about it. We need to talk.'

'There's nothing to talk about!' Philip speared a piece of bacon with his fork and smeared it with yolk from the fried egg before raising it to his mouth. He chewed angrily then swallowed before continuing. 'I'm sorry about that business with the river. I know it was all a dreadful nuisance. But it was just an aberration. It won't happen again.'

'No, Phil, it's not that,' Anna protested. 'Or, well, of course that comes into it. But that's just a symptom, not the underlying problem. I mean we need to talk about us.'

'You've made it abundantly clear that there isn't any *us* anymore,' Philip muttered. 'I know I'm only here on sufferance, and you'd all prefer me to go back to live with Mum. And if Marcus has become this reformed character that you say he is, you won't even need me as a child-minder, will you?'

'Marcus will be going back to uni in September,' Anna pointed out. 'But it's not about childcare. I've offered to pay someone to look after Donna when Jess and I are both working.'

'So, you won't need me at all!' Philip muttered into his coffee cup. 'Thanks a lot!'

'No!' Anna took a deep breath in an effort to hold down her rising anger and frustration. 'I *meant* so that you'd be free to expand the business as much as you like – if that's what you want. But it's up to you. You've got to start making some of the decisions, instead of always saying you'll do whatever I want. I thought marriage was supposed to be a partnership.'

'And you made it abundantly clear that our marriage was over! You said you'd never be able to trust me again!'

'Oh Phil! I'm sorry! I know I haven't been being very fair to you since you came back. It was just ... Oh! I don't know!'

'Oh yes you do! You've been through it often enough,' Philip said bitterly. 'I should've consulted you before making plans to moves us all down to Devon. I don't appreciate how important your job is to you. I'm a murderer for wanting you to have an abortion. I-'

'I never said that!' Anna protested.

'But you thought it, didn't you? And you didn't contradict Jess when she said it.'

'Jess sees everything in black-and-white. When she's older, she'll understand that things are more complicated. Look, Phil, I never thought that about you. I knew you were just ... you were just worried about the commitment of having another child, especially one with disabilities. And you thought I was going to expect you to put your career on hold again to look after her. And I'm sorry that I wasn't more understanding at the time. Can't we have a go at making a fresh start?'

'Because you don't want to feel responsible if I make a better job of topping myself next time?'

'No!' Anna squealed indignantly. Then more calmly, 'No. It's just ... that made me realise how much I still cared about you. And how unreasonable I've been, not giving you a chance to start over again. And ... and how lucky I am to have a second chance. I've got a funeral to go to this afternoon. A young man, just turned twenty-one, hanged himself because he thought all the people who cared about him would be better off without him. and he was so, so wrong!'

**

Father Damien inspected his vestments in the vestry mirror, adjusting the purple stole so that it hung down evenly on both sides. At a funeral mass it was particularly important that everything should be as close to perfection as a mere mortal man could achieve. It was an occasion that would stick in the minds of the family for ever. Satisfied that he was suitably well turned out, he checked his watch for the last time and then made his entrance.

He was surprised and relieved to see that the church was full – unusually so. Even the seats in the "Welcome Area" at the side were occupied, something that normally only happened at Christmas and Easter. The unfortunate circumstances of Rory's death appeared to have stimulated, rather than dulled, the desire among his flock to attend the service and show support for his family. There had been no need to fear criticism from them of his decision to allow full Catholic burial rites to a confirmed victim of suicide.

As he walked solemnly to take up his place at the centre of the sanctuary, he noted with pleasure that Jamie was sitting alongside Emma on the front pew.

The family, including Ellie and her parents, filled the first two rows. Behind them, in the place where a pew had been shortened to make space for his wheelchair, sat Jonah with Bernie, Peter and Lucy. Then there was a group of people whom he did not recognise – more distant family members, he supposed. Near the back, a cluster of younger people looked rather uncomfortable, as if they were finding it all very unfamiliar and strange. Perhaps they were friends of Rory and Jamie from university. The remaining seats appeared to be filled with regular – and some less regular – members of St Cyprian's congregation, obeying his injunction at the services on the previous Sunday to attend if they could to show support for the family. And right at the back, standing by the door looking a little uncomfortable, as if they were unsure about being there at all, were two people whom he did not recognise: a brown-skinned man, whose face looked somehow familiar, and an older woman.

As he stood there silently scanning the congregation, the low murmur of conversation gradually died down and everyone turned their eyes towards him.

'Welcome!' he proclaimed. 'We have come together today to remember Rory Quinn, a much-loved son, brother, and friend, and to pray for the peaceful repose of his soul. We begin by bringing forward symbols of the faith that he shared with his family and our church family here at St Cyprian's.'

He looked down at the coffin, which had been placed on trestles at the foot of the sanctuary steps at the start of the Vigil the previous evening, and then towards Patrick and Martina Quinn, who got up and walked solemnly forward carrying between them a large white cloth. They spread it carefully over the coffin, smoothing it down on both sides.

'The pall reminds us of baptism,' Damien said, nodding towards them to return to their places, as Rory's brother Brendan advanced, carrying a wooden crucifix, which he placed on top of the coffin, pausing to genuflect towards the altar before following his parents back to the front pew.

'The cross reminds us that Jesus died for us,' Damien continued, 'and that through Him the dead will be raised to eternal life.'

Finally, Róisín approached bearing a large leather-bound Bible with ornate gold writing on its cover. She laid it on the coffin, opening it at Psalm 23.

'The Bible reminds us that God's word endures for ever and God's promises can be relied upon.' Damien told the congregation. 'And now, let us remember Rory as we celebrate this mass together. In the name of the Father, and of the Son, and of the Holy Spirit.'

'Amen,' the congregation responded.

'The grace of our Lord Jesus Christ and the love of God and the fellowship of the Holy Spirit be with you all.'

'And also with you.'

The service continued smoothly. Jamie read the approved lesson from the Book of Wisdom, 'But the souls of the righteous are in the hand of God, and no torment will ever touch them. In the eyes of the foolish they seemed to have died, and their departure was thought to be an affliction, and their going from us to be their destruction; but they are at peace ...'

After the gospel reading, Damien gave a short homily, trying to strike a balance between acknowledging the shock and trauma of Rory's sudden and tragic death and offering hope for the future. He was grateful to escape back into the ritual of the mass, which he could recite without needing to agonise over whether his words were the right ones to comfort and encourage rather than to rub salt into open wounds.

The familiar liturgy appeared to give comfort to the grieving family who were able to lose themselves for a short time in the rhythm of the words and the beauty of the music, a highlight of which was a solo performed by a gifted member of the congregation, Precious Sibanda, whose singing voice never failed to move her listeners.

At the end, Rory's coffin was carried out to the waiting hearse, followed by his family: Patrick and Martina side-by side, then Emma holding her grandmother's arm, his brother and married sisters with their spouses, and finally Ellie and Jamie in a strangely appropriate partnership.

Damien waited at the door, greeting people as they left and directing them to the Parish Centre at the back of the church, where refreshments, prepared by Deirdre and a small band of helpers from among the ladies of the church, were waiting for them. He was to accompany the family to the cemetery for the burial.

'Anna! Andy! Don't rush off!' Jonah's voice, directed at the two strangers who had loitered at the back of church and had not come forward to receive communion, jogged Damien's memory. Of course! That was where he had seen the dark-skinned man before: he had been Jonah's sergeant, years ago, when he had investigated the discovery of a long-dead body hidden beneath the church organ. He must have been part of the team looking into Rory's death. Presumably the woman with him was a police officer too.

'Jonah!' Anna greeted her ex-colleague warmly. 'What are you doing here?'

'Attending a funeral. What does it look like?' Jonah smiled back. 'We only live round the corner, remember. The Quinns are our neighbours. Come round the back and have a cup of coffee and some of Deirdre's raisin cookies. She'll be tremendously disappointed if anyone goes off without trying any of her baking, and you'll be missing a treat!'

'And, of course,' Bernie added, leaning forward over his shoulder, 'he wants to pump you for information about the trial and why the defendants changed their pleas.'

'And what convinced you that Rory's death *was* suicide, after all,' Lucy chimed in.

They made their way across the paved courtyard, enclosed on three sides by the church, the presbytery and, on the far side, a single-storey brick building, which constituted the Parish Centre. Jonah's wheelchair glided easily up the ramp to the double doors, which had been left wide open to encourage people in, and in the hope that a through draught might lessen the sweltering heat.

'The suicide question was simple, in the end,' Anna told Lucy. 'It turns out Rory did write a note, after all.'

'Yes, we know all about that, but what about the ladder?' Lucy asked, picking up two paper plates and placing one on the small tray-table attached to Jonah's wheelchair. '*He* couldn't very well have put it away after he hanged himself!'

'It turned out that was a misunderstanding,' Anna explained. 'All that really happened was that he kicked it away as he jumped and his father found it on the ground and put it back up again to get him down.'

'Now tell us about the trial,' Jonah urged impatiently. 'Why did they suddenly change their pleas?'

'I really have no idea,' Anna sighed. 'We all turned up at court on Friday morning expecting to see Ruby talking us through the forensic evidence, and after a lot of people in wigs flapping about and muttering to each other, the defence lawyers all said their clients wanted to plead guilty to everything except murder. Presumably something must have gone on in the background, but I don't know what.'

'It's a pity they couldn't have decided to plead guilty before poor Gabriel Sibanda had to give evidence,' Peter observed. 'It must have been a dreadful experience for him, being cross-examined by three barristers.'

'That was his mother singing *Be not afraid*,' Bernie told Anna. 'They're Catholics and members of St Cyprian's. Gabriel sometimes plays the organ for services.'

'Yes, I recognised her,' Andy nodded.

'But the trial,' Jonah persisted. 'The press reports said that the prosecution agreed to accept it was manslaughter, not murder. Was there any more to it than that?'

'Honestly,' Anna insisted, adding two egg sandwiches to her plate and reaching for a piece of quiche, 'I don't know any more than you do about any legal machinations that may have gone on. The case was adjourned while the prosecution considered the new pleas. Then it re-convened and they said they were willing to drop the murder charge and accept that the incident was an *unlawful and dangerous act of manslaughter*. Then the defence counsels went into a huddle and eventually came back and said OK, and that was that. The defendants were bailed and sentencing will be tomorrow.'

'Will you be there?' Jonah asked.

'No. Andy's going with his father, so I'll leave him to report back to me on that. Monisha Chowdhury has a reputation for giving harsh sentences for crimes against children, and of course there's the racial element, so I'll be surprised if any of them get away without a custodial sentence.'

'Yakubu thinks *he* ought to be able to decide what penalty Wyatt gets for stabbing his son,' Andy informed them. 'I told him he'd be allowed to read out his victim statement in court and the judge would take it into account. I just hope he doesn't get carried away and say things he shouldn't. I don't trust him to stick to the script.'

The friends settled down at one of the small tables dotted around the room, each with a small vase of flowers in its centre, courtesy of Margaret Kenny, another stalwart of St Cyprian's congregation. After about forty minutes, Andy started to wonder if he ought to get back to the police station. It was all very well showing solidarity with the family of a young man whose death they had been investigating, but there were other serious incidents that needed police attention – not to mention plenty of paperwork still required for the coroner in readiness for the inquest into Rory's death. He was just getting to his feet and preparing to make his excuses to Jonah and his friends when the Quinn family arrived back.

Anna got up at once and went over to them, almost colliding with Deirdre who was intent on directing them to the refreshment table, where there were still plenty of sandwiches, vol-au-vents and mini-quiches, not to mention her famous raisin cookies and a delicious rhubarb cake.

'Mr Quinn?'

Patrick gestured to his family to go with Deirdre, then turned to face Anna. 'Inspector Davenport?'

'I'm sorry if I'm intruding on your grief, but I thought you should know: we've informed the CPS and the coroner that there are no grounds for suspecting that anyone other than your son was involved in his death,' she told him. 'And you don't need to worry about any action being taken in relation to your ... having overlooked a few things in our initial interview with you.'

'Thank you.' The relief on Patrick's face was unmistakable. 'I feel such a fool, deceiving you like that. I'm only glad it didn't lead to someone being charged for killing him. That was such a stupid thing that I said about it having to be murder. Poor Jamie! He tells me you questioned him as if you thought he might have done it.'

'We did, I'm afraid. And you and your family were on our list of suspects too,' Anna told him gravely. 'We had to consider all possibilities.'

'When I could have cleared everything up for you right away.' Patrick sighed. 'I just can't apologise enough. It was ... it was ... well, I just can't explain it. I must have been insane!'

'I think every parent goes a bit insane when they lose a child suddenly,' Anna replied. 'And suicide! It's so difficult to imagine how someone close to you could have wanted to end their own life. Try not to beat yourself up about it.'

***

'Choose whatever you like; this is my treat,' Yakubu told them, as they picked up the menus in the small Italian restaurant that Amanda Lepage had selected as neutral territory for a reunion. Determined not to permit Yakubu the chance of a tête-a-tête, she had insisted on bringing Andy with her; and he had invited

Esther for moral support and in the hope that the presence of an outsider would force his mother to moderate her behaviour towards Yakubu.

For a few minutes they all buried their heads in the conveniently large menus, glad of the excuse not to speak or to make eye contact with their companions. Andy stole a sideways glance at Esther, who looked back and slipped her hand under the table to give his knee a gentle squeeze of solidarity.

Amanda had ordered a bottle of red wine, which Andy refused on the grounds that he was driving and Yakubu waved away in silence. Andy wondered whether his mother were deliberately trying to draw attention to their religious differences by offering Yakubu alcohol, which she must have known he would feel compelled to decline.

The waiter returned and they gave their orders. After handing back the menus, they were forced to attempt conversation.

'Would anyone like some bread?' Amanda asked, picking up the basket of rolls that lay in the centre of the table and offering it round. Andy and Esther each took one, but Yakubu shook his head. 'Butter?' Amanda enquired, still playing the part of host.

Andy took the glass bowl containing curls of butter and passed it to Esther. They both broke their rolls in half and spread butter over the interior, conscious of his mother's eyes on them as she determinedly avoided looking up at Yakubu's face.

'This looks like a nice place,' Esther said, desperately making conversation. 'I hadn't come across it before.'

'Some of us from work went here last Christmas,' Amanda told her. 'It *is* very good, and the prices are very reasonable.'

'I remember the first time we went out for a meal together, Mandy,' Yakubu said, leaning across the table towards her. 'It was at that little place in the covered market. You had sausage and chips and a milkshake.'

'Your memory is better than mine,' Amanda replied, refusing to engage in reminiscences.

'I suppose Oxford must have changed a lot since you were a student here?' suggested Esther.

'In some ways yes, and in others hardly at all,' Yakubu responded, taking his eyes off Amanda and smiling wistfully towards Esther.

'That's Oxford for you!' Andy observed with a nervous laugh. 'Stuck in the past and at the same time at the cutting edge of innovation.'

'Yes,' his mother agreed, eagerly grasping the opportunity to keep the conversation away from anything more personal. 'I had a striking example of that at work the other day. A new way of analysing archaeological remains to assess their age, bringing together researchers from four or five different disciplines across Humanities, Science and Social Science. Being based in the Radcliffe Science Library, I don't usually meet people from the Classics Faculty. They're doing some absolutely fascinating work in the Middle East and North Africa.'

'I always thought Classics was just Latin and Greek,' Andy commented, also glad of the neutral topic.

'Oh no, it's all about ancient history and archaeology too,' his mother told him.

'Your work in the library must be very interesting,' Yakubu said. 'And you must meet some interesting people.'

'Yes,' Amanda agreed. 'Only the other day I had a mathematician from Ukraine in, asking about some journal articles she needed. She was here on a research grant when the war started. Her family are all still stuck in Kiev. They couldn't escape because her mother is too old to travel.'

'That must be awful for her!' exclaimed Esther. 'She must be so worried for them.'

'Yes,' agreed Amanda. 'She told me that the block of flats where her husband lives with their two little girls was hit in an air raid and burned down. They only narrowly escaped with their lives. And, of course, the children have been completely traumatised by it. She said she keeps having nightmares of them running down the stairs, unable to breathe in all the smoke. It must have been so frightening for them. Oh! I'm sorry!' she looked up and caught Yakubu's eye for the first time that evening. 'I forgot that was how your family ...'

'No, no. Do not distress yourself. It was a long time ago.' He waved his hand dismissively.

'But something like that, you never really get over, do you?' Amanda insisted earnestly. 'And it was insensitive of me to have forgotten, especially now that you've lost your son too. Andy told me about the trial,' she continued before Yakubu could come back with the inevitable reminder that Jibrilu was not his only son. 'You must be relieved that it's over, but were you disappointed with the sentences. I thought the judge was rather lenient – considering the things they said to that poor child.'

'I think the worst thing was that they didn't plead guilty until after he'd had to go through the whole thing again in court,' Esther said with feeling. 'It must have been terrifying for him being questioned by their lawyers.'

'He was very brave,' Yakubu nodded. 'I admired him very much.'

'And you must be very proud of your son for stepping in to defend him,' Esther replied. 'That was very courageous too. I am glad that the man who killed him will go to jail, but I don't understand why the others who were with him have been set free.'

'The judge gave them the maximum level of Community Service,' Andy pointed out, 'and they're being sent on a course to educate them about inappropriate behaviour towards minority groups.'

'But that girl!' Esther exclaimed. 'I saw her on the news afterwards, posing for the cameras, with her bright red lips and her low-cut blouse. She was enjoying all the attention!'

'I agree,' Yakubu said sadly. 'It was disappointing to see that she did not have any remorse – or any sense of decorum. I am pleased to see that you understand modesty,' he added, smiling towards Esther. 'I am not bigoted when it comes to women's dress, but I do think that there are reasonable limits that should be observed.'

Their food arrived and, for a few minutes, conversation lapsed while they poured glasses of water and handed round the condiments.

Yakubu ate a few mouthfuls of his risotto, then put down his fork and looked thoughtfully towards Amanda.

'Mandy,' he said earnestly. 'I have something important to say to you before I go back to Nigeria. I know that I do not have any right to ask you for anything. Andy has finally made me understand how much I hurt you, for which I have nothing but the deepest regret.'

Amanda looked up briefly, then lowered her head again and made herself busy with her spaghetti carbonara.

'I return home tomorrow,' Yakubu went on. 'And I may never return to England. I am sure that this fact will be a great relief to you.' He sighed sadly and looked round at Andy and Esther, before continuing, 'but I will never – I can never – forget you. I do not wish to forget the times that we spent together all those years ago. And I cannot regret them either. And especially, I cannot – I will not – I must not – forget the wonderful young man who was the result of my encounter with you.'

THANK YOU

Thank you for taking the time to read *Just Another Suicide*. If you enjoyed it, please consider telling your friends or posting a short review. Word of mouth is an author's best friend and much appreciated. Thank you,

Judy

ACKNOWLEDGEMENTS

I would like to thank many Facebook friends, especially those from the *Pesky Methodist* group, for their support and encouragement and for suggesting ideas for my books.

Every effort has been made to trace copyright holders of any quotations from writing other than my own. The publishers will be glad to rectify in future editions any errors or omissions brought to their attention.

DISCLAIMER

This book is a work of fiction. Any references to real people, events, establishments, organisations or locales are intended only to provide a sense of authenticity and are used fictitiously. All the characters and events are entirely invented by the author. Any resemblances to persons living or dead are purely coincidental.

Many of the locations and institutions that feature in this book are real. Their inhabitants and employees, however, are purely fictional. In particular:

- Neither Holy Cross nor Lichfield colleges exist;

- None of the police officers depicted here are based on real people in Thames Valley Police or any other police service.

MORE BOOKS FROM JUDY FORD

This is the second of the Davenport and Lepage series of novels. The first, **Just Another Knife Crime**, tells of Andy's first murder investigation following his promotion to the rank of Inspector. It is here that we first encounter Yakubu Danjuma and begin to learn of his secret relationship with Andy's mother.

Many of the characters in this book feature in the fourteen **Bernie Fazakerley Mysteries**:

1.   **Two Little Dickie Birds**: a murder mystery for DI Peter Johns and his Sergeant, Paul Godwin.
2.   **Murder of a Martian**: Peter and Jonah solve a double murder and Peter meets Martin Riess for the first time.
3.   **Grave Offence**: Peter investigates an assault and a suspicious death, while Jonah is in rehab in the spinal injuries centre.
4.   **Awayday**: a traditional detective story set among the dons of Lichfield College.
5.   **Death on the Algarve**: a mystery for Bernie and her friends to tackle while on holiday in Portugal.
6.   **Mystery over the Mersey**: a murder mystery set in Liverpool.
7.   **Sorrowful Mystery**: Jonah investigates a child abduction and Peter embarks on a new journey of faith.
8.   **In my Liverpool Home**: Bernie and her friends return to Liverpool to investigate a suspicious death in Aunty Dot's Care Home.
9.   **Organ Failure**: a body is discovered under the organ in St Cyprian's Church and Jonah is called in to investigate.
10. **Rainbow Warrior**: One of their friends is injured in a hit-and-run incident and Jonah is convinced that this is attempted murder.
11. **Admission of Innocence**: Father Damien calls Peter and Jonah out of retirement to solve a murder case and prevent a miscarriage of justice.
12. **Lethal Mix**: Three of Lucy's student friends are injured in an anti-Muslim hate crime in Liverpool. Jonah, Peter and

Bernie assist Merseyside Police to bring their attacker to justice.

13. **A Secret Gardener?** Bernie's friend Martin discovers a body in the Fellows' Garden of his Oxford College.

14. **Crowd of Witnesses**: Jonah decides to write his memoirs, beginning with a murder investigation from 1982.

Andy Lepage's colleagues from Thames Valley police also appear in five other novels:

- **Changing Scenes of Life**: Jonah Porter's life story, told through the medium of his favourite hymns.

- **Despise not your Mother**: the story of Bernie's quest to learn about her first husband's past.

- **Weed Killers**, **Lost in Lockdown**, and **Victim Statements** form a trilogy of novels about the aftermath of the murders of two young men.

And there's a book of short stories, in which Peter Johns narrates his side of the story:

- **My Life of Crime**: the collected memoirs of DI Peter Johns. This includes some episodes that appear in other books, but told from a new perspective, as well as some completely new stories.

You can find all these on Judy Ford's **Amazon Author page:** https://www.amazon.co.uk/-/e/B01935B1M.

Visit the Bernie Fazakerley Publications **Facebook page:** https://www.facebook.com/Bernie.Fazakerley.Publications.

Follow Judy Ford on **Twitter**.

GLOSSARY OF UK POLICE RANKS

Uniformed police

Chief Constable (CC) – Has overall charge of a regional police force, such as Thames Valley Police, which covers Oxford and a large surrounding area.

Deputy Chief Constable (DCC) – The senior discipline authority for each force. 2nd in command to the CC.

Assistant Chief Constable (ACC) – 4 in the Thames Valley Police Service, each responsible for a policy area.

Chief Superintendent ('Chief Super') – Head of a policing area or department.

Police Superintendent – Responsible for a local area within a police force.

Chief Inspector (CI) – Responsible for overseeing a team in a local area.

Police Inspector – Senior operational officer overseeing officers on duty 24/7.

Police Sergeant – Supervises a team of officers.

Police Constable (PC) – 'Bobby on the beat'. Likely to be the first to arrive in response to an emergency call.

Police Community Support Officer (PCSO) – A uniformed civilian member of the police service.

Crime Investigation Department (CID) – Plain clothes officers

Detective Superintendent (DS) – Responsible for crime investigation in a local area.

Detective Chief Inspector (DCI) – Responsible for overseeing a crime investigation team in a local area. May be the Senior Investigating Officer heading up a criminal investigation.

Detective Inspector (DI) – Oversees crime investigation 24/7. May be the Senior Investigating Officer heading up a criminal investigation.

Detective Sergeant (DS) – Supervises a team of CID officers.

Detective Constable (DC) – One of a team of officers investigating crimes.

These descriptions are based on information from the following sources:

[1] Mental Health Cop blog, by Inspector Michael Brown, Mental Health co-ordinator, College of Policing.
https://mentalhealthcop.wordpress.com/, accessed 31st March 2017.
[2] Thames Valley Police website,
https://www.thamesvalley.police.uk, accessed 31st March 2017.

ABOUT THE AUTHOR

Like her main character, Bernie Fazakerley, Judy Ford is an Oxford graduate and a mathematician. Unlike Bernie, Judy grew up in a middle-class family in the South London stockbroker belt. After moving to the North West and working in Liverpool, Judy fell in love with the Scouse people and created Bernie to reflect their unique qualities. She has worked in academia and in the NHS.

As a Methodist Local Preacher, Judy often tells her congregation, "I see my role as asking the questions and leaving you to think out your own answers." She carries this philosophy forward into her writing and she hopes that readers will find themselves challenged to think as well as being entertained.

Printed in Great Britain
by Amazon

24424788R00165